American Theater and Drama Research

An Annotated Guide to Information Sources, 1945–1990

IRENE SHALAND

McFarland & Company, Inc., Publishers
Jefferson, North Carolina, and London

British Library Cataloguing-in-Publication data are available

Library of Congress Cataloguing-in-Publication Data

Shaland, Irene, 1955–
    American theater and drama research : an annotated guide to
information sources, 1945–1990 / Irene Shaland.
        p.   c.m.
    Includes index.
    ISBN 0-89950-626-7 (lib. bdg. : 55# alk. paper) ∞
    1. Theater – United States – History – 20th century – Bibliography.
2. American drama – 20th century – History and criticism –
Bibliography.   I. Title.
Z1231.S53   1991
[PN2266.3]
016.792′0973′09045 – dc20   91-52741
                                                              CIP

Manufactured in the United States of America

McFarland & Company, Inc., Publishers
  Box 611, Jefferson, North Carolina 28640

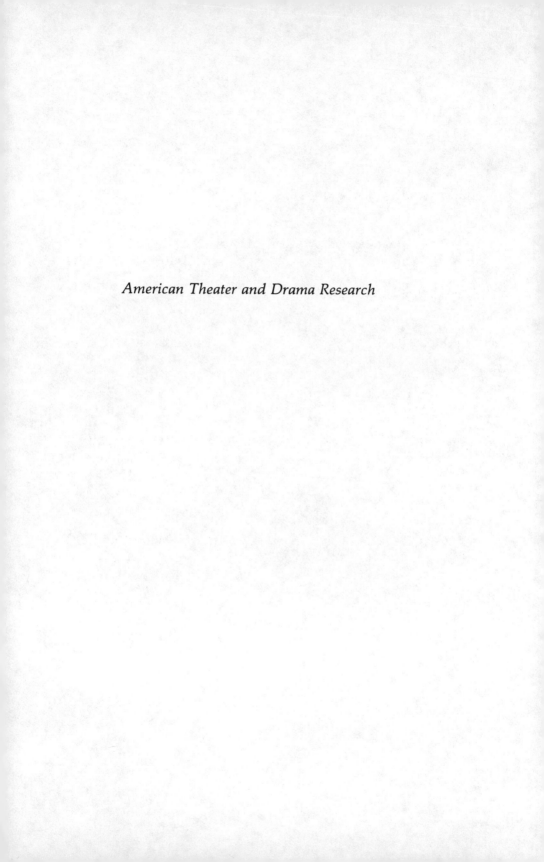

American Theater and Drama Research

For Alex
for so many things

Table of Contents

Acknowledgments

This work could not have been written without the encouragement and help I have received from Doctor Lois Buttlar (School of Library Science, Kent State University, Kent, Ohio). It was her continued interest and advice that enabled me to see my project through to the end.

I also wish to express my gratitude to my friend Gail Reese (Head of Reference, University Libraries, Case Western Reserve University) and Rosario Poli (Reference Librarian) for their wise help in my research.

My friends and colleagues from the NASA Lewis Research Library have also helped me significantly with their understanding, support, and professional advice during my working on this book.

Finally, my husband Alex has helped me tremendously by both continuing to believe in the importance of my work and by patiently correcting all the technical problems I encountered while using my computer.

Without these people, the effort would have taken far longer, and may have never been completed.

Irene Shaland
Cleveland, Ohio
Spring 1991

Introduction

An Overview

This *Guide* seeks to provide both student and researcher in the theater arts with a basic list of general and specialized sources of reference and bibliographical information on American theater and drama after World War II. In the time period from 1945 to the present, the problem of a researcher is not scarcity of sources on American theater and drama but their overabundance. In such a wilderness, guides are needed. The great variety of sources on American plays, theaters, and playwrights raises the need to organize them.

There are other available guides and bibliographies that offer research assistance in the fields of drama and theater. However, none provides the same approach and coverage of current literature on this most important period in the history of American theater as the present work does.

This is not a comprehensive bibliography: as a playwright seldom writes "curtain" to the play without a feeling that it could be improved, a bibliographer can also never say that the job is finished. However, the *Guide* attempts to include all relevant and important sources of information, published after 1965, that will assist and direct both student and researcher in this field of study.

As theater reference works, including bibliographies, have multiplied greatly, it seemed imperative to cover both new works and the most usable ones from the past. There are several previous works (see pages xii–xiii) that to greater or lesser degrees have attempted systematic coverage of many aspects of American theatre, chief among them *Bibliography of the American Theater*, Chicago: Loyola University Press, 1965 (a work that is not annotated). The decision was made in the present work to begin with the sources published after 1965. The closing date is roughly December 1989 (however, some significant sources published in the first half of 1990 are also included).

Some limits have to be placed on the types of books that are admitted to the bibliography. The listings are restricted to books published in the United States; all books are in English. No plays or collections of plays are included. While reference books on musical theater are listed, books that deal with musical theory or composition are not. Books written about the techniques of acting and directing are excluded also. The major concern of the *Guide* is the history of American drama and theater after World War II. The emphasis of this bibliography is on the reference and information sources dealing with the historical and aesthetical development of American theater and drama; with the works of major dramatists such as Eugene O'Neill, Tennessee Williams, Arthur Miller, Edward Albee, William Inge; with ideological and social conditions in respect to theater; and with various political and philosophical influences, etc. Along with reference sources arranged by categories (guides, bibliographies, encyclopedias, directories, handbooks, biographical tools, etc.), the *Guide* also includes all major periodicals associated with the field, all relevant databases that could be searched, and all major theater related organizations, associations and research centers.

Theater research is a highly diversified field of study and requires a considerable level of skill in the use of library resources. The value of the *Guide* is meant to be determined by its usefulness to the researcher. The organization of material first by subject and then by categories attempts to clarify the purpose and content of the entries.

All works cited were examined closely. Annotations for each work are factual, critical, and comparative when appropriate. Occasionally, material from a work's introduction is quoted. Information provided in each entry includes author, title, place of publication, publisher, copyright date, and pagination.

Existing Reference Works

American Playwrights Since 1945: A Guide to Scholarship, Criticism, and Performance. Philip C. Kolin, ed. Westport, CT: Greenwood Press, 1989. 610pp.

This excellent book is an invaluable resource for anyone studying contemporary American drama. Being many books in one — a bibliography, a stage history, a critical survey of scholarly works about the playwrights — this guide concentrates on the state of scholarship on forty major American dramatists. A researcher interested in the historical and aesthetical development of American theater, its different political and philosophical aspects, has to use a number of additional sources.

Bibliographic Guide to Theater Arts. Annual. Boston: G. K. Hall 1975–   .

G. K. Hall's *Bibliographic Guides* are comprehensive annual subject bibliographies. They bring together publications cataloged by the Research Libraries of the New York Public Library with additional entries from Library of Congress MARC tapes for thorough subject coverage. This source attempts to include material on all periods; the word "theater" is interpreted in its broadest sense and covers the stage, cinema, radio, television, night club performances, the circus, vaudeville, theater criticism, biography, and material on individual theaters. Although this useful source covers current literature, its too-broad coverage and complete lack of annotations cannot provide sufficient help for a researcher in the particular time period.

Bibliography of the American Theater. Carl J. Stratman, ed. Chicago: Loyola University Press, 1965. 397pp.

This systematic compilation attempts to be as inclusive as possible for stage and theater activity in the United States. However, its arrangement by state and city could be found confusing. The source is not current, and annotations are limited to periodical articles.

A Guide to Reference and Bibliography for Theater Research. Claudia J. Bailey, ed. Columbus: Ohio State University Press, 1983.

This annotated guide is the one most competitive to the present work. It is an indispensable tool for selecting material for theater and drama research. However, its coverage of literature on American theater after 1945 is insufficient, and the guide does not provide information on sources published after 1980.

The Humanities: A Selective Guide to Information Sources. Ron Blazek and Elizabeth Aversa, eds. Littleton, Colo.: Libraries Unlimited, 1988.

This excellent book is planned as a text rather than a research tool. Though it includes good annotations and provides information on important bibliographies, dictionaries, directories, encyclopedias, etc. (prior to 1987) on theater, it is not concerned with particular periods and the chapter on theater is just one of many sections on different fields of the humanities.

International Bibliography of Theatre: 1982. New York: American Society for Theatre Research, 1982.

This book is the accumulation of a wide-ranging databank of international theater research references. It does not cover literature after 1982, and it is not annotated, though some entries do have brief abstracts.

Performing Arts, 1876–1981; Books. New York: R. R. Bowker, 1981.

This is a comprehensive bibliography of over a hundred years of United States publishing in the performing arts as cataloged by the Library of Congress. This volume provides a historical perspective of literature in all of the performing arts; and though it could be a very good tool for reference or acquisitions, it is difficult to use for a researcher in a particular time period because of its broad coverage and lack of annotations.

Performing Arts Books in Prints: An Annotated Bibliography. New York: Ralph Newman Schoolcraft, 1973.

Though this guide presents good descriptive information on all books concerned with the performing arts, including literature on theater and drama, it cannot be used as an up-to-date source.

Performing Arts Research: A Guide to Information Sources. Marion K. Whalon, ed. Detroit: Gale Research, 1976.

This annotated guide attempts to cover many aspects of research in theater arts, including literature on drama. Although a very useful tool, it is not up-to-date.

As can be seen from this brief description of the relevant and competitive literature, none of the available sources offer research assistance in the field of American theater and drama after 1945 with up-to-date and descriptive information.

The Methodology of the Present Work

In collecting material for this *Guide* all of the above sources were thoroughly consulted; the most significant material from these tools was consolidated with additional and more current publications. However, the first step in compiling the *Guide* was to investigate such obvious bibliographical tools as:

American Reference Books Annual, 1965–
Book Review Index, 1965–
Cumulative Book Index (CBI), 1898–
Subject Guide to Books in Print, 1965–

The following LC subject headings were used: American Drama — Bibliography; American Drama; Drama — 20th Century; Theatre — United States. After checking these sources, and gathering an initial bibliography, a database computer search was undertaken (one of the DIALOG databases, LC MARC subject coverage, files 427, 426). Each book was examined and its overall theme and major premise were taken into account in placing it in a particular category.

Overall, this *Guide* attempts to provide a clear overview of the most useful retrospective and current sources to reference and research, collection assessment and development in the stated area of the American theater and drama.

Part I. General Reference Sources

1. Literature and Drama

Guides and Bibliographies

1. Adelman, Irving and Rita Dworkin. *Modern Drama: A Checklist of Critical Literature on 20th Century Plays*. Metuchen, N.J.: Scarecrow, 1967. 370pp.

   This is a selective survey of the critical literature of the 20th century drama in more than 800 books and periodicals. The compilers stress critical articles rather than reviews of productions. Information is arranged by author and title of play. Bibliography of reference sources is included. However, lack of clear organization reduces the book's usefulness, especially for a researcher of any specific national drama.

2. Birney, Alice L. *The Literary Life of Jesus: An International Bibliography of Poetry, Drama, Fiction, and Criticism*. (Garland Reference Library of the Humanities Series). New York: Garland, 1989. 187pp.

   The emphasis of this bibliography is on American and British contemporary works, though there are entries from other countries, and items included range from the beginning of the Christian era to 1984. The 1,424 entries of the bibliography are arranged alphabetically by author, and the work consists of four sections: General Works, Poetry, Fiction, and Drama. The author demonstrates the fascination with Jesus that has persisted through the twentieth century, turning her bibliography into a chronicle of changing perceptions of Christ and supporting the view that each generation reinterprets Jesus in its own image. The book has an author/editor index. The majority of entries are not annotated, however, those that are have clear, concise, and helpful annotations. The broad focus of this source makes it useful for those students and researchers of modern American drama who are interested in religious aspects of contemporary theater.

3. Blackmore, Ruth. *Index to American Reference Books Annual, 1980–1984: A Cumulative Index to Subjects, Authors, and Titles*. Littleton, Col.: Libraries Unlimited, 1984. 402pp.

   This detailed source directs researchers to the reference tools dealing with American theater and drama.

1

4. Breed, Paul F. and Florence M. Sniderman. *Dramatic Criticism Index: A Bibliography of Commentaries on Playwrights from Ibsen to the Avant-garde*. Detroit: Gale Research, 1972. 1022pp.

   This tool serves as a guide to American and foreign playwrights and play reviews in nearly 630 books and 200 periodicals. There are 1,200 entries arranged by the dramatist's name, with a general section followed by an alphabetical listing of works. The commentaries cited under each heading may range from major articles and chapters of books to a few pages from a longer work. There are three indexes: titles of the plays, names of critics (lists play title and playwright criticized), and book titles. Though being admittedly selective, the index proves to be a helpful reference tool.

5. Carpenter, Charles A. *Modern Drama Scholarship and Criticism 1966–1980: An International Bibliography*. Buffalo, N.Y.: University of Toronto Press, 1987, 1986. 587pp.

   The author claims his book to be a "bibliographical precis of the entire discipline of modern drama" that offers "a worldwide picture of all the playwrights, topics, and approaches." This international bibliography is considerably more than a convenient checklist of critical works: there are more than 27,000 entries in a classified, selective list of publications covering a 15-year period of modern drama studies. The author emphasizes drama and dramatists rather than performances and performers. Bibliography is arranged by nationalities of the playwrights: American drama, British and Irish drama, French drama, etc. Within each national group, individual playwrights are listed alphabetically. There are also classified subheadings under each author's name: "by," "reference," "about," etc. The bibliography's breadth, comprehensive coverage, and clear organization make this tool a very useful reference source for a researcher in modern world or American drama.

6. Cohen, Ralph et al. *New Literary History: International Bibliography of Literary Theory and Criticism*. Baltimore, Md.: Johns Hopkins University Press, 1989. 188pp.

   This is a new annual bibliography, the editors of which state a goal of comprehensive coverage. Country/language of origin is the basis of this tool's organization; then material is subdivided by type of theory. The range and depth of the bibliography's various sections are enormous, and there are many listings not found in the *MLA International Bibliography*. Some researchers in modern American literature and drama may find this source useful, while some may just enjoy the fascinating browsing this bibliography provides. However, there is no subject index, and only the English language section has cross-references.

7. Coleman, Arthur and Gary Tyler. *Drama Criticism*. Denver: Alan Swallow, 1966–71. 2v.

Volume 1 is a bibliography of critiques since 1940 of English and American plays, while volume 2 is a checklist of critical works since 1940 of classical and continental drama. All interpretations are in English and appeared in 1,500 books and 1,000 periodicals, but the plays are from different countries. Volume 2 has two sections: "Plays by Shakespeare" and "Plays Other than Shakespeare." All entries are arranged alphabetically by playwright, then by title of play. Sources in which criticism was found are listed. The material included is of "critical nature" rather than biographical, plot outlines, historical or staging. However, along with the checklist from *Modern Drama* by Adelman and Dworkin, this tool is a useful source for researchers involved in the critical analysis of modern plays.

8. *Contemporary Literary Criticism: Excerpts from Criticism of the Works of Today's Novelists, Poets, Playwrights and Other Creative Writers.* Detroit: Gale Research, 1973– .
   This multi-volume work serves as a guide to selections from criticism on contemporary authors, including dramatists, living or deceased, since 1960. Each volume has cumulative index and covers approximately 200 writers. Original critical sources are cited. Volume 50, 1988, 539pp., is edited by Sharon K. Hall, and entitled *Contemporary Literary Criticism: Yearbook 1987. The Year in Fiction, Poetry, Drama, and World Literature and the Year's New Authors, Prizewinners, Obituaries, and Works of Literary Biography.* The volume provides outstanding coverage of the 1987 significant events, and is arranged into five major categories: "The year in Review," "New Authors," "Prizewinners," "Obituaries," and "Literary Biography." With its distinguished essays and fact-filled bibliographies, this series makes a first-rate information source. For a researcher in modern American drama this well-indexed and handy reference tool, which becomes more valuable with the publication of each new volume, might serve as a useful source that provides an overview of the critical reception given to a dramatist.

9. Fletcher, Steve. *The Book of 1000 Plays.* New York: Facts on File, 1989. 352pp.
   This source provides the researcher with a list of plot summaries for the longest running plays over the past 80 years in London's West End and on Broadway, and for the most popular plays on Off Broadway and in British theaters. The entries include title, author, date and place of first performance, a brief synopsis of the plot, and dramatis personae. The book does not, however, give any information on original cast, statistics, or production. It also does not include criticism. Students and scholars of the American modern drama may use this source for a quick reminder of plots and characters.

10. Hunter, Frederick J. *Drama Bibliography: A Short-Title Guide to Extended*

*Reading in Dramatic Art for the English-Speaking Audience and
Students in Theatre.* Boston: G. K. Hall, 1971. 239pp.

This work includes books published through 1970 and covers drama
and theater from the Greek and Roman period to the present.There are
more than 3,000 entries in classified arrangement: reference sources,
periodicals, materials about dramatic literature, theater history and
criticism, techniques of theater, biography and autobiography, and
dance. Indexed by personal names. Entries are not annotated, however,
the work provides adequate bibliographic data and good coverage of
modern American theater and drama.

11. Magill, Frank N. *Magill's Bibliography of Literary Criticism: Selected
    Sources for the Study of More than 2,500 Outstanding Works of
    Western Literature.* Englewood Cliffs, N.J.: Salem Press, 1979. 4 v.

    This tool provides citations of critical studies in monographs and
    journals. Arranged alphabetically by the author's name. Each entry
    gives a list of titles of individual works. There is a title index in the last
    volume. With its broad chronological coverage, this bibliography can
    be used for research in modern American drama, though the same
    author's *Critical Survey of Drama* proves to be the first and the wisest
    place to look for answers.

12. Modern Language Association of America. *MLA International Bibliog-
    raphy.* New York: Modern Language Association, 1921–   . Annual. Ti-
    tle and coverage vary.

    These annual supplements to *Publications of the Modern Language
    Association of America* present extensive compilations of books and ar-
    ticles in the fields of language and literature, including drama. There is
    a classified arrangement with national and chronological subdivisions.
    This source is a good starting point in search of bibliographies on any
    modern American playwright.

13. Patterson, Margaret C. *Literary Research Guide.* 2d ed. New York:
    Modern Language Association of America, 1984. 559pp.

    This tool is annotated and arranged by format and type of literature.
    Covers reference sources relevant to the study and research of different
    national literatures with the emphasis on English and American
    literature. Author-title indexes as well as those of editors, periods,
    genres, and subjects make this guide a convenient reference tool and
    easy to use.

14. *The Reader's Adviser: A Layman's Guide to Literature.* 13th ed. New York:
    Bowker, 1986–88. 6v.

    The Reader's Adviser is a selective, annotated bibliography that
    covers titles from different subject fields. Major emphasis is, however,
    on British and American books in the humanities. Extensive sections on
    drama are in the second volume, entitled *The Best in American and*

British Drama and World Literature in English Translation and edited by Maurice Charney.

15. *Roth's Index to Literary Criticism: Providing Access to the Over 1,200 Critical Essays and Selections Contained in CoreFiche: Literary Criticism.* Great Neck, N.J.: Roth Publishing, 1988. 206pp.

     The index is designed to help a researcher or a student of literature and drama find necessary critical articles, monographs, etc., on the subject of interest. The work is arranged in four main sections: a checklist of titles, a subject index, an author and title index, and a contents of the works indexed. *Roth's Index* is meant for use with a companion set of microfiche, *CoreFiche: Literary Criticism.*

16. Salem, James M. *Drury's Guide to Best Plays.* 4th ed. Metuchen, N.J.: Scarecrow, 1987. 480pp.

     The emphasis of this updated and revised edition, as in the previous editions, is on playwrights and their plays. Over 1,500 non-musical plays from the Greek and Roman classics to recent Broadway hits are listed, and only those that appear in English (translated or not) are identified. Entries provide authors in alphabetical order, brief summary of each play, date of first production or publication, information about number of acts, cast, set, and royalty fee. The *Guide* brings coverage up through the 1984–85 theatrical season. There are number of very valuable indexes: "Cast Index" covers plays containing from one to more than forty characters; "Index of Selected Subjects" classifies plays according to their subjects; there is also a list of prize-winning drama. Though objective in its selectivity, the *Guide* is a very useful reference tool for those doing research in drama or producing plays, as well as for those who purchase them for libraries.

17. Shipley, Joseph T., ed. *The Crown Guide to the World's Great Plays: From Ancient Greece to Modern Times.* Rev., updated ed. New York: Crown, 1984. 866pp. 1st ed. (1956) had title: *Guide to Great Plays.*

     Though Shipley's consideration of "great" is subjective, *The Crown Guide* is an authoritative and excellent source of information on drama. The emphasis is on the new types of drama such as theater of the absurd, for example. Modern American masters such as Tennessee Williams, Arthur Miller, Edward Albee, Sam Shepard, etc. receive good coverage. For each of the total 750 entries is given plot, facts about the play's origin and significance, stage history, notes on cast, and excerpts from reviews. This easy-to-use tool is alphabetically arranged by author and has a detailed index of titles.

18. Slavens, Thomas P., ed. *The Literary Adviser: Selected Reference Sources in Literature, Speech, Language, Theatre, and Film.* Phoenix, Ariz.: Oryx, 1985. 196pp.

     This work is an annotated bibliography for 650 reference sources and attempts to embrace these different fields in a comprehensive manner. Coverage is international with the emphasis on primarily American and British titles. It follows a classified arrangement with geographical divisions. The work is supplemented with the set of indexes providing easy access through author, title, and subject. This tool proves to be a useful source for information on major reference works.

19. Wood, Patrick W. and Naomi Caldwell-Wood, eds. *Checklist of Bibliographies Appearing in the "Bulletin of Bibliography, 1897-1987"*. Littleton, Col.: Libraries Unlimited, 1989. 150pp.

This useful reference tool indexes every bibliography, book or drama review, editorial and bibliographical note that ever appeared in the *Bulletin of Bibliography* from 1897 through 1987. This cumulative index to every issue of the *Bulletin of Bibliography* could be a good starting point in search of bibliography on modern American drama.

Indexes to Plays

20. Hoffman, Herbert H. *Recorded Plays: Indexes to Dramatists, Plays, and Actors*. Chicago: American Library Association, 1985. 139pp.

The main section of this source is an alphabetical list of playwrights' names with the provided bibliographical data of the recorded play and when available, actors' names. A second section is arranged by plays' titles, and the third section gives names of the actors. Though most of the play recordings are 33 1/3 rpm phonodiscs, other media — 16mm films, tapes, videocassettes — are included. The source also provides information helpful for locating these recordings. Hoffman's index might be useful for those researchers who are interested in identifying and locating rare play recordings.

21. Keller, Dean H. *Index to Plays in Periodicals*. Revised and expanded ed. Metuchen, N.J.: Scarecrow, 1979. 824pp.

This expanded edition includes nearly 10,000 plays appearing in 270 periodicals through 1976. The book is arranged in such a way as to make location of a play quite simple. There are two major sections. The first one provides author's name, dates, title of the play, brief summary of the plot, number of acts, and bibliographical data of periodical. The second section is a listing of titles, which are numbered to correspond with authors' entries. The book provides an international coverage. Keller's *Index* is a well-designed, valuable identification tool, a good finding aid for plays published in periodicals.

22. Leonard, William T. *Theatre: Stage to Screen to Television*. Metuchen, N.J.: Scarecrow, 1981. 2v.

This unusual source provides selection of over 300 plays that after their productions on the British and American stage became subjects for both movie and television adaptations (Shakespeare, Gilbert and Sullivan, and the Greek classics excluded). Entry is by title of the play with a brief summary of the plot, followed by a survey of criticism on the original and subsequent productions, background on the playwright, and cast listings for production and its two adaptations. The book is indexed by authors, composers, lyricists, and librettists. Having all this information together in two volumes might be helpful for a researcher who seeks to find out about a play's life in a media other than theater.

23. NCTE Liaison Committee. *Guide to Play Selection: A Selective Bibliography for Production and Study of Modern Plays.* 3d ed. New York: Bowker, 1975. 292pp.

   In spite of its title, this work is actually an index to plays compiled by the National Council of Teachers of English Liaison Committee with the Speech Communication Association and the American Theatre Association. This tool provides index to nearly 850 modern plays (with the emphasis on British and American drama) which are described in the first section. A brief summary and comments on staging needs are indicated. Information on royalties is also included. The second part is a listing of short plays, full-length plays, musical plays, plays by black playwrights, etc. This useful source provides author and title indexes, a topical index, and a "player index" with the listing of titles according to the number and sex of the characters.

24. Ottemiller, John H. *Ottemiller's Index to Plays in Collections: An Author and Title Index to Plays Appearing in Collections Published Between 1900 and 1985.* 7th ed. Revised and enlarged by Billie M. Conner and Helene G. Mochedlover. Metuchen, N.J.: Scarecrow, 1988. 564pp.

   This useful source covers plays from all periods and places if published in collections in England and the United States from 1900 to 1985. The index furnishes over 10,000 citations to nearly 3,700 plays by nearly 2,000 authors, among them many modern American dramatists. The author index provides an author's name, his birth and death dates, name of play, first production date, and an acronym representing the collection in which the play is to be found. Full bibliographic information on the collections are included in "The List of Collections Analyzed and the Key to Symbols." There is also a title index. This old favorite among reference librarians index provides immediate solutions for a researcher who needs a certain play but finds it missing or out in a library.

25. Patterson, Charlotte A. *Plays in Periodicals: An Index to English Language Scripts in Twentieth Century Journals.* Boston: G. K. Hall, 1970. 240pp.

   This index provides access to more than 4,000 plays appearing in 97 periodicals during the period 1900–1968. Title entries are arranged alphabetically and include the author (or translator, if appropriate), the number of acts, the size of cast, and the bibliographical data for a periodical. There are also a "Cast Analysis Index" and author index. Patterson's *Index* may serve as an identification tool if Keller's — which gives twice as much coverage — is unavailable.

26. *Play Index*. New York: H. W. Wilson, 1949/1952.

This is a comprehensive work and it covers all types of plays, including American modern drama, from all types of sources, either separately published or parts of collections. Generally about 4,000 plays are covered in each volume. All plays are in English, but translations are included. Each volume consists of four parts: the main list, arranged by author, title, and subject; a list of the collections indexed; cast analysis, which lists plays under gender of cast and number of characters; and finally, there is a directory of publishers. Particularly helpful in this useful source are the dictionary catalog arrangement and the subject indexing. The latest volume edited by Juliette Yaakov and John Greenfieldt indexes nearly 4,000 plays published during the five-year period 1983–1987 and even includes some plays published before 1983, but omitted from the previous volumes. All seven volumes of the *Play Index* series are the source of invaluable information for all those seriously interested in contemporary theater.

27. Samples, Gordon. *The Drama Scholars' Index to Plays and Filmscripts: A Guide to Plays and Filmscripts in Selected Anthologies, Series and Periodicals*. Metuchen, N.J.: Scarecrow, 1986. 3v.

This index fulfills a purpose for those researchers who seek either an unusual play or a well-known play in an unusual version or places. Several foreign and American periodicals are indexed for the first time in this work. The cut-off date for this index is 1983. The information is arranged in alphabetical order by playwrights and titles of plays. At the end of the third volume there is a complete "Title List of Anthologies Indexed in Volumes 1, 2, and 3," and an index of publishers. Provides good coverage on American modern drama, amassing information not readily available from any other source.

28. Samples, Gordon. *How to Locate Reviews of Plays and Films*. Metuchen, N.J.: Scarecrow, 1976. 114pp.

This index is annotated and serves as an identification tool to other indexes, checklists, bibliographies, and other sources of reviews and critiques of plays and films. There are separate sections for each genre, and each section is subdivided by type of reference tool. The entries within these divisions are arranged in chronological order by period covered. Some researchers may find it useful, though coverage for modern American drama is insufficient, and there are inaccuracies.

29. Sharp, Harold S. and Margorie Z. Sharp. *Index to Characters in the Performing Arts*. Metuchen, N.J.: Scarecrow, 1966–73. 6v.

This source covers non-musical plays in the first two volumes, while operas and musicals are listed in the next two. Volumes five and six are devoted to ballets and radio and television plays. The index is actually a dictionary of major and minor characters in stage works from earliest times to 1965. There are cross-references to productions and a list of symbols identifying title, type of production, number of acts, author, name of theater, and date and place of first performance.

Dictionaries

30. Courtney, Richard. *Dictionary of Developmental Drama: The Use of Terminology in Educational Drama, Theater Education, Creative Dramatics, Children's Theater, Drama Therapy, and Related Areas.* Springfield, Ill.: Charles C. Thomas Publishing, 1987. 153pp.

The author of this dictionary offers 956 terms of the vocabulary used in the area of educational drama. Significant terms from anthropology, psychology, and sociology are also included. Some students and scholars interested in modern American drama, including children's and educational drama, may find this source useful. However, the compiler does not provide clear criteria for the choice of entries, and many definitions seem too abbreviated. A brief concluding list of references and journals is included.

31. Hodgson, Terry. *The Drama Dictionary.* New York: New Amsterdam Books, 1989. 432pp.

The author's intention "is to provide useful working definitions of terms used in the theater and by theater critics" and also to bridge a "regrettable gap between the practical theater and those who read and write about drama." The dictionary contains more than 1,300 entries that provide definitions and illustrate dramatic theory and practice. There are also 31 line drawings. The language is clear and concise. The illustrations are very helpful. Some entries are three-quarters of a page, the majority of entries are eight or ten lines in length. This book is a single source of useful information on dramatic practice, theory, and criticism. With its use of cross-references and even short bibliographies, this dictionary provides coverage that seems very thorough.

Encyclopedias

32. *Benet's Reader's Encyclopedia.* 3d ed. New York: Harper & Row, 1987. 1091pp.

Expanded and revised, this edition of Benet's encyclopedia contains more than a thousand entries, the scope of which includes brief biographical essays on artists, musicians, writers, playwrights, philosophers, etc. Plot and character synopses are also provided. Among the newly added entries are the ones on Neil Simon, Sam Shepard, and the theater of the absurd. The source also provides detailed descriptions of literary and artistic movements, awards, and schools, as well as explanations of myth, folklore, and legends. Though, unfortunately, this encyclopedia has no illustrations, it is a useful and comprehensive source.

33. Cantor, Norman. *Twentieth-Century Culture: Modernism to Deconstruction*. New York: P. Lang, 1988. 452pp.

Written by a distinguished New York critic and historian with the astounding erudition, this book is an incomparably thorough one-volume encyclopedia of 20th-century culture. The author does not intend to cover only the arts and literature, but he also encompasses science, psychology, education, etc. — all intellectual aspects of modern society. While the book suffers from a lack of discrimination, and there are some sharply drawn opinions to disagree with, it could be used by many researchers in modern theater and drama as a source of information on cultural and intellectual background.

34. Gassner, John and Edward Quinn. *Reader's Encyclopedia of World Drama*. New York: Crowell, 1969. 1030pp.

This single volume ready-reference work focuses on drama as literature and not on the performance aspects. Coverage is given to the plays, their authors, and literary characteristics. The entries fall into four general categories: national drama, playwrights, plays, and genres. This source examines the development of drama in individual countries from its origin to its most contemporary forms. Significant playwrights are treated in separate entries which include biographical sketches, brief bibliographies, and some critical evaluations. Plays receive critical commentaries and synopses. All entries are signed. There is an appendix of basic documents on dramatic theory. No indexes are included. This book provides sufficient coverage of American drama after 1945 and is useful for any reader interested in drama in general as well as in American modern drama given in the context of the world dramatic history.

35. *McGraw-Hill Encyclopedia of World Drama*. Hochman, Stanley, ed. 2d ed. New York: McGraw-Hill, 1984. 5v.

Encyclopedia's coverage of bibliographical materials far exceeds that of such one-volume works as, for example, *The Reader's Encyclopedia Of World Drama* by Gassner. The primary emphasis is on dramatists, with individuals receiving the majority of the entries. The second edition of this work is thoroughly revised and updated. International in scope, *Encyclopedia* presents detailed information on the achievements of playwrights throughout theater history. The work also examines national, regional, and ethnic drama of countries throughout the world and provides comprehensive material on different dramatic traditions, dramatic genres, influential theater companies, etc. The work is well illustrated (more than 2,800 photographs and drawings). General index can be found in Volume 5. Useful and up-to-date entries make this tool an invaluable reference work for teachers, critics, theater historians — any reader interested in the history of world or national drama.

36. Matlaw, Myron. *Modern World Drama: An Encyclopedia*. New York: Dutton, 1983, 1972. 960pp.

    Though the content entirely reflects the author's own taste and preferences, the tool provides rather comprehensive coverage of modern drama of individual countries. It includes four types of alphabetically arranged articles: summary articles on drama; biographical sketches for playwrights; entries for specific dramatic works (some plays with full plot outlines, many without), including notes on publication; and definition for technical terms for recent theater movements. There are general and character indexes. The European playwrights receive more detailed coverage than do Americans. Avant-garde dramatists are not treated as fully as the realists. Such important modern American playwrights as Sam Shepard or Israel Horovitz receive no entries at all. As a tool for research in modern American drama it should be used with caution; however, could be valuable for undergraduate studies.

37. Wynar, Bohdan, ed. *ARBA Guide to Subject Encyclopedias and Dictionaries*. Littleton, Col.: Libraries Unlimited, 1986. 570pp.

    This useful reference tool offers information on subject encyclopedias and dictionaries, including those dealing with American theater and drama. It provides detailed reviews of over 1,300 subject encyclopedias and dictionaries, most of which are taken from *ARBA*.

Handbooks

38. Anderson, Michael, Jacques Guicharnau, Kristin Morrison, et al. *Crowell's Handbook of Contemporary Drama*. New York: Crowell, 1971. 505pp.

    This convenient one-volume tool is a comprehensive, alphabetically arranged listing of playwrights, plays, terms, movements and national events considered influential in the development of world drama since 1945. The emphasis of this work is on written drama rather than theater. The *Handbook* includes surveys of modern drama in various countries in long overview studies; biographical sketches and critical essays on the work of many dramatists; descriptive and critical evaluation of important plays; and brief presentation of theories and movements. Especially important is the coverage given to avant-garde plays and playwrights. Though no index is provided and bibliographic information is sparse, the *Handbook* is an authoritative and useful source for research in American theater for critical appraisal of modern drama and dramatists.

39. Birch, David. *Language, Literature, and Critical Practice: Ways of Analyzing Text*. New York: Routledge, 1989. 214pp.

    The author draws together various critical theories of present and recent past times. The monograph is well documented, and includes a thorough bibliography. It could be used by a student or scholar of modern literature and drama as a handbook on different ways of analyzing text.

40. Pfister, Manfred. *The Theory and Analysis of Drama*. John Halliday, translator. New York: Cambridge University Press, 1988. 339pp.

    This book was originally published in Germany in 1977; however, in acknowledgment of the growth of theater semiotics in the last ten years, its English translation was substantially revised. The monograph serves as an easy to consult handbook which aim is to outline a systematic general theory of drama, to identify basic parameters (such as closed and open dramatic forms), and examine the range of possibilities with reference to specific dramatic texts. This source proves to be a valuable contribution to dramatic theory, and a necessary reading for students and researchers in the field of dramatic criticism.

41. Vaugh, Jack A. *Drama A to Z: A Handbook*. New York: Frederick Ungar Publishing, 1978. 239pp.

    Though the compiler of this book disclaims completeness; the purpose of the work is to serve as a general source of information and a reference tool for a student of the drama or for any reader interested in dramatic literature. Entries arranged alphabetically and attempt to cover drama from Aristotle to the present. May be used for undergraduate studying.

Biographical Sources

42. Beacham, Walton, ed. *Research Guide to Biography and Criticism: World Drama*. Washington, D.C.: Research Publications, 1986. 742pp.

    This tool is designed as a companion to the *Research Guide to Biography and Criticism: Literature* (1985). It is limited to 146 dramatists from the ancient Greeks to modern authors, but only to those who are considered "the most studied" by the compilers. Each entry provides a dramatist's brief biography, evaluation of selected biographies with an overview of biographical sources, an annotated list of selected criticism, and a list of a playwright's works that is often incomplete. Though some researchers in American modern drama may find this source helpful, it has to be used with caution.

43. Combs, Richard. *Authors: Critical and Biographical References: A Guide to 4,700 Critical and Biographical Passages in Books*. Metuchen, N.J.: Scarecrow, 1971. 221pp.

This guide provides a researcher with an access to biographical and critical selections in nearly 500 published collections. Over 1,400 authors are analyzed. There is an author index to the collections. Though coverage on modern American playwrights is not broad enough, the guide may be used as one of the biographical sources.

44. *Contemporary Authors: Autobiography Series.* Vol. 7. Zadrozny, Mark, ed. Detroit: Gale Research, 1988. 429pp.

Volume 7 of this unique autobiography series represents writers who, as in the main *Contemporary Authors* set, fall into a broad range of categories, including literary and drama criticism, nonfiction, film, television, and drama. Before this series, there have been no brief autobiographies of current writers and playwrights collected in one source. Each autobiographical essay is accompanied by photographs supplied by the writer and contains a bibliography of his works. The index provides adequate access to the names and titles mentioned in this and previous volumes. This tool reveals the writers' and playwrights' sources of creativity and inspiration, and it is an interesting and unusual supplement to already existing reference tools for literary biography and criticism.

45. *Contemporary Authors/Contemporary Authors New Revision Series.* Detroit: Gale Research.

This classical reference source is an outstanding tool that encompasses authors in every field, including drama. The series provides detailed biographical and bibliographical information combined with interviews with authors. *Contemporary Authors* are edited by Susan M. Trosky. Volumes 1–129 are in print. *New Revision Series* has 29 volumes in print, and the editors are Hal May and James L. Lesniak.

46. *Critical Survey of Drama: English Language Series.* Magill, Frank N., ed. Englewood Cliffs, N.J.: Salem Press, 1985. 6v.

This six-volume set is a part of the 45-volume Salem Press genre series, and is carefully researched, skillfully constructed, and well-written. It contains individual articles on playwrights from all periods of American, British, Irish, Canadian, African, Afro-American, West-Indian, and Australian drama. Essays are arranged alphabetically by the dramatist's name. Each essay provides dates of birth and death, list of the playwright's plays as well as survey of his publications other than drama; a biographical sketch; and an extensive critical analysis of the dramatist's development. There is also a bibliography of criticism about the author and his work. A comprehensive index provides easy access to the information making this tool extremely useful for research in any aspects of American as well as other English language drama.

47. *Critical Survey of Drama. Supplement.* Magill, Frank N., ed. Englewood Cliffs, N.J.: Salem Press, 1987. 408pp.

This publication extends coverage to important playwrights who were not covered in earlier volumes of both the English language and Foreign language series. Almost all included dramatists are from the twentieth century, most of them are active. Arrangement and format are consistent with that of earlier volumes. Both of Magill's tools are invaluable sources for any researcher looking for the best textual, critical, and biographical information about American or other world's outstanding playwrights.

48. *Dictionary of Literary Biography*. Detroit: Gale Research, 1989. 3v.

49. *Dictionary of Literary Biography: Documentary Series*. Detroit: Gale Research, 1989. 7v.

50. *Dictionary of Literary Biography Yearbook*. Detroit: Gale Research, 1989.
    This series of biographical dictionaries is a valuable source of information on specific genres, nationalities, and time periods in all of literature and drama. Author entries in the *Dictionary of Literary Biographies* are arranged in volumes covering specific genres or eras. This tool proves students and researchers with invaluable resource material: specially written comprehensive essays on individual writers and playwrights, photographs and illustrations. Cumulative indexing in each volume makes it easy to locate the article on the particular writer, scholar, or dramatist.
    Each volume of the *Documentary Series* concentrates on the major figures of a particular literary period, movement, or genre. Each entry contains chronicle of a writer's or a playwright's career and includes letters, notebooks, diaries, interviews, contemporary reviews, etc. Each volume is well illustrated and provides pictures from the authors' lives, facsimiles of their manuscripts, title pages, etc.
    The *Yearbook* series provides an up-to-date information. Each volume is heavily illustrated and contains detailed biographies of writers and playwrights and bio-critical discussions. It also includes a list of literary awards and honors, a checklist of contributions to literary history and biography, a necrology, and a cumulative index to all previous volumes.

51. Kirkpatrick, D. L., ed. *Contemporary Dramatists*. 4th ed. Chicago: St. James Press, 1988. 785pp.
    This book may be qualified as one of the major biographical research sources. It provides a great amount of information for every major contemporary dramatist in a logical and readily accessible form. The biographies of over 400 living playwrights writing in English are the subject of this directory. Supplemental section contains information on screenwriters, radio and television writers, music librettists, and theater groups. Each entry consists of a biography, a complete survey of

chronologically arranged published and produced plays, a bibliography of all other works, and a critical essay. Sometimes information on location of manuscript collections, critical studies and bibliography, theatrical activities, agents, addresses, etc. is included when available. The volume contains a title index.

52. McNeil, Barbara. *Author Biographies Master Index: A Consolidated Index to More than 845,000 Biographical Sketches....* 3rd ed. Detroit: Gale Research, 1989. 2v.

    This invaluable, timesaving source covers all eras and countries, and indexes biographies of major literary figures (more than 400,000 different authors found in about 700 editions of 290 English-language biographical dictionaries) including modern American playwrights plus those of minor authors and dramatists about whom it is often difficult to find information. There are no cross-references for pseudonyms, variant spellings, or forms of entry. However, this is a thorough and handy reference tool.

53. McNeil, Barbara and Amy L. Unterburger, eds. *Abridged Biography and Genealogy Master Index: A Consolidated Index to More than 1,600,000 Biographical Sketches..."* Detroit: Gale Research, 1988. 3v.

    This biographical source covers more than 1,600,000 biographical sketches in 115 biographical dictionaries and, as the *Author Biographies Master Index*, is based on the larger *Biography and Genealogy Master Index*, 8 vols, of the same publisher. Coverage is very wide, and includes artists, musicians, mass media and show business personalities, political figures, scientists, writers, and playwrights. It is a current biographical reference tool.

54. Seidel, Alison P. *Literary Criticism and Authors' Biographies.* Metuchen, N.J.: Scarecrow, 1978. 209pp.

    This author guide to critical and biographical materials about prominent writers and playwrights is similar in its coverage and organization to the one by Combs, but it is more updated. Each entry is provided with a brief annotation. It can be used as a finding aid in research in modern American dramatists, though unfortunately, some standard biographical sources are omitted.

55. Seymour-Smith, Martin. *Who's Who in Twentieth Century Literature.* New York: Holt, Rinehart, and Winston, 1976. 414pp.

    This comprehensive guide is arranged alphabetically by author and covers nearly 700 modern writers and dramatists with the emphasis on the American and British authors. Even Sigmund Freud is included because of his tremendous influence on literature and drama. Each entry provides brief biography of a writer or a playwright, critical analysis of his works, important influences on his writing, and selected bibliography. This useful biographical source gives a researcher not only standard biographical information on an author but also summarizes key ideas and traces significant movements in modern literature and drama. There are many cross-references but, unfortunately, this tool is unsatisfactorily indexed.

56. Stein, Rita, Friedhelm Rickert, and Blandine Rickert. *Major Modern Dramatists*. New York: Ungar, 1984–86. 2v. (Library of Literary Criticism).

     This first genre-oriented set in series provides easily accessible excerpts of drama criticism. All excerpts are in English, some of them translated specially for this compilation. Volume 1 covers American, British, Irish, German, Austrian, and Swiss dramatists, while volume 2 extends the coverage to French, Belgian, Russian, Polish, Spanish, Italian, Norwegian, Swedish, and Czech playwrights. The purpose of the set is to provide an overview of the dramatists from the beginning of his career up to the present time through excerpts from reviews, articles, and books. It is a good but not an indispensable source; and its usefulness for a researcher in American drama is greatly reduced by insufficient coverage of domestic playwrights. There are just seven Americans and such important dramatists as Sam Shepard, David Mamet, and David Rabe are omitted.

57. *Writers Directory 1988–90*. 8th ed. Chicago: St. James Press, 1988. 1045pp.

     All writers listed in this directory have at least one book published in English and are from many countries, including the United States. This edition is completely revised and expanded and provides bio-bibliographical entries for more than 15,000 writers, including playwrights. Each entry consists of personal and career data, a chronological list of publications, and present address. This source also includes a separate section that lists authors by writing categories.

58. Wynar, Bohdan S., ed. *ARBA Guide to Biographical Dictionaries*. Littleton, Col.: Libraries Unlimited, 1986. 444pp.

     This comprehensive work reviews more than 700 dictionaries, encyclopedias, and other reference biographical resources, including those that provide biographical material on modern American writers and playwrights.

2. Theater Arts

Histories and Critiques

59. Berthold, Margot. *A History of World Theatre*. Translated by Edith Simmons. New York: Ungar, 1972. 733pp.

 The book by a professor of theater history at the University of Munich provides a scholarly, worldly view with a European perspective in a history of the theater from the ancient time to the trends and developments of the twentieth century. The author treats American theater too briefly, especially in sections on Broadway and experimental theater, thus reducing the book's usefulness for a researcher in modern American stage. However, it still might be a good source of information for those interested in historical, anthropological, and aesthetic influences in theater history.

60. Bradby, David and David Williams. *Director's Theater*. Chicago: St. Martin Press, 1988. 275pp.

 This monograph is important in its tracing the director's development as a central creative force in modern theater from the 19th century to the present. The authors present the range of functions assumed by postwar directors, such as Joan Littlewood, Peter Stein, Robert Wilson, Roger Planchon, Ariene Mnouchkine, Jerzy Grotowski, and Peter Brook, and discuss their working techniques and philosophies. Though not directly related to the history of modern American theater, this book with its succinct summaries and view on the director as a joint author of the production could be a valuable source for anybody seriously interested in the development of modern theater.

61. Brockett, Oscar G. *History of the Theatre*. 5th ed. Boston: Allyn & Bacon, 1987. 779pp.

 This successful, scholarly book provides a good overview of the theater from the primitive times to the present. Unlike Berthold's *History*, Brockett gives sufficient coverage of the American theater which he treats as an outgrowth of European influences. Scenic and performance practices, stage architecture, theatrical conditions, etc. are discussed. There is a list of major bibliographical sources and an alphabetical index. Brockett's book is one of the best one-volume general theatrical histories that, also gives an overview on the American theater, including its modern period.

17

62. Cheney, Sheldon. *The Theatre: Three Thousand Years of Drama, Acting, and Stagecraft.* Revised and reset illustrated ed. New York: McKay, 1972. 710pp.

    This book is generally considered as a standard reference source on the history of international theater and drama. In two chapters — "The Theatre in Decline: War, Commercialism, and Other Evils" and "Absurdity and Defilement with Bright Interludes, 1950–1970" — Cheney provides good coverage on modern trends and movements in European and American theater.

63. Cottrell, Tony. *Evolving Stages.* Chicago: St. Martin's Press, 1990. 198pp.

    This is a historical and literary overview of the Western theater in the twentieth century presented by a drama teacher and a playwright. Though the work is oriented toward a theater goer rather than a scholar, anyone seriously interested in contemporary theater may find this lively and polemical historical study an enjoyable reading.

64. Devin, Diana. *Mask and Scene: An Introduction to a World View of Theater.* Metuchen, N.J.: Scarecrow, 1989. 221pp.

    This book presents a fresh overview of theater history, the survey of historical and modern theater which is direct and informative. The author intends to direct reader's attention to those historical conventions that have continued and have found universal application today as she stresses contemporary sociopolitical concerns expressed in modern theater. The book consists of several sections: the first one on the function of theater, and the following sections treating the play, the playing space, the performance, scenic effects, masks and costumes, music and sound, etc. The book is well illustrated, and includes suggested research topics and a good general bibliography. It could be used as a useful source on theater history by both emerging and established theater scholars.

Guides and Bibliographies

65. Bailey, Claudia Jean, ed. *A Guide to Reference and Bibliography for Theatre Research.* 2d rev. and exp. ed. Columbus: Ohio State University, 1983. 149pp.

    This is an annotated guide to a broad range of materials in the field. The book is divided into two major sections. The first part, "General Reference" covers standard tools, national bibliographies, library catalogs, general periodical indexes, dissertations list, etc.; while the second, "Theatre and Drama" deals with more specialized materials. Arrangement in both parts is classified with entries by author, geographical location, and time period. General theater history is included in the section of bibliographies. About 650 titles published through the fall of 1979 are included with the majority of them on American and British theater. The guide is useful to the beginning student as well as the scholar. However, for a researcher in contemporary American theater the coverage of this time period is not sufficient enough.

66. Baker, Blanch. *Theatre and Allied Arts: A Guide to Books Dealing with the History, Criticism, and Technique of the Drama and Theatre and Related Arts and Crafts*. New York: B. Blom, 1967. 536pp.

Although this reference book was compiled and first published in the fifties, it is still a useful basic theater bibliography for both librarians and specialists. The guide is divided into three main parts. The first one is entitled, "Drama, Theatre, and Actors"; the second part is "Stagecraft and Allied Arts of the Theatre"; and the third section is called "Miscellaneous Reference Material." Each part is subdivided by subject and by geographical location. The arrangement of main entries is alphabetical by the author name. The information provided includes author, title, place of publication, publisher, date, pagination, etc. The guide is indexed.

67. Banham, Martin, ed. *The Cambridge Guide to World Theater*. New York: Cambridge University Press, 1989. 1104pp.

The purpose of this source is to offer a "comprehensive view of the history and present practice of theater in all parts of the world," as it is stated in the introduction. The book is encyclopedic in scope and world-wide in its breadth. The vast array of topics covered does not imply a surface treatment of these topics. All entries are signed, many of them are full- or multi-page in length. The information is presented in one alphabetical listing and includes historical and contemporary theater, stage and television, theater and show business people, etc. There are also entries covering such non-common topics as academic theater in the U.S., gay theater, theatrical education in the U.S., animal imper-sonification, popular theater and popular entertainment, carnivals, shadow puppets, censorship in the theater, sound, theories of drama, etc. This is a very useful reference tool which updates and seems to ex-pand considerably such standard sources as *The Oxford Companion to the Theater* (4th edition, 1984, Phyllis Hartnoll, editor) or *The Everyman Companion to the Theater* (by Peter Thomson, 1985).

68. *International Bibliography of Theatre*. New York: Theatre Research Data Center, Brooklyn College, City University of New York, 1985– . Annual.

This is a comprehensive reference tool that establishes a functional computerized classification system for the total field of theater on an in-ternational basis. This work is sponsored by The American Society for Theatre Research and The International Association of Libraries and Museums of the Performing Arts, in cooperation with the International Federation for Theatre Research. The year 1982 was covered in the 1985 book, while 1983 coverage was issued in 1986. The work identifies periodical coverage in various languages as well as books published in different countries. Entries are classified by subject with the subject index usually comprising two-thirds of the volume. The five-column "Taxonomy of the Theatre" serves as a table of contents and provides a structure for the arrangement of the 1,275 bibliographic entries. The listings not only include English translations of the titles of foreign-language articles and complete citations with indications of illustrations or notes, but also the content of each article is briefly summarized and its country and time period is identified. There are three indexes that provide access to the "Classed Entries": "The Document Author Index," "The Document Geography Index," and "The Subject Index." This source might greatly assist a theater scholar in any specific period in locating literature about playwrights, actors, directors, critics, etc.

69. Kienzle, Siegfried. *Modern World Theatre: A Guide to Productions in Europe and the United States Since 1945*. Translated by Alexander and Elizabeth Henderson. New York: Ungar, 1970. 509pp.

This work — a translation from the German *Modernes Welttheater* (1966) — describes and provides brief evaluative comments for 563 plays and their productions from the original version plus 15 which were added for the American one. Approximately 26 countries are represented with the majority of the plays from Germany, France, England, and the United States. Only the plays produced for the first time after 1945 are included. Entries are arranged alphabetically by playwright and play title. Information given includes the dates and location of publication, genre, time and place of the first performance, the action, and the locale. There is a title index. A useful source for a researcher in contemporary theater looking up a masterplot and the opening performance's date and place.

70. *Performing Arts Books, 1876–1981: Including an International Index of Current Serial Publications*. New York: Bowker, 1981. 1656pp.

This comprehensive source may serve as a basic tool for collection assessment and development as well as for reference and research. The bibliography, arranged by the Library of Congress subject headings, equally covers all aspects of performing arts, including "legitimate" theater and lists more than 50,000 titles with complete cataloging information for each. Scholars in American theater can compare entries for works on single subjects published over a period of time. The subject index includes 12,000 Library of Congress headings and is accessed with the aid of author and title indexes. Although this bibliography is not annotated, the Subject Area Directory helps the user to find the range of information included. There is also a listing of serials with a separate subject and title index.

71. Schoolcraft, Ralf Newman. *Performing Arts Books in Print: An Annotated Bibliography*. New York: Drama Book Specialists, 1973. 761pp.

The listings are restricted to books readily available in the United States at the year of the source's publication, and, with few exceptions, to materials in English. The work covers all aspects of performing arts, including literature on theater and drama. There are two major sections: works in print that were published prior to December 1970 and books published during 1971 with some additions. Each section is further subdivided by subject: books on theater and drama, books on technical arts of the theater, etc. Subject parts are in turn subdivided by geographical area, time period, etc. Good descriptive annotations make this book a valuable source.

72. Whalon, Marion K. *Performing Arts Research: A Guide to Information Sources*. Detroit: Gale Research, 1976. 280pp.

Designed as an "evaluative, annotated bibliography," the guide covers resources on many facets of the performing arts, including literature on theater. The cut-off date for bibliography was 1973. Arrangement is in seven main parts by format categories, such as: guides; dictionaries, encyclopedias, and handbooks; directories; etc. Entries provide complete bibliographic information with brief annotations that are merely descriptive. The work is indexed by authors, subjects, and titles. The guide suffers from organizational problems: it is difficult to locate a work on a particular time period, for example. However, it provides a great deal of information in one volume.

Library Catalogs

73. Angotti, Vincent L. *Source Materials in the Field of Theatre: An Annotated Bibliography, Subject Index and Guide to the Microfilm Collection*. Ann Arbor, Mich.: University Microfilms, c1973, (1967). 73pp.

This is a catalog of theater materials: books, periodicals, manuscripts, etc., that belong to various libraries or collections and are available on microfilm. Complete bibliographic information is provided and the annotations consist of a summary and critical interpretation of each text. There is also a subject index.

74. *The Center for Research Libraries Handbook 1987*. Chicago: Center for Research Libraries, 1987. 161pp.

This guide is published irregularly since 1969, and its purpose is to represent a convenient overview of the collections of the Center for Research Libraries. This Center is a cooperative venture of 150 research libraries (including those for research in humanities and theater) across the United States. This *Handbook* is a descriptive listing, arranged by subjects and categories, which characterizes the nature and the size of the collection. There is also a subject index. From a collection of 3.5 million volumes, the Center lends books to its members. Any institution that supports research or has a research library is eligible to join. This guide may be an important source for those academic libraries that do heavy interlibrary loan in support of scholarly research.

75. Hoblitzelle Theatre Arts Library. *A Guide to the Theatre and Drama Collections at the University of Texas*. Austin: Humanities Research Center, University of Texas, 1967. 84pp.

    Compiled by curator Frederick J. Hunter, this book is a catalog of the special collections in theater arts at the University of Texas. The guide may serve as a finding tool to those researchers in American theater who try to locate an obscure book not listed in conventional sources.

76. New York Public Library. Research Libraries. *Catalog of the Theatre and Drama Collections*. Boston: G. K. Hall, 1967–76. 51v.

    This is a massive reproduction of the card catalog of the New York Public Library outstanding collection of theater and drama materials established in 1931. Parts I and II were published in 1967. Part I is a "Drama Collection" (twelve volumes) consisting of two sections: a six-volume "Cultural Origin List" groups plays by language; and the six-volume "Author List" brings together editions, phonodiscs, promptbooks of plays, etc. Part II is a nine volume "Theatre Collection." It provides subjects, authors, and titles in alphabetical order and also includes periodicals. Part I covers editions of some 120,000 plays in Western languages (including translations); Part II contains about 121,000 entries for more than 23,5000 volumes of works relating to all aspects of the theater. Part III is a "Non-book Collections." It consists of 30 volumes and provides comprehensive coverage for such materials as programs, photographs, portraits, reviews, press clippings, scrapbooks, etc. — total 700,000 cards. There is an annual publication since 1975, *Bibliographic Guide to Theatre Arts*, produced by the same publisher, that serves as a supplement to the Library's *Catalog of the Theatre and Drama Collections* and provides information for newly acquired material. These sources give a researcher access to the comprehensive and unique collection with a wealth of reference and resource materials for a scholar.

77. *Performing Arts Resources*. New York: Drama Book Specialists, 1974–   . Annual.

    This is an annual publication sponsored by the Theatre Library Association in order to facilitate the search for materials on theater and other areas of performing arts and to provide a series of articles on special theater collections. In each volume there are articles describing the location, identity, and content of various collections of the performing arts. The scope of the publication also includes unpublished manuscripts, historical documents, and out-of-print materials. This is a useful tool for researchers in theater looking for unusual sources.

78. *Special Collections in College and University Libraries*. New York: Macmillan, 1989. 639pp.

    This guide could be a useful source for those scholars or academic libraries that do not have access to current editions of Lee Ash's *Subject Collections* (6th ed., 1985) or *Directory of Special Libraries and*

Information Centers (1963–   ). At any rate, published in 1989, this tool provides the most up-to-date information about special collections in academic libraries. Arrangement is alphabetical by institution within each state. Each entry includes names and descriptions of collections, general holdings, addresses, telephone numbers, and listings of key library administrators. There are subject and institutional indexes.

79. Young, William C. *American Theatrical Arts: A Guide to Manuscripts and Special Collections in the United States and Canada*. Chicago: American Library Association, 1971. 166pp.

    This guide lists the collections of 138 institutions, most of them in the United States. Arrangement is alphabetical by state and then by institution. The entries cover manuscripts, playbills, theater history documents, posters, promptbooks, letters, diaries, brochures, contracts, photographs, recordings, etc. – all of them are primary source materials on the theatrical arts (legitimate theater, vaudeville, burlesque, etc.). All entries are numbered and the tool is indexed by persons and by subjects. Most entries indicate the number of pieces in the collection. Many of the covered collections have not been cataloged and do not appear in the Library of Congress union list of manuscripts or in any other national listing. This guide is a very valuable aid for a scholar in American theater in his inquiry and research.

Dictionaries

80. Bowman, Walter P. and Robert H. Ball. *Theatre Language: A Dictionary of Terms in English of the Drama and Stage from Medieval to Modern Times*. New York: Theatre Arts, 1976. 428pp.

    This useful reference source focuses only on the "legitimate" theater and provides concise definitions of theatrical language employed in the Great Britain and the United States.

81. Lounsbury, Warren C. and Norman Boulanger. *Theatre Backstage from A to Z*. 3rd ed. Seattle, Wash.: University of Washington Press, 1983. 213pp.

    The authors intended to "present an alphabetized explanation of the terminology and methods peculiar to technical theater." The terms selected for this dictionary are adequately defined and the explanations are concise. The entries cover the following topics: lighting, sound, set construction, scene design, properties, backstage responsibilities, etc. Entries are cross-referenced, and there are good illustrations throughout the entire volume. The work begins with a detailed historical essay on the evolution of theater backstage technology. The authors also provide a helpful list of theatrical equipment manufactures and a selected bibliography on scene design and lighting. The language is clear and concise, but the descriptions of processes are sometimes too superficial for a professional, when in order to gain entry to information a professional knowledge of technical theater terminology is presupposed. However, as a whole, this is a helpful reference work, and both the theater historian and technical theater professional should find many uses for this dictionary.

82. Packard, William, David Pickering, and Charlotte Savidge, eds. *The Facts on File Dictionary of the Theater*. New York: Facts on File, 1989. 556pp.

This dictionary contains 5,000 essays on a variety of topics: plays, historic dramatic styles, innovations and genres, technical terms, theatrical organizations, biographies of producers, directors, playwrights, actors, actresses, theatrical companies, school, and associations. The coverage is international, though emphasis is on British and American theater. The compilers focus on the contemporary stage, and provide a very good coverage of today theater (Off Off Broadway, for example), modern drama, critics, and technical terms. The arrangement is alphabetical, and there are extensive cross-references. However, a bibliography for further reference is a regrettable omission. Because of its generally broad scope, this tool is a useful source for brief, factual quarries and verification of basic information.

83. Trapido, Joel, ed. *An International Dictionary of Theatre Language*. Westport, Conn.: Greenwood Press, 1985. 1032pp.

This comprehensive reference source includes over 15,000 terms with approximately 10,000 drawn from the English-speaking theater, while the remaining 5,000 came from 60 different languages. The editors included only those foreign terms that were used in English-language publications. Excluded are terms from the mass media, and from other forms of entertainment not fully theatrical, such as the circus, magic shows, or night clubs. The work is straight-forward: the terms are defined, but seldom explained. The entry consists of the heading, language of origin, meaning, and definition. Some entries also have citations to sources of additional definitions or include a brief discussion. The work contains extensive bibliography and cross-references. The volume includes an interesting essay by Trapido on the history of theater dictionaries and glossaries. This one-volume dictionary seems to be an excellent research tool, an indispensable aid for theater students and scholars.

Encyclopedias

84. Esslin, Martin, ed. *The Encyclopedia of World Theatre*. New York: Scribner, 1977. 320pp.

Martin Esslin, noted theater critic, has prepared, revised, and updated this one-volume reference work based on the German *Friedrichs The-*

aterlexikon (1969). The present book is an expansive encyclopedia of persons associated with all aspects of the theater, plays, playhouses, terms, trends, and national surveys. There are about 2,000 entries, many of which contain bibliographical references. The information provided is concise. Coverage is better for European theater, though Esslin deleted many German-oriented titles in favor of those of more importance for a researcher in English-speaking theater. The 400 black-and-white illustrations add visual dimension and compliment the varied entries. There are explanations of abbreviations, cross-references, and an index of play titles. Covering both historical and current aspects of theater, this is an excellent tool for a researcher.

85. Hartnoll, Phyllis, ed. *The Oxford Companion to the Theatre*. 4th ed. New York: Oxford University Press, 1985, 1983. 934pp.

Since its initial edition in 1951 Hartnoll's work has been an old standard in the reference department. In the fourth edition such topics as ballet and opera were dropped and cuts were made in the area of stage technology. However, the work does an excellent job in its focus on the "legitimate" theater. Though the long survey articles on the theater in individual countries were somewhat reduced, the book's coverage on American modern theater is better than in Esslin's *Encyclopedia*. Coverage is given on a variety of new topics, especially in the field of contemporary American theater, such as "Chicano Theatre" and "Chicago." The work is illustrated. There are bibliography and cross-references. For a researcher looking for concise and brief factual information rather than for comprehensive surveys, Hartnoll's *Oxford Companion* remains a very useful tool.

Directories

86. Heys, Sandra, comp. *Contemporary Stage Roles for Women: A Descriptive Catalog*. Westport, Conn.: Greenwood Press, 1985. 195pp.

This directory opens with a short introductory essay dealing with the problem of stereotypes, improving roles, and redesigning male roles for women. This source presents about 200 plays with approximately 800 roles for women. The directory consists of two main parts. The first one lists plays alphabetically by title. The information provided includes author, date of publication, summary of the plot, number of male and female characters, and a list of female roles, each of them categorized as lead, supporting, short, etc. In the second part, the plays are classified by the ages of the characters and character types, such as heroic, comic, etc. The description also includes unusual physical characteristics of roles. The author specifies the criteria for selection of the plays: women have substantial roles, plays are artistic and dramatically sound, and there are no negative female stereotypes. In addition, the author provides a list of agents and publishers with addresses and a bibliography. The book includes index of characters and index of dramatists. This directory is a convenient and useful tool for actors, producers, directors, and also for those researchers in contemporary theater interested in genre distribution of roles in the play.

87. Kullman, Colby H. and William C. Young, eds. *Theatre Companies of the World*. Westport, Conn.: Greenwood Press, 1986. 2v.

This is a comprehensive directory of theater companies around the world. Theater companies are defined as permanent acting groups under contract for a specific period each year who perform a season of plays that includes nonmusical productions. Part-time companies without regular contracts, such as mime, puppetry, etc., are included also if they best represent the tradition of theater in various regions. Each entry provides the name and address, significance of the company, its history, including names of founders, philosophy of production, names of dramatists working with the company, important productions, etc. Though this important source allows a user to develop a comprehensive picture of theater climate in each country, the usefulness of the tool for a researcher in modern American theater is limited because the U.S. entries are very selective.

88. Slide, Anthony, Patricia K. Hanson, and Stephen L. Hanson, comps. *Sourcebook for the Performing Arts: A Directory of Collections, Resources, Scholars, and Critics in Theater, Film, and Television*. Westport, Conn.: Greenwood Press, 1988. 227pp.

The bulk of the directory is comprised by the two major sections. The first one, arranged alphabetically by state, profiles institutions with major collections in theater, television, radio, and film. Each entry consists of a name, address, telephone number, and a description of holdings. The second section offers brief biographies of scholars, critics, historians, archivists, and librarians in the areas of theater, film, radio, and television. There is also a third part of this directory that provides basic information on bookshops, journals, publishers, film and television studios, television networks, U.S. film commissions, and international film commissions. It is a comprehensive source that attempts to bring together a variety of useful information in the areas of the performing arts previously available only through searching many different reference tools. Unfortunately, only two major sections of the directory are indexed.

Biographical Sources

89. Bryan, George B. *Stage Lives: A Bibliography and Index to Theatrical Biographies in English*. Westport, Conn.: Greenwood Press, 1985. 368pp.

The work attempts to be all-inclusive, and covers almost 3,000 entries: 2,500 individual and 200 collective biographies of nearly 4,000 theater personalities from the ancient Greeks to modern Americans. Coverage provided is international, but only works written in English are included. "Stage Lives" are those of playwrights, actors, directors, musicians, designers, producers, critics—all kind of people who are significant to live theater. There is a very good index that gives stage names of theatrical personalities, their actual names, married names, dates of birth and death, areas of their creative work, etc. The source may prove a useful aid to a research in any specific period of theater. However, there are some unfortunate omissions, like Peter O'Toole's biography, for example. Bryan's index is better used as a supplement or extension to such important biographical sources as Wearing's *American and British Theatrical Biography . . .* (1979) or *Performing Arts Biography Master Index* (1982).

90. *Contemporary Theatre, Film, and Television: A Biographical Guide Featuring Performers, Directors, Writers, Producers, Designers, Managers, Choreographers, Technicians, Composers, Executives, Dancers, and Critics in the United States and Great Britain.* O'Donnell, Owen and Linda S. Hubbard, eds. Detroit: Gale Research, 1984– . 7v.

This work expands and supersedes two of the same publisher's long-running series of biographical reference sources, *Who's Who in the Theatre* and *Who Was Who in the Theatre*. It adds new categories of persons included, as indicated in the subtitle, because of the expansion of activities of theatrical personalities across media boundaries. The work is modeled on the Gale's *Contemporary Authors,* and each volume includes new biographies of new and established talents. However, there is no attempt to update previous entries. Each volume contains about 250 photographic portraits and provides about 700 biographical entries of people active in the field at the present time and of those who are not but played an important role in their media. With the volume seven, the series now contains over 3,800 biographies and 1,400 photographs. Information provided is often obtained from the biographies or their agents. The emphasis of the series is on the United States. Entries provide personal data, education, debut dates, credits, awards, etc. However, the entries vary widely in length and content with the resulted unevenness in the information level. There is a cumulative index in the last volume that covers all previous volumes and also the last volumes of *Who's Who in the Theatre.* The series is now published biannually, enhancing its reference value. This publication is an important reference tool for those researchers who need background biographical information.

91. Herbert, Ian, Christine Baxter and Robert E. Finley, eds. *Who's Who in the Theatre: A Biographical Record of the Contemporary Stage.* 17th ed. Detroit: Gale Research, 1981. 2v.

Though historically this source was limited to theater personalities associated with the London stage, in the 17th edition there is a greater coverage on Americans. About 2,400 prominent living persons active in the literary and artistic areas of the theater are included. This guide brings coverage up to the end of the 1979–80 theater season. Volume 2 is the "Playbills" volume and includes playbills from both London and New York. Even with the existing new Gale's publication, *Contemporary Theatre, Film, and Television...*, *Who's Who in the Theatre* remains a monumental research tool.

92. Kaplan, Mike, ed. *Variety: International Showbusiness Reference*. New York: Garland, 1983. 877pp.

This source provides all kinds of information about people and events of the entertainment world. There are brief biographies of 6,000— mostly contemporary—theatrical personalities; lists of people who were winners or nominees for the Oscar, Tony, Emmy, and Grammy Awards; 50 top Nelson shows for the period of 20 years, 1960–80; the Pulitzer Prize plays, etc. There are no Off Broadway play listings, and the Broadway play listings do not provide the length of the run. The film and TV credits for stage personalities cover only 1976–80 period. This source is far from being a comprehensive tool, and though the more obscure play or biographical details of a stage personality, the more they are being sought, some researchers in modern American theater may still find use for this compilation.

93. McNeil, Barbara and Miranda Herbert, eds. *Performing Arts Biography Master Index: A Consolidated Index to Over 270,000 Biographical Sketches of Persons Living and Dead, as They Appear in Over 100 of the Principal Biographical Dictionaries Devoted to the Performing Arts*. 2d ed. Detroit: Gale Research, 1982. 701pp.

This is an expanded edition of the 1979 Gale publication, *Theatre, Film and Television Biographies Master Index* with the coverage increased by more than double of the number of citations to sketches in biographical dictionaries. A wide spectrum of the performing arts, including "legitimate" theater, is represented. The entries include birth and death dates and page citations in the source. The biographical dictionaries cited in the *Index* are considered by the editors to be readily available in most libraries, making this book a valuable and practical aid in research in any specific type of theater.

94. *Who Was Who in the Theatre, 1912–1976*: A Biographical Dictionary of Actors, Actresses, Directors, Playwrights, and Producers of the English-Speaking Theatre. Detroit: Gale Research, 1978. 4v.

This set contains more than 4,100 entries in a single alphabetical listing and provides brief biographical information, person's original name, education, credits, favorite parts, interests, and last address known. The source includes all individuals listed in the first 15 editions of *Who's Who in the Theatre*. Death dates are given through 1976. Though the entries appear reasonably informative, this source could be more valuable for minor theatrical personalities rather than for major ones on whom individual biographies were written.

Dissertations

95. Black, Dorothy M. *Guide to Lists of Master's Theses*. Chicago: American Library Association, 1965. 144pp.

    This guide presents a classified (by subjects) and briefly annotated list of Master theses written in the United States and Canada through 1964. Works on drama and theater are included and have special references.

96. *Comprehensive Dissertation Index*. Ann Arbor, Mich.: University Microfilms International, 1988. 5v.

    This powerful tool provides fast access to current research information in all subject areas, including drama and performing arts. It contains citations of nearly 34,000 doctoral dissertations written in North America Universities, plus 2,300 British dissertations and 2,600 dissertations worldwide. There are three ways to locate information — by subject, by author, and by a keyword. Each entry includes dissertation title, author, degree, year, school name, number of pages, and location of the abstract in *Dissertation Abstract International*. A publication number for full-text ordering is also provided. This useful source helps a scholar and a student of modern theater to be in the forefront of research developments in the humanities and the arts.

97. *Comprehensive Dissertation Index, 1861–1972*. Ann Arbor, Mich.: Xerox University Microfilms, 1973. 37v.

    If the previous source provides access to current research information, this comprehensive index offers historical perspective and records practically all doctoral dissertations written in American universities over the course of more than hundred years. Languages and literature are covered in volumes 29–30. There are numerous entries for playwrights and their plays. Volume 31 presents dissertations on theater (pp. 591–961) and other fields of the performing arts (pp. 269–589). This multi-volume work is a computer-generated index to such sources as *Dissertation Abstracts International*, *American Doctoral Dissertations*, etc. Access is made easier by an index of keywords selected from the dissertation titles and arranged under broader subjects. There are regular supplements and also five- and ten-year cumulations.

98. *Dissertation Abstracts International*. Ann Arbor, Mich.: University Microfilms, 1956– . Monthly.

    The author and subject indexes cumulate annually in this source which is not comprehensive. Institutions where the dissertations were written contributed information selectively. Only the abstracted dissertations were included.

99. Merenda, Merilyn D. and J.W. Plichak. *Speech Communications and Theater Arts: A Classified Bibliography of Theses and Dissertations, 1973–78.* New York: Plenum, 1979. 326pp.

This useful source provides a classified by categories and subjects list of theses and doctoral dissertations written in the areas of speech and theater arts. The work is indexed.

Part II. Major Information Sources in American Theater After 1945

3. Literature and Drama

Histories and Critiques

100. Abbot, Anthony S. *The Vital Lie: Reality and Illusion in Modern Drama*.
Alabama University Press, 1989. 239pp.

In his scholarly monograph, the author examines the complex dimensions of these seeming polarities, which, finally, become one — illusion and reality. The theme reality versus illusion is extremely important for understanding contemporary American drama, and is the one that connects all Western drama, from the Greeks through its modern forms. The author discusses such major theatrical figures as Eugene O'Neill, Arthur Miller, Tennessee Williams, Edward Albee and the absurdists; and he emphasizes the philosophical and the theatrical meaning of their works. The book is carefully prepared and well researched, and — with the systematic treatment of the theme illusion versus reality — offers a comprehensive modern historical survey of contemporary drama. *The Vital Lie* may be used by a student or scholar as an important source for better understanding of contemporary American drama, the one that brings a reader closer to the very definition of the modern.

101. Adler, Thomas P. *Mirror on the Stage: The Pulitzer Plays as an Approach to American Drama*. West Lafayette, Ind.: Purdue University Press, 1987. 350pp.

Though not a standard reference source, Adler's book may serve as a well-researched survey of contemporary American drama. The author does not repeat the previous works on Pulitzer Prize plays, such as John Toohey's *A History of the Pulitzer Prize Plays* (1967), John Hohenberg's *The Pulitzer Prize: A History of the Awards* (1974), or Jane Bonin's *Major Themes in Prize-Winning American Drama* (1975). He also does not group the plays around common themes, but rather provides a scientific analysis of individual dramas and of the major trends in the development of contemporary American drama. Researchers in American theater and drama after 1945 may consult this work for distinguished comments on America's most important plays. The book has an index and a bibliography.

31

102. Auslander, Philip. *The New York School Poets as Playwrights: O'Hara, Ashbery, Koch, Scuyler, and the Visual Arts*. New York: P. Lang, 1989. 179pp. (Literature and the Visual Arts Series, Vol. 3).

This interesting study provides a researcher or a student of the history of contemporary American theater with a critical introduction to a little-known but important body of drama. The author analyzes the New York School of poets, which forms, from his point of view, an intriguing chapter in the history of the American literary and theatrical avant-garde. Their works are discussed in the general cultural context of the fifties and sixties when visual and literary arts collaborated and exchanged ideas. The first part of the monograph presents an account of the New York School in transition and the theory of Pop Art. The second part gives the cultural background through a brief discussion of the contemporary theatrical milieux in which the poets and artists worked. Chapters three, four, five, and six present individual poets as playwrights, and the concluding chapter presents a concept of postmodernism in drama. In the appendix the author included a chronology of events in the history of New York School, contemporary painting, poetry, and theater, which provides a useful overview of the cultural atmosphere. This book is a good source for studying an interesting period in the history of contemporary drama.

103. Bigsby, C.W.E. *A Critical Introduction to Twentieth-Century American Drama*. New York: Cambridge University Press, 1982–1985. 3v.

This work is a useful critical guide in three volumes. Volume 1 deals with the 1900–1940 time period. Volume 2 takes up in 1940 and contains a scholarly analysis of the plays by Tennessee Williams, Arthur Miller, and Edward Albee. Volume 3 presents theatrical development outside of New York and is called "Beyond Broadway." In his synthesis of contemporary American drama, the author clearly relates the works of each playwright to the major trends in art, philosophy, psychology, and politics (the McCarthy hearings) during his time. Fine scholarship and clarity of ideas make this work an important tool for research in modern American drama and theater. A bibliography and indexes are included.

104. Bigsby, C.W.E. *Confrontation and Commitment: A Study of Contemporary American Drama, 1959–1966*. University of Missouri Press, 1969. 187pp.

Among the playwrights analyzed in this important study of contemporary American drama are Arthur Miller, Edward Albee, James Baldwin, Leroi Jones, and Lorraine Hansberry. According to the author, two concepts are the most meaningful for the generation after the World War II: confrontation and commitment; and with this approach, he provides an analysis of the development of contemporary American drama. The book includes a bibliography and an index.

105. Bock, Hedwig and Albert Wertheim. *Essays on Contemporary American Drama*. Munich: M. Hueber, 1981. 302pp.

This book is a collection of scholarly essays written by acknowledged American and European theater and drama critics. The essays cover the aesthetical and historical development of the contemporary American drama. Among the playwrights discussed are such major figures of the history of American theater as Tennessee Williams, Arthur Miller, Edward Albee, Arthur Kopit, Sam Shepard, David Rabe, and others. There are essays that provide a general overview of important plays and movements in contemporary black, Chicano, or feminist theater. A useful annotated bibliography is also provided.

106. Bogard, Travis, Richard Moody, and Walter J. Meserve. *American Drama*. New York: Barnes & Noble, 1978. 324pp.

This book belongs to the series,"The Revels History of the Drama in English." A detailed historical analysis of the development of American drama is preceded by a chronological table of major historical and theatrical events from the very beginning of American theater to 1975. There are also a bibliographic essay and indexes.

107. Brater, Enoch, ed. *Feminine Focus: The New Women Playwrights*. New York: Oxford University Press, 1989. 283pp.

This is a collection of critical essays analyzing plays written by contemporary women dramatists. The coverage is international with the special emphasis on modern American drama. Out of many possible approaches to discussing the feminist drama, the editor intends to pursue the interest women playwrights show in deromanticizing and "earthing" the traditional images of women in contemporary theater. This collection of essays offers an interesting view on modern drama, and may be used by historians of American theater for understanding nontraditional aspects of modern American plays.

108. Cohn, Ruby. *New American Dramatists, 1960–1980*. New York: Grove Press, 1982. 186pp.

Beginning with Neil Simon's *Golden Boy* and concluding with Sam Shepard's plays, the author discusses 30 published American playwrights, among them Arthur Kopit, Terence McNally, Lannford Wilson, David Rabe, David Mamet, and others. Although the book's major concern is explication rather than analysis, it is nevertheless an important introduction to new voices in contemporary American drama.

109. Counts, Michael L. *Coming Home: The Soldier's Return in Twentieth-Century American Drama*. (American University Studies. Series IV. English language and Literature) New York: P. Lang, 1988. 228pp.

This interesting and highly original study sheds new light on the history of the twentieth-century American drama. The author analyzes historical and sociological impact of 55 plays and their productions which depict the return of the soldier from war. The book is divided into four sections: a select history of the homecomer drama, a background on the wars which produced these plays, a discussion of the plays, and a conclusion. There is a useful bibliography and an index.

110. Demastes, William W. *Beyond Naturalism: A New Realism in American Theater*. (Contributions in Drama and Theater Studies Series). New York: Greenwood Press, 1988. 174pp.

In his valuable monograph, the author re-emphasizes the flexibility and significance of the realistic approach in contemporary American drama. Demastes offers a well balanced and often insightful analysis of modern American dramatists, such as Fuller, Henley, Mamet, Norman, Rabe, Shepard, and others, and intends to show how they are transcending the naturalistic forms of their predecessors. From the author's point of view, these playwrights share the outlook of the absurdists but use surface realism to express their understanding of life. New realistic plays of the American theater, the author insists, offer a view on modern existence as too complex for easy social solutions, and depict human actions and language as too ambiguous and without any logic. The book includes a comprehensive bibliography and is well indexed. It is also well illustrated with black-and-white production photographs. *Beyond Naturalism* is a useful source for understanding the important aspects of contemporary American drama.

111. Downer, Alan Seymour, ed. *American Drama and Its Critics: A Collection of Essays*. Chicago: University of Chicago Press, 1975. 258pp.

This book is a collection of critical essays on American drama written from the beginning of the twentieth century to 1965. Even more than 20 years after its publication, this work still can be used by researchers in contemporary American theater and drama. The essays are arranged to show the historical development of American drama and the changes of its critics' attitudes and approaches.

112. Eddleman, Floyd Eugene. *American Drama Criticism: Interpretations, 1890–1977*. 2d ed. Hamden, Conn.: Shoe String Press, 1979. 488pp.

113. Eddleman, Floyd Eugene. *American Drama Criticism: Supplement I to the Second Edition*. Hamden, Conn.: Shoe String Press, 1984. 255pp.

114. Eddleman, Floyd Eugene. *American Drama Criticism: Supplement II to the Second Edition*. Hamden, Conn.: Shoe String Press, 1989. 269pp.

The historical development of twentieth-century American drama is covered here through the sources of critical writings. These are critiques and reviews of American plays that appeared in some 200 books and monographs and in more than 400 periodicals between 1890 and 1977. The period after 1945 receives a detailed coverage. Supplement I to the second edition was published by the same publisher and under the same title in 1984, and continued coverage through 1983 (about 1,300 interpretations were added). Supplement II appeared in 1989 and continued coverage through 1988. The work is arranged by dramatist, and books and articles about individual plays are listed under the playwright's name. Interviews, biographies, and non-dramatic works of playwrights are excluded. The dates of first production are noted. There are indexes of critics and of adapted authors and works. The compiler included "see" references to help keep clear the numerous variations in spelling and joint authorships. This source is one of the most comprehensive listings of critiques and interpretations of contemporary American drama.

115. Elliot, Emory, ed. *Columbia Literary History of the United States*. New York: Columbia University Press, 1988. 1263pp.

This work is not comprehensive, and it is less a history than a collection of critical essays covering many facets of American literature and drama from the different contemporary points of view. The book is divided into five broad time periods, each with a different editor. Each section deals with major American writers and dramatists and with literary movements and genres. The book includes an excellent index, but it lacks the detailed bibliography. Researchers in modern American theater and drama may use this book as a helpful source providing quite diverse contemporary views.

116. Freedman, Morris. *American Drama in Social Context*. Carbondale: Southern Illinois University Press, 1971. 143pp.

In this scientific study the author explores the ways in which contemporary American drama (among others: Albee, Kopit, Miller, Jones) reflects the social values of the time. The book also deals with the essential qualities of modern American tragedy and of playwriting as an art. There are selected bibliography and an index. Freedman's book may serve as a useful source of information for a researcher in modern American drama.

117. Gould, Jean. *Modern American Playwrights*. New York: Dodd, Mead, 1966. 302pp.

This is a well-researched survey of contemporary American drama. Such playwrights as Edward Albee, Arthur Miller, and Tennessee Williams are studied at length. The book is well illustrated with photographs. It includes an index and a bibliography.

118. Harriott, Esther. *American Voices: Five Contemporary Playwrights in Essays and Interviews*. Jefferson, NC: McFarland, 1988. 189pp.

The author of this monograph presents theater as an important reflection of American society. She approaches contemporary American theater as public art that intends to make a cultural statement through a particular generation. From the author's point of view, the five playwrights she chose — Charles Fuller, David Mamet, Marsha Norman,

Sam Shepard, and Lanford Wilson—are representatives of the modern theater in this country for their image of America as a violent and unstable society. These dramatists are analyzed within the context of the development of American theater and drama. The interviews with writers add a personal touch to the critical essays about them. Though the scope of this scientific monograph is smaller than, for example, *In Their Own Words* by David Savran (1988), which includes 20 playwrights, or *Interviews with Contemporary Women Playwrights* by Kathleen Betsko and Rachel Koening (1987), which consists of 30 interviews, Esther Harriott's book offers a fresh look at the contemporary drama and is an important source useful for anybody involved in studying modern American theater. The monograph has an adequate bibliography.

119. Herman, William. *Understanding Contemporary American Drama*. Columbia, S.C.: South Carolina University Press, 1987. 271pp.

The author covers the development of American drama from 1964 to 1984 and concentrates on five individual dramatists: Sam Shepard, David Rabe, David Mamet, Ed Billins, and Lanford Wilson. The book includes an index and selective bibliography. Though this work is mostly intended for a lay person, some researchers in contemporary American theater may find it useful.

120. Jay, Gregory S., ed. *Modern American Critics, 1920–1955*. Detroit: Gale Research, 1988. 384pp.

Academic audience will find this reference tool very useful. The book is devoted to the analysis of the major works of modern American critics who flourished between 1920 and 1955, such as Kenneth Burke, Cleanth Brooks, Van Wyck Brooks, T. S. Eliot, H. L. Mencken, Lewis Mumford, Ezra Pound, John Crowe Ransom, Allen Tate, Edmund Wilson, and other important critics significant for their cultural, not just literary or dramatic commentaries. The author also included a bibliography of the critic's writings, a selected list of studies about the critic, and the location of his papers. This handy tool is a part of the "Dictionary of Literary Biography" series (vol. 63), and some of the essays are interconnected with other volumes in series.

121. Lenz, Gunter H., Harmut Keil and Sabine Brock-Sallah, eds. *Reconstructing American Literary and Historical Studies*. Chicago: St. Martin Press, 1990. 435pp.

This collection of essays is not directly related to the history of the contemporary American drama. However, the book might be of interest and considerable help to a researcher or a student in this field. This source provides critical view on the recent efforts in American literary and historical studies, incorporating various studies on different genres and innovative research methods and strategies. The authors also analyze the cultural meaning of women or ethnic writings in literary or historical studies and the scope and objectives in any serious research in literature and history.

122. Lewis, Allan. *American Plays and Playwrights of the Contemporary Theatre: Revised Edition*. New York: Crown Publishers, 1970. 270pp.

The author provides an in-depth study of modern American drama, analyzes new themes and forms, new trends and movements, giving a background for every contemporary development. Among the playwrights discussed are Albee, Grotovski, Horovitz, Kopit, Miller, Scisgal, and others. The book includes an index.

123. Marranca, Bonnie. *American Playwrights: A Critical Survey*. New York: Drama Book Specialists, 1981. 238pp.

The book focuses on New York City playwrights, and the author selects eighteen dramatists who represent the Off Broadway theater since the 1960s. A brief introductory essay is provided for each playwright along with the analysis of his individual plays. The author also gives an assessment of each dramatist's creative development and their place in contemporary American drama. There is no bibliography, and the treatment of material is often too brief. However, some researchers in modern American theater may find this book useful, especially in regards to the history of the New York experimental theater companies, where several of these dramatists' careers developed.

124. Meserve, Walter, ed. *Discussions of Modern American Drama*. New York: D.C. Heath, 1966. 150pp.

This book is a collection of essays that provide a picture of the development of modern American drama after 1945, its new forms and themes. The authors are foremost American playwrights and critics: Lionel Trilling, Harold Clerman, Robert Brustein, Mary McCarthy, Eugene O'Neill, Tennessee Williams, and Edward Albee. These essays may be a valuable source for a researcher in modern American theater.

125. Palmer, Richard H. *The Critics' Canon: Standards of Theatrical Reviewing in America*. (Contributions in Drama and Theater Studies Series). New York: Greenwood Press, 1988. 183pp.

This is a well-written book, which purpose, as the author states, is to demonstrate "the ways of critics to theatre practitioners, the ways of theatre to inexperienced reviewers." Palmer explains the nature of reviewing (without distinguishing between criticism and a review), obligations of the reviewer to his readers, theatergoers, and the journalistic professional consideration. The author also analyzes all important aspects of the theater show being reviewed, such as the script of the play, the actors and the acting, the direction, etc. The book includes examples of theater reviews of the 1986–87 season. It is an interesting reading for anybody who loves and cares about modern theater, and also a useful source for theater professionals and students and researchers of contemporary American theater and drama.

126. Porter, Thomas E. *Myth and Modern American Drama*. Detroit: Wayne
State University Press, 1969. 285pp.
This careful, detailed, and interesting study may be of use to a student
or a researcher of modern American theater and drama. The author
brings together an enormous body of critical writing; and in his analysis
of major contemporary plays (such as *Mourning Becomes Electra* by E.
O'Neill, *Death of a Salesman* and *The Crucible* by A. Miller, *A Streetcar
Named Desire* by T. Williams, *Our Town* by T. Wilder, *Who's Afraid
of Virginia Woolf?* by E. Albee, and some others) attempts to develop
a critical approach to the concept of myth in modern drama. The author
offers some sharp insights and links the plays with the cultural atmosphere of their time.

127. Savran, David. *In Their Own Words: Contemporary American Playwrights*. New York: Theatre Communications Group, 1988. 320pp.
The author, who is the head of a drama department in one of the
Canadian universities, interviewed twenty contemporary playwrights,
including Christopher Durang, Charles Fuller, John Guare, David
Mamet, Marsha Norman, David Rabe, August Wilson, Lanford
Wilson, and some others. The author precedes each interview with a
brief critical essay on a playwright. The purpose of the book is to illuminate the state of contemporary American drama, and the political
and social awareness of modern theater. The playwrights express their
own opinions, talk about the progress of their careers, and their working methods, providing an extremely interesting picture of today's
theater.

128. Schlueter, June, ed. *Feminist Rereadings of Modern American Drama*.
Rutherford, N.J.: Fairleigh Dickinson University Press, 1989. 253pp.
This interesting book is a collection of critical essays written by
women-theater scholars. They discuss—from the feminist point of
view—plays of five major American playwrights: Eugene O'Neill, Arthur Miller, Tennessee Williams, Edward Albee, and Sam Shepard. The
essays are arranged not in chronological order or by any literary aspect,
but by a playwright. Representing rereadings, in feminist terms, of most
important plays in modern American drama, these scholarly essays
offer an interesting and new approach to drama criticism.

129. Schroeder, Patricia R. *The Presence of the Past in Modern American
Drama*. Cranbury, N.J.: Associated University Presses, 1989. 148pp.
The author of this interesting scientific monograph analyzes the
historical development of contemporary American drama from an
unusual point of view: a unique relationship of drama to time; a por-
trayal of the past as a crucial problem for a playwright; the playwrights'
methods for connecting past to the present. The author explores the
vision of the past as the one that prompted innovation in American

dramatic form. The book deals mostly with four major playwrights: Eugene O'Neill, Thornton Wilder, Arthur Miller, and Tennessee Williams. The author's scholarship is careful; the footnotes and bibliographies also show the author's wide knowledge of biographies and published critical works. The book includes helpful selected bibliography on the subject, and an index.

130. Shewey, Don, ed. and compl. *Out Front: Contemporary Gay and Lesbian Plays.* New York: Grove Press, 1988. 564pp.

This book is an anthology of plays. However, because of the detailed introduction and because of the book's subject matter, it may serve as a helpful source of up-to-date information for those scholars of contemporary American drama who are interested in gay theater. This anthology presents a milestone of gay culture, because gays and lesbians use the theatrical stage as a public medium for considering their own issues and presenting their points of view to the general audience. In his introduction, the editor and compiler analyzes the history of American gay theater and its naturalistic, documentary, parodic, or farcial dramas. There is useful bibliography and notes on contributors.

131. Simard, Rodney. *Postmodern Drama: Contemporary Playwrights in America and Britain.* Lanham, Md.: University Press of America, 1984. 163pp.

The author offers an interesting point of view on the development of modern English-speaking drama. He brings up the concept of a postmodern aesthetic that distinguishes itself from the modern one and is a "synthesis of realism and absurdism." Within the context of this definition, he discusses in details the works of Edward Albee, Sam Shepard, David Rabe, and of some British playwrights, such as Harold Pinter and Tom Stoppard. Focusing on the difficult task of defining a theatrical phenomenon which is still in the process of self-definition, Simard offers an unusual angle for looking at contemporary drama.

132. Weales, Gerald. *The Jumping Off Place: American Drama in the 1960's.* New York: Macmillan, 1969. 306pp.

This book is a study of American drama during 1960s. The author discusses playwrights Tennessee Williams, Arthur Miller, Edward Albee, LeRoi Jones, James Baldwin, Robert Lowell, Lawrence Ferlinghetti, Joseph Heller, and others. The value of this well-researched work is also in its sense of time: it is written not from the distance of twenty years but in 1969, from the "1960s" point of view.

Guides and Bibliographies

133. Altick, Richard D. and Andrew Wright. *Selective Bibliography for the Study of English and American Literature.* 6th ed. New York: Macmillan, 1979. 180pp.

This is a selective bibliography of research materials in English and American literature, including drama. Arrangement of the entries is by categories. The book includes author and title indexes.

134. Bateson, Frederick W. and Harrison T. Meserole. *A Guide to English and American Literature*. 3d ed. New York: Gordian Press, 1976. 334pp.
       This is a guide to resource material in research in English and American literature and drama. Entries arranged chronologically by historical periods and then by categories, such as general reference works, bibliographies, monographs dealing with literary and dramatic criticism and scholarly research. The guide is indexed.

135. Bonin, Jane F. *Prize-Winning American Drama: A Bibliographical and Descriptive Guide*. Metuchen, N.J.: Scarecrow, 1973. 222pp.
       This work gives a chronological record of plays which won significant American theater prizes from 1917/18 through 1970/71 season. The author provides a historical background for each play, brief summary of the plot, performance history, notes on critical reception, and selective bibliography of criticism. The book includes an index.

136. Bracken, James K., ed. *Reference Works in British and American Literature*. Vol. I: *English and American Literature*. Englewood, Col.: Libraries Unlimited, 1990. 252pp.
       Vol. II: *English and American Writers*. Englewood, Col.: Libraries Unlimited. To be published in 1991. 400pp. (Reference Sources in the Humanities Series; James Rettig, ed.).
       Volume I of the set deals with British and American literature and drama and includes more than 500 well annotated entries, which cover general and specialized research guides, encyclopedias and dictionaries, handbooks, historical studies, indexes and abstracts, general and specialized bibliographies, biographical sources, periodicals, and major associations and research centers. Annotations are evaluative and helpful in understanding the bibliographic control of the literature covered by the source. There are also extensive cross-references to other works. Volume II is going to cover more than 500 individual English and American writers and playwrights historical studies, guides and bibliographies, encyclopedias and dictionaries, and other reference tools. The set will provide a critical bibliographic guidance to the many reference works on English and American literature and drama.

137. *Contemporary Authors: Bibliographical Series*. Vol. 3: *American Dramatists*. Matthew Roudane, ed. Detroit: Gale Research, 1989. 484pp.
       It is an indispensable source for students and scholars in modern American drama since 1945. Volume 3 of the series provides in-depth treatment of the scholarship concerning major contemporary American

dramatists. The editors included bibliographies on seventeen playwrights; among them Edward Albee, Amiri Baraka, Lorraine Hansberry, Beth Henley, David Mamet, Carson McCullers, Arthur Miller, Sam Shepard, Tennessee Williams, and Lanford Wilson. Each entry includes a bibliography of works by and about the playwright, as well as an essay analyzing the most significant secondary sources. The editors stated the purpose of the source as being a guide "to the best of critical studies about major playwrights," and the included bibliographical essays do help a student or a scholar to evaluate the mass of critical material.

138. Coven, Brenda. *American Women Dramatists of the Twentieth Century: A Bibliography.* Metuchen, N.J.: Scarecrow, 1982. 237pp.

This is a bibliography on 133 American women playwrights selected on the basis of at least one successfully produced play on or Off Broadway. Among the dramatists included are such important figures in American theater as Lorraine Hansberry and Lillian Hellman, and also other less-known women playwrights involved in feminist theater. The book consists of two main sections: the first one includes general reviews of women's drama; and the second section is a bibliography itself. The information provided in this section includes birth and death dates; an alphabetical list of play titles (full bibliographic and publication data is given); brief biographical information; and selected criticism. The bibliography is indexed. This is an important source in research in contemporary American women playwrights.

139. Gohdes, Clarence. *Bibliographical Guide to the Study of the Literature of the U.S.A.* 5th ed. Rev. and enl. Durham, N.C.: Duke University Press, 1984. 255pp.

This book provides bibliography of research material in the field of American literature and drama. Entries are arranged by categories. Most of the entries have brief annotations. Unfortunately, bibliographical descriptions do not always include pagination or publisher. Material listed in the book covers in 35 chapters many specific and related subject areas of the field. It is a useful source in research in modern American drama.

140. Gohdes, Clarence. *Literature and Theatre of the States and Regions of the U.S.A.: A Historical Bibliography.* Durham, N.C.: Duke University Press, 1967. 276pp.

The author provides a historical bibliography of material dealing with the history of local theater, drama, fiction, and poetry. The cut-off date is 1964. The listing includes numerous books, chapters from books, anthologies, monographs, pamphlets and periodical articles. Entries are arranged by states and geographical regions. Some researchers in modern American theater and drama may find some useful material in this source.

141. Harris, Richard H. *Modern Drama in America and England, 1950–1970: A Guide to Information Sources*. Detroit: Gale Research, 1982. 606pp.

Each part — American and English drama — has two sections. The first section is a listing of relevant bibliographies and selected critical writings which includes both books and articles. The second is a list of writings by and about playwrights. Here, entries are arranged alphabetically by dramatist's name; and each entry includes published plays, selected nondramatic works (unfortunately, their genre is rarely indicated), published bibliographies, and criticism of the playwright's plays (most of the critical writings have brief annotations). The book is indexed. It is a valuable source for a researcher in modern American drama, especially, for identification of works written about lesser-known playwrights.

142. Kennedy, Arthur G. and Donald B. Sands. *A Concise Bibliography for Students of English*. 5th ed. Stanford, Calif.: Stanford University Press, 1972. 300pp.

This is an important and useful guide to major research sources in English and American literature and drama. Arrangement is by categories. There are three main sections: Literature — includes general reference sources and critiques on literature and drama in the Great Britain, United States and Canada; Book — provides bibliographies, periodicals, major publishers; and Profession — indicates literary scholarship and allied fields. The book includes several useful indexes for authors, editors, translators, and also subject and periodical indexes.

143. King, Kimball. *Ten Modern American Playwrights: An Annotated Bibliography*. New York: Garland Publishers, 1982. 251pp.

This book is an annotated bibliography of primary and secondary works dealing with the following contemporary American dramatists: Edward Albee, Amiri Baraka, Ed Billins, Jack Gelber, Arthur Kopit, David Mamet, David Rabe, Sam Shepard, Neil Simon, and Lanford Wilson. There are some important omissions, and the book is indexed only by the last name of the critics. Also the arrangement of material is somewhat confusing. For example, entries listed under the titles of the individual plays do not include criticism and dissertations that have to be looked up under the general section on a playwright. However, some researchers in modern American drama may find this bibliography a helpful source of some data.

144. Kolin, Philip C., ed. *American Playwrights: A Research Survey of Scholarship, Criticism, and Performance*. Westport, Conn.: Greenwood Press, 1989. 608pp.

This book is an excellent guide to the state of scholarship on forty major American dramatists. The guide also includes a bibliography, a stage history, an assessment of critical works about each dramatist, and a detailed analysis of future research studies on each playwright. The essays are written by experts in contemporary American drama, and focus on such important figures as Tennessee Williams, Arthur Miller, Edward Albee, David Rabe, David Mamet; women playwrights Wendy Wasserstein, Beth Henley, Marsha Norman; black dramatists James Baldwin, Ed Billins; and many others. Each essay provides information on the dramatist's achievements; primary bibliography; a stage history of his plays; evaluation of secondary materials, and future research opportunities. Among the first of its kind, this guide is an invaluable resource for anyone studying modern American theater and drama.

145. Long, E. Hudson. *American Drama from its Beginnings to the Present*. New York: Appleton-Century-Crofts, 1970. 78pp.

The book is intended as a guide to selected major research sources in the field of American drama published from the beginning of the twentieth century to the 1960s. The work consists of the following sections: bibliographies, anthologies, histories, actor and producer accounts, theatrical groups, periods, geographical regions, genres, and studies of individual playwrights. There are no annotations. The value of this guide is greatly reduced also by the uneven coverage.

146. Ousby, Ian, ed. *The Cambridge Guide to Literature in English*. New York: Cambridge University Press, 1988. 1109pp.

This book is not related to *The Cambridge Guide to English Literature* but the latter appears to be a revision of the former, for each of the sources contains much of what was not included in the other. For example, *The Cambridge Guide to English Literature* attempts to cover English language literature all over the world; while *The Cambridge Guide to Literature in English* does not cover translations, though its title implies that it also deals with the works translated into English. In spite of its limitations, *The Cambridge Guide to Literature in English* is a helpful ready-reference source, especially for students and researchers of contemporary American drama. It is a handy tool for checking the most important works of a writer or a playwright, biographical data, definitions of literary and dramatic terms, descriptions of genres, identification of literary allusions, etc.

147. Ryan, Pat M. *American Drama Bibliography: A Checklist of Publications in English*. Fort Wayne, Indiana: Fort Wayne Public Library, 1969. 240pp.

This checklist includes English language listings of biography, criticism, and history of American playwrights and their plays. Reviews of the plays are seldom emphasized. There are three main divisions: history and reference, general background, and individual authors. There are no indexes. Some of the researchers in modern American drama may be able to use this checklist to fill a gap left by more general bibliographies of American literature.

148. Salem, James M. *A Guide to Critical Reviews: Part I, American Drama, 1909–1982*. 3d ed. Metuchen, N.J.: Scarecrow, 1984. 657pp.

This book is a bibliography of reviews of non-musical American plays. The author provides citations for 2,500 plays by 350 authors. Entries are arranged alphabetically by the dramatist's name, then follows the list of plays in alphabetical order and citations to each play, also alphabetically arranged by the critic's name. The production history is given for each play: opening date, number of performances, length of the run, where the play was first staged, etc. There are few useful appendixes: birthplace and dates of birth and death for each of the dramatists; number of performances for each of the plays; lists of awards — Tony, New York Drama Critics' Circle, and Pulitzer. The value of this guide is somewhat reduced by the author's focusing almost exclusively on New York and by his omitting some important plays that were staged only Off Broadway and reviewed only in the *Village Voice*. However, Salem's guide is an indispensable tool for serious research in the developments of certain playwrights, in tracing the historical changes in content and style of modern American drama, etc.

149. Schweik, Robert C. and Dieter Riesner. *Reference Sources in English and American Literature: An Annotated Bibliography*. New York: Norton, 1977. 258pp.

This is a useful bibliography of selected reference sources for research in English and American literature and drama. The authors provide brief annotations for all entries. The book is indexed by subjects and by personal names. Though not so detailed as two-volume set of *Reference Works in British and American Literature* (edited by James Rettig, 1990–91), this book could be helpful as a quick ready-reference source.

Bibliographies on Individual Playwrights

Edward Albee

150. Amacher, Richard and Margaret F. Rule. *Edward Albee at Home and Abroad*. New York: AMS Press, 1973. 95pp.

151. Green, Charles Lee. *Edward Albee: An Annotated Bibliography, 1968–1977*. New York: AMS Press, 1980. 150pp.

Amacher's and Rule's book is a bibliography that covers works by and about Albee from 1958 to 1968. Green's bibliography is the second one on Albee published by the same publisher, and its purpose is to supplement and update the first. Green lists Albee's works since 1945 and some annotated critical material about the playwright from 1958 to 1977. Nevertheless, the focus of this bibliography is on the period from 1968 to 1977. There are two main sections in the second bibliography: primary and secondary sources. Critical works of scholarly nature —

monographs and periodical articles—make up the bulk of the bibliography. There are also interviews and biographies. All entries are annotated. Green also provides a list of manuscripts and special collections in major academic libraries. Both bibliographies are indexed.

152. Giantvalley, Scott. *Edward Albee: A Reference Guide*. Boston, Mass.: G. K. Hall, 1987. 459pp.

The author of this easy-to-use bibliographical guide intends to "provide a richly detailed overview of the critical reputation of a major American writer as he approaches his fourth decade of public scrutiny." The bibliography is well-compiled and comprehensive. It includes the standard academic criticism written about Albee in the U.S. and other countries, as well as reviews and interviews from daily newspapers, entertainment press, and popular magazines. All the material by and about Edward Albee is arranged alphabetically within the year of publication. The book has a good index that proves a means of finding items by author, subject, and publication. Among all existing reference sources for research in Albee as a playwright, this guide is perhaps the most comprehensive and detailed.

153. Tyce, Richard. *Edward Albee: A Bibliography*. Metuchen, N.J.: Scarecrow, 1986. 212pp.

This bibliography consists of the following sections: chronology of initial productions of the plays; initial publications of the plays; early writings by Albee (lists a number of less-known periodicals); general critical works about Albee (includes books and monographs, chapters from books, periodical articles, and interviews); theses and dissertations (over 150 citations); critiques and reviews of individual works. The cut-off publication date is 1985. There are also some foreign reviews and criticism of Albee's plays. The bibliography has a comprehensive index. It is an important source for research in Albee as a dramatist.

William Inge

154. McClure, Arthur F. *William Inge: A Bibliography*. New York: Garland, 1982. 93pp.

This bibliography includes an introduction—a well-researched essay about William Inge as a midwestern playwright. The two main sections are Inge's published works and criticism. The author's intention in compiling the second part was to show different attitudes of critics to Inge's works; he does not provide a comprehensive listing. Arrangement is by genres, dates, and works' titles. Not all the entries are annotated. An index is included. This is a valuable tool for a researcher interested in William Inge.

Arthur Miller

155. Hayashi, Tetsumaro. *An Index to Arthur Miller Criticism*. 2d ed. Metuchen, N.J.: Scarecrow, 1976. 151pp.

The first edition of this work was published in 1969. The book consists of two main sections: primary sources and secondary sources. The cut-off date for the bibliography is 1974. Only English language critical material is considered. Included are the list of unpublished master's theses, interviews, and the chronology of Miller's works. The book is indexed. Hayashi's bibliography could be a very valuable source for a researcher interested in Arthur Miller, but unfortunately, it suffers from inconsistency of treatment and errors.

Clifford Odets

156. Cooperman, Robert. *An Annotated Bibliography of Criticism, 1935–1989*. Westport, Conn.: Meckler, 1989. 168pp.

Though most of his plays Odets (1906–1963) wrote before 1945, the best of his later dramas were done during the forties and the fifties (such as *The Big Knife*, 1949, *The Country Girl*, 1950, or *The Sweet Smell of Success*, 1957). This is the first comprehensive bibliography of Odets. The book consists of a bibliographic essay, chapters covering published works of the playwright, production of his plays, screenplays, teleplays, annotated bibliography of Odets' scholarship, biographical materials, critical monographs, journal articles, dissertations, materials from the Un-American Activities Committee, etc.

Eugene O'Neill

157. Atkinson, Jennifer M. *Eugene O'Neill: A Descriptive Bibliography*. University of Pittsburgh Press, 1974. 410p.

At the time of this book's publication, no one had previously attempted to bring together a descriptive record of O'Neill's complete published works. This excellent bibliography aids both a person looking for information about a particular play and a person interested in the published books. Section A of the book includes all O'Neill's plays, broadsides, or special publications and describes all first printings of the playwright's plays in America. There is also a supplement that lists in alphabetical order published acting scripts. O'Neill's material appearing for the first time in books by other authors (letters, interviews, etc.) is included in Section B. In the Section C the author lists chronologically material written by O'Neill published in periodicals, newspapers, or theater bills. Sections D, E, and F include respectively promotional blurbs by O'Neill, his material quoted in auction or bookdealer catalogues, and catalogues of his plays in collections and anthologies. The Appendix contains adaptations of O'Neill's works by other authors. This bibliography admirably filled the gap in O'Neill's scholarship, and is still one of the important sources for research in this great American playwright.

158. Miller, Jordan Y. *Eugene O'Neill and the American Critic: A Bibliographic Checklist*. 2d ed. Hamden, Conn.: Archon Books, 1974. 553p.

This excellent source provides a detailed and comprehensive picture of domestic criticism of O'Neill. The cut-off date of this bibliography is 1972. The book contains a chronology of the playwright's life and works and their major productions; then follow almost 400 pages of citations to criticism. The author cites first general criticism, then criticism for individual plays. Information on graduate research on O'Neill is also provided. The book is indexed. Miller's work is one of the most significant reference sources for research in Eugene O'Neill.

159. Smith, Madeline, and Richard Eaton. *Eugene O'Neill: An Annotated Bibliography*. New York: Garland, 1988. 320pp.

This is an excellent source for identifying the broad range of material written about Eugene O'Neill from 1973 to 1985. The authors updated Miller's book, *Eugene O'Neill and the American Critic* (the cut-off date of that bibliography was 1972) and expanded its American coverage to broader international scope. All entries are arranged alphabetically by year and annotated (though the annotations of foreign-language publications are rather weak). The volume is divided into parts covering books and sections of books, dissertations, periodicals on both English and foreign languages, English-language productions and reviews, audio and film recordings, television and radio adaptations, editions of primary works, translations, and fictional presentations of the playwright's life. The book is indexed. Though there is no introduction (that would have been of interest), this reference tool is the most updated and one of the most important for research in the great playwright's works.

David Rabe

160. Kolin, Philip C. *David Rabe: A Stage History and a Primary and Secondary Bibliography*. New York: Garland Publishing, 1988. 273pp.

In his important book, Philip C. Kolin, who is a Professor of English at the University of Southern Mississippi and the Founding Co-Editor of *Studies in American Drama, 1945–Present*, presents the first study of Tony Award-winning playwright David Rabe. This reference work is the product of exhaustive and scholarly research. It consists of a chronological stage history which includes Rabe's plays performed in the United States and abroad. The primary bibliography lists chronologically Rabe's plays, interviews, and his nondramatic works, such as early poetry, fiction, and his writings for the newspaper, *New Haven Register*. The secondary bibliography is also chronological, and provides a listing of criticism and reviews on Rabe's plays. A combined name and subject index, giving both the page number references and the bibliography item number references, is also supplied. It is an invaluable tool for scholars interested in this playwright, as well as those readers concerned with the history of modern American drama.

William Saroyan

161. Foard, Elisabeth C. *William Saroyan: A Reference Guide*. New York:
     G.K. Hall, 1989. 207pp.
     Although most of Saroyan's dramatic works were done before World
     War II, some of his major plays that celebrate his favorite ideas (such
     as *The Cave Dwellers*, 1957, or *Sam, the Highest Jumper of Them All*,
     1960) are important for understanding contemporary American theater.
     This reference book is a good starting point for research in Saroyan. The
     compiler wrote an introduction where she discusses the life and works
     of the playwright. The reference guide itself covers secondary publica-
     tions from 1934 through 1986. Each of the 1,100 entries is briefly an-
     notated, with some annotations presenting the text of the original. The
     arrangement is chronological, with an alphabetical listing by author
     within individual years. Within each year there are two major divisions:
     books and shorter writings. Unfortunately, neither foreign materials
     nor dissertations have been included. The author and subject indexes
     provide ample access to the entries.

Sam Shepard

162. King, Kimball. *Sam Shepard: A Casebook*. (Garland Reference Library
     of the Humanities, 861; Casebooks on Modern Dramatists, 2) New
     York: Garland, 1989. 176pp.
     This reference source covers every phase of Shepard's career, his
     plays, their structure, themes, and characters. The last essay written by
     Tommy Thomson describes his experience of collaborating with
     Shepard, and ends this creative and often insightful book with a per-
     sonal reminiscence. The bibliography includes an annotated survey of
     major criticism on this one of the most impressive living American
     playwrights. It is a very useful source for researching Sam Shepard's
     dramas.

163. Gunn, Drewey Wayne. *Tennessee Williams: A Bibliography*. Metuchen,
     N.J.: Scarecrow, 1980. 255pp.
     This useful bibliography consists of two main sections. The first one
     includes publications by Tennessee Williams in chronological order:
     collections of his plays, plays in anthologies, plays that were produced
     without having appeared in print, poetry, essays, works in periodicals,
     recordings, and translations. Some of the early items that Williams
     published under his given name, Thomas Lanier Williams, are also in-
     cluded. In the second section, the author traces the history of Williams'
     plays with notes on composition and textual variants. Here, entries are
     arranged alphabetically by the play's name. The rest of the bibliography
     deals with Williams' manuscripts, production of his plays, and the ma-
     jor critical works on Williams: monographs, articles, bibliographies,
     and dissertations. It is an extremely useful tool for a researcher interested

in Williams' precise bibliographical information, full production record of his plays, and variations of the works. The bibliography is complete with an index.

164. McCann, John S. *The Critical Reputation of Tennessee Williams: A Reference Guide*. Boston, Mass.: G. K. Hall, 1983. 430pp.

This is an annotated bibliography of critical works written about Tennessee Williams. The author includes books, chapters from books, articles from national periodicals and metropolitan press. The book has an adequate index. Together with Gunn's bibliography, McCann's work is an excellent source for a researcher involved in Williams' studies.

Indexes

165. *Index Guide to Modern American Literature and Modern British Literature*. New York: Ungar Publishing, 1988. 144pp.

This is a useful reference tool that provides a comprehensive index and an easy access to the first five volumes of *Modern American Literature* and of *Modern British Literature*. The index consists of two major sections. The first one covers authors (about 830 of them total) and the second section provides an index to the critical literature (some 3,500 studies).

166. Toohey, John L. *A History of the Pulitzer Prize Plays*. New York: Citadel Press, 1967. 344pp.

This is an index to plays that won a Pulitzer Prize. Arranged chronologically by years and then alphabetically under the play's title, this index provides a brief summary of each play, information on original cast, length of run, selected bibliography of reviews, etc. Though twenty years old, this index may still be useful for some researchers in modern American drama. The source is indexed.

Biographical Sources

167. *Concise Dictionary of American Literary Biography*. Detroit: Gale Research, vols. 5 and 6, 1987.

Volume 5, entitled *The New Consciousness, 1941–1968*, and volume 6, *Broadening Views, 1968–1987*, devoted to a single historical period and each cover 30–40 authors from all genres, including playwriting. Both of these volumes are a handy source of biographical-critical information on the best modern American writers and playwrights. Each entry includes a discussion of life, the works and ideas of the author, an annotated bibliography of secondary sources that may help a student or a researcher to go on to further study, and a "contextual map" showing graphically how this particular writer or a dramatist fits into the cultural, social, and literary context of his time.

168. Kaye, Phyllis J., ed. *National Playwrights Directory*. 2d ed. Waterford, Conn.: O'Neill Theater Center, 1981. 507pp.

This is a biographical directory to about 500 living American playwrights. Each entry includes, whenever possible, a photograph of the biographee, personal and career information along with a listing of play titles (with indication of production and availability of scripts), and synopses of selected works. Nearly all entries were updated by the playwright just before the press time. The book, complete with an index for all plays, included along with the designation of the plays in the special tape and film research collection of The New York Public Library. This is an important tool for any researcher in modern American theater seeking to locate scripts, plays, and playwrights.

169. MacNicholas, John, ed. *Twentieth-Century American Dramatists*. Detroit: Gale Research, 1981. 2v.

This work is a part of Gale's Dictionary of Literary Biography series. Among the 76 American playwrights of the twentieth century are Edward Albee, James Baldwin, Lillian Hellman, Arthur Miller, William Saroyan, Neil Simon, Tennessee Williams, and Paul Zindel. Arrangement is alphabetical by the playwright's name. Each entry begins with the list of playwright's works, then followed a critical essay about their life and works. There are two bibliographies at the end of each entry: primary—provides a list of the dramatist's works, and secondary—includes major critiques about this playwright. There are numerous illustrations: photographs of the dramatists, examples of their typescripts, playbills of their major productions, etc. The editor also includes three valuable appendixes: "Trends in Theatrical Productions"; "Major Regional Theaters"; and "Books for Further Reading." This Gale's publication is an important source of biographical information for any researcher in modern American drama.

170. Unger, Leonard, ed. *American Writers: A Collection of Literary Biographies*. New York: Scribner, 1974. 4v.
_____. Supplement. 1979. 2v.

This work began as a collection of biographical essays, *Pamphlets on American Writers (1959–1972)* originally published at the University of Minnesota. Supplements in two volume update this source to 1979. These six volumes provide bibliographical and biographical information to many contemporary American writers and playwrights along with the discussion of each author's literary works.

Dissertations

171. Hayashi, Tetsumaro, ed. *Arthur Miller and Tennessee Williams: Research Opportunities and Dissertation Abstracts*. Jefferson, N.C.: McFarland, 1983. 133pp.

In the first part of this work, professor of literature from the Ball State University, Thomas M.Tammaro offers suggestions on further research opportunities for scholars interested in Arthur Miller or Tennessee Williams. The second part lists abstracts of dissertations written about these playwrights or their plays from 1952 to 1980. Each dissertation entry provides the author's name, title, university, date, and also a number for the same dissertation in *Dissertation Abstracts* or *Dissertation Abstracts International*. Included is a checklist for each playwright that provides plays, fiction, radio scripts, essays, etc. The book also has two indexes—one for Miller and another one—for Williams. Both indexes list authors of dissertations, subjects, titles, and universities. Hayashi's is a valuable research tool for those involved in studying Miller or Williams.

172. Howard, Patsy C., comp. and ed. *Theses in American Literature, 1896–1971*. Ann Arbor, Mich.: Pierian Press, 1973. 307pp.

The source provides information on Master's theses in American literature and drama written during a 75 year period. It is not comprehensive because the basis for selection was one of availability. The arrangement is alphabetical by the name of American writer or playwright. Under each entry the theses are also alphabetized by the name of the thesis' author. The information provided includes complete title for the thesis, degree, institution (most of the institutions are in the United States), date, number of pages, etc. Included are the author and theses' author indexes.

173. Woodress, James. *Dissertations in American Literature, 1891–1966*. Rev. ed. Durham, N.C.: Duke University Press, 1968. 185pp.

This work provides a classified list of doctoral dissertations on American literature and drama written mainly in the United States from 1891 through 1966. Drama entries are numbered from 2926 through 3281. Unfortunately, there are no annotations.

4. Theater Arts

Histories and Critiques

174. Bartow, Arthur. *The Director's Voice: Twenty-One Interviews.* New York: Theatre Communications Group, 1988. 382pp.

    The author has done a very good job in gathering interviews from a diversified array of stage directors working in the contemporary American theater. Emphasis is upon directors influenced by or themselves representative of avant-garde theater, such as experimentalists and reconstructionists. The book also tends to focus on those directors who used to or continue to work in regional theaters. Each of the 21 presented directors' histories is included along with an interview. This book introduces insights, via questions and answers, into the art of major American stage directors. It also illuminates the current trends in contemporary theater. This collection of interviews may be an important source for any scholar, student, or anyone interested in modern American theater.

175. Bedard, Roger L. and C. John Tolch., eds. *Spotlight on the Child: Studies in the History of American Children's Theatre.* New York: Greenwood Press, 1989. 207pp.

    This book is a good source for studying and research in the history of the American children's theater. In the introduction the authors provide a review of early concepts in the field and the evolution of present-day theories and thoughts. Followed is the collection of historical and critical essays written by leading authorities in this area. The book illuminates different facets of the rich history of American theater for children and focuses on its historical development.

176. Bentley, Eric, ed. *Thirty Years of Treason.* New York: Viking, 1971. 991pp.

    This book is a collection of excerpts from hearings before the HUAC — House Committee on Un-American Activities, 1938–1968, focused exclusively on confrontations with artists and dramatists. There are excerpts from the testimonies of such important figures in American culture as Hallie Flanagan, Lillian Hellman, Elia Kazan, Arthur Miller, Clifford Odets, Joseph Papp, Jerome Robins, even Ronald Reagan, and many others. The editor provides material from contemporary newspapers that include articles on hearings, and also writes his own explanatory notes. The book includes several appendixes and index. Not a standard reference tool, Bentley's collection of excerpts is a unique and valuable information source for a researcher in American theater of this period.

177. Berkowitz, Gerald. *New Broadways: Theatre Across America, 1950–1980*. Totowa, N.J.: Rowman & Littlefield, 1982. 198pp.

This is a historical study of provincial American theaters during the period of thirty years. The author provides detailed critical survey of major regional theatrical companies. The book includes a bibliography and an index. Berkowitz's study is a helpful source of information for any researcher interested in history of contemporary regional theater.

178. Broun, Heywood H. *A Studied Madness*. Sagaponack, N.Y.: Second Chance Press, 1979. 298pp.

Though this reprint of the 1965 edition (published by Doubleday) is not a comprehensive historical account of the American stage during the sixties, Broun's well-written, philosophical book — even twenty years later — might be a useful source for any researcher interested in New York theater of this period. It is a charmingly witty, intelligent and philosophical view of the Broadway world described by an actor who knew it well from inside.

179. Brown, John Russel and Bernard Harris, eds. *American Theater*. New York: St. Martin's Press, 1967. 228pp.

This book is the result of collaboration of ten foremost critics and theater scholars, such as John Gassner, Gerald Weales, Brian Way, and others. It remained in print for over 20 years, but is now out of print. There are different topics discussed in relation to modern American theatrical history: realism in contemporary American theater, European influences, Edward Albee, theater of the absurd, etc. Each chapter forms a comprehensive analysis of the particular theme and provides a selective bibliography. The book is indexed.

180. Brustein, Robert. *Seasons of Discontent: Dramatic Opinions, 1959–1965*. New York: Simon & Schuster, 1965. 322pp.

Not a history in traditional sense, Brustein's book is an analytic record of a half-decade of professional American theater. The author views theater in the context of modern American life and culture. The history of contemporary American stage comes alive from the essays in this book. Brustein analyzes the theater of the absurd, Edward Albee's plays, dramas of Tennessee Williams, European influences brought by foreign companies, etc. This concrete, production-by-production look at the American stage as it functioned during the sixties, is a fascinating historical document by itself. The book is indexed.

181. *Changing Scenes: Theater in the South*. Durham, N.C.: Institute for
     Southern Studies, 1986. 120pp.
         This unique study is published in one of the issues of the *Southern Ex-
     posure* (vol. 14, 3.4) and dedicated to the history and development of
     the American theater and drama in the South. This collection of essays
     consists of few parts: "People's Theater"; Acting on the Issues";
     "Theaters"; "Playwrights"; and "SE Contest Winners." The articles ex-
     plore the roots of theatrical forms as well the works of the playwrights
     of the current movements. Excluded are the community and university
     theaters as well as well known playwrights, such as Tennessee Williams
     and Carson McCullers. The authors reflect in their essays the diversity
     and range of style and subjects in contemporary Southern drama. The
     book as a whole is an important source for studying the history of the
     American theater.

182. Conolly, L.W., ed. *Theatrical Touring and Founding in North America*.
     Westport, Conn.: Greenwood Press, 1982. 245pp.
         This is a scientific historical study of American and Canadian theater
     from the beginnings around 1700 to 1980. The period after 1945 is very
     well presented. The book is a collection of essays dealing with various
     subjects in North American theater history. There are an index and a
     bibliography.

183. Durham, Weldon B. *American Theatre Companies, 1931–1986*. West-
     port, Conn.: Greenwood Press, 1989. 605pp.
         This indispensable work surveys the fifty-year period in which the
     American theater has undergone one of the major changes in its history:
     the process of decentralization and the shift from Broadway to regional
     theaters. The wide range of theater types — workers' theater, art theater,
     experimental groups, children's companies, ethnic theater, etc. — are
     profiled in 78 entries. This section is entitled "Profiles" and provides in-
     formation on facilities, personnel, management policies, repertories,
     etc. Each entry also contains a bibliography of sources and a guide to
     archives for further research. The work is well indexed by personal
     names and by play titles. There are also two useful appendices that list
     theater companies chronologically and geographically, state-by-state.
     This reference source is a valuable research aid providing information
     not readily available elsewhere.

184. Gard, Robert E., Marston Balch, and Pauline Temkin. *Theatre in
     America, Appraisal and Challenge*. Madison, Wis.: Dembar Educa-
     tional Research Services, 1968. 192pp.
         This interesting historical document is an appraisal of the contem-
     porary (by the end of the sixties) American stage that was undertaken
     by the National Theatre Conference. It is an analysis of what is being
     done on Broadway, in various New York theaters, in the Educational
     theater, on the provincial stage, etc. The book provides an interesting

view of the changes on the American stage since the end of World War II. There are bibliography and an index.

185. Gottfried, Martin. *A Theatre Divided: The Postwar American Stage.* Boston, Mass.: Little, Brown, 1969. 330pp.

This is an interesting socio-political study of the American theater after World War II done from the point of view of the sixties. The author places Broadway, as a theatrical industry on the extreme right wing of the political theatrical spectrum. New repertory resident companies together with Off and Off Off Broadway are placed at the left wing of this scheme. The author's analysis of interaction between these two wings provides a picture of the particular intellectual climate of the time that could be of interest for a researcher involved in studying the American stage of the sixties.

186. Hagen, Uta. *Respect for Acting.* New York: Macmillan, 1973. 227pp.

The famous actress in her book makes a statement of the problems an actor faces in the contemporary American theater. Part one deals with the actor's concept of himself and his art; part two offers specialized exercises, and part three discusses the problems of rehearsal, style, and communication. Although the author addresses it to professional actors, anyone seriously interested in the history of modern theater should find Hagen's book stimulating and informative: it is a fine document of the Stanislavski-oriented school of American acting that came into being after World War II.

187. Hart, Lynda, ed. *Making a Spectacle: Feminist Essays on Contemporary Women's Theatre.* University of Michigan Press, 1989. 347pp.

The editor selected essays that present a wide spectrum of contemporary performance criticism and illuminate important trends in modern American theater. The first group of articles addresses the role of women in the contemporary American ethnic theater (such as Margaret Wilkerson's essay "Music as Metaphor: New Plays of Black Women"). The second group of essays is called "Reformulating the Question" and explores the strategies and ideas of Beth Henley, Pam Gems, Marsha Norman, and others important for the modern American theater women playwrights. The other two groupings of articles — parts three and four — deal with contemporary trends in Chicano and Japanese American feminist theater; with Sue-Ellen Case's (who, by the way, is an editor of the *Theatre Journal*) essay on an aesthetics of "camp"; studies of such significant women playwrights as Caryl Churchill, Megan Terry, and Michelene Wandor. The book in general proves to be a useful reference source for all those who want to study the trends in modern American feminist theater.

188. Henderson, Mary C. *Broadway Ballyhoo: The American Theater in Posters, Photographs, Magazines, Caricatures, and Programs.* New York: H. N. Abrams, 1989. 184pp.

This is a well-researched and well-written comprehensive, illustrative two-century history of American theater by an author of the award-winning *Theater in America* (1973). It is an invaluable and inspirational source for a researcher or a student of the history of American theater. The theater of the post-war time received a good coverage. The book consists of the following parts: Preface and Acknowledgments; Posters; Photographs; Magazines; Caricatures; and Programs. A bibliography, an index, and a list of major collections of American theatrical paper add to the usefulness of this book.

189. Hobgood, Burnet M. *Master Teachers of Theatre: Observations on Teaching Theatre by Nine American Masters.* Southern Illinois University Press, 1988. 212pp.

The subjects covered in this book include children's drama, theatrical interpretation, drama as literature, stage movement, and directing. The authors (such as theater historian Oscar Brockett, acting teacher Robert Benedetti, designer Howard Bay and others) are highly creative and original in their approaches to the material; and they all illuminate a sense of the high calling that theater teaching can be. The essays provide important insights into understanding of current trends in contemporary American theater. Theater practitioners and teachers may find this book a useful source with much here to think over and profit from. Students and researchers wishing to know more about areas of theater study will also benefit from this fine collection of essays.

190. Jenkins, Ron. *Acrobats of the Soul: Comedy and Virtuosity in Contemporary American Theatre.* New York: Theatre Communications Group, 1988. 179pp.

The author intended to study the artists who reflect in wondrous ways "the complexity of our cultural environment" while breaking down the barrier between performer and his audience. Though not a comprehensive and exhaustive survey, this book may serve as a reference source or a good starting point for all those students and researchers interested in comedy and comedians in contemporary American theater. The profiles of the artists are faithful and detailed. The author proves that American comic theatrical genre is used by the performers to subversively attack the oppressive elements of everyday life. With surprisingly clear descriptions of routines and performances, the author covers such important and prominent artists and groups as puppeteer Paul Zaloom (his "theater of trash"); Stephen Wade who is an oral historian and banjoist; the Flying Karamazov Brothers, the Big Apple Circus and its clowns; Le Cirque du Soleil (clown Denis Lacombe); Avner the Eccentric, a clown-juggler-rope-walker; monologist Spalding Gray; clown Bill Irwin; the Pickle Family Circus; etc. Although not a traditional reference tool, Jenkins study might serve as a useful source introducing a researcher to the important aspect of modern American theater and to these innovative performing artists who synthesize popular entertainment traditions and experimental theater techniques to fight off the dehumanizing tendencies of the contemporary life.

191. Kerman, Alvin B.,ed. *The Modern American Theatre*. Englewood Cliffs, N.J.: Prentice-Hall, 1967. 183pp.

     Not a historical reference source in traditional sense, this book, anyway, may be of use for some researchers who are concerned with the development of American theater after the World War II. In this collection of essays, foremost critics, directors, and playwrights, including Kenneth Tynan, Allan Kaprow, Robert Brustein, and Edward Albee, consider the historical development, range, and variety of American theater. Among the topics discussed in details are Broadway musical as a genre, existential Theater of Choice, works and productions of Edward Albee, William Inge, Arthur Miller, Thorton Wilder, Tennessee Williams, and others. A bibliography and an index are included.

192. Keyssar, Helene. *Feminist Theatre*. New York: Grove Press, 1985. 223pp.

     The author presents a concise and comprehensive study of feminist theater in Britain and the United States and illustrates the influence of the social climate during the sixties on the women's theater. The focus of the book is upon such important figures as Caryl Churchill, Pam Gems, Megan Terry, Michelene Wandor, Ntozake Shange, and others. Keyssar's scholarly monograph is a useful source for studying the history of contemporary feminist theater and the ways of its development into the experimental and political art.

193. Laufe, Abe. *Anatomy of a Hit: Long-Run Plays on Broadway from 1900 to the Present Day*. New York: Hawthorne Books, 1966. 350pp.

     Though "the present day" in this title means the beginning of the sixties, Laufe's detailed study of plays that had runs of more than 500 performances may be a useful source of information for a theater historian interested in the development of modern American stage. The author analyzes qualities important for a commercial success and studies plays from the initial idea to opening night and the critics' attitudes towards the production. The book is indexed.

194. Leiter, Samuel L. *Ten Seasons: New York Theatre in the Seventies*. New York: Greenwood Press, 1986. 245pp.

     This is an important scientific study of the previous decade in New York theater which the author views as an indicator for theatrical trends throughout the United States. Leiter discusses various activities on, Off, and Off Off Broadway: actors and acting styles, directors and different approaches to directing the show, theaters and theatrical groups, trends and artistic movements. The author also provides informational tables in most of his chapters. Extensive bibliographies follow each chapter. The book includes a index. This historical study is a useful source for a researcher in contemporary American theater.

195. Lewis, Emory. *Stages: The Fifty Years Childhood of the American Theatre*. Englewood, N.J.: Prentice-Hall, 1969. 290pp.

    The author provides a detailed scientific study of the development of American theater from 1915 to the 1960s. Decade after decade, he analyzes actors, acting styles, directors, producers, scenic designers, costumers, plays and playwrights. The period after World War II receives a detailed coverage. The book includes an index.

196. Little, Stuart W. *Off-Broadway: The Prophetic Theatre*. New York: Dell, 1974. 323pp.

    This book may be a helpful source of historical information for a researcher in American theater from the fifties to the early seventies. The author provides a historical study of the Off Broadway theater from the production of Tennessee Williams' *Summer and Smoke* in 1952 to the beginning of the seventies. There is also a useful list of Off Broadway Award Winners from 1955 to 1971. The book includes detailed title and name indexes.

197. Loney, Glenn Meredith. *Twentieth-Century Theatre*. New York: Facts on File, 1983. 2v.

    This book is a chronological, year-by-year, record of theatrical developments in the United States and Great Britain from 1900 to 1979. The arrangement of data is first by year, then, within each year, by activity, with dates running from January 1 to December 31. Notable· events in theater are subdivided into the following categories: "American Premieres," "British Premieres," "Revivals and Repertoires," "Birth/Death/Debuts," "Theatre Productions." There is a source bibliography for each year at the end of the second volume. Several useful indexes are also included: names, production titles, awards, etc. There are many illustrations. Loney's book is a very helpful source for a researcher in modern theater who needs to find a particular date, identify a personality, or to locate an event.

198. McConachie, Bruce A. and Daniel Friedman, eds. *Theatre for Working-Class Audiences in the United States, 1830–1980*. Westport, Conn.: Greenwood Press, 1985. 264pp.

    This is a collection of thirteen essays, the authors of which generally employ a post-positivist, sociological approach to theater history to analyze the historical development of the theater for working-class people. Interpreting not only the plays' subject matter but their production ingredients and dramatic structure in light of workers' experiences, the essays bring into focus the significant meaning of the audience's involvement in the theatrical process. Unfortunately, not all of the essays are the same quality. Discussions on the ethnic (Italian or Yiddish) theater provide descriptive rather than interpretive history. A final essay (written by Friedman) utilizes data that the editors compiled from questionnaires sent to workers' theaters operating in the 1980s. The volume also includes the list of these theaters in alphabetical order. This book is a very useful source for research in one of the important aspects of contemporary American theater: another layer of America's rich, multifaced and democratic theatrical heritage.

199. Mordden, Ethan. *The American Theatre.* New York: Oxford University Press, 1981. 365pp.

This is a history of the American theater written with a keen sense of historical perspective. More than half of the book deals with the period after World War II. Energetic yet scholarly in style, the book provides more than adequate coverage of the last few decades with plays and their productions perceptively analyzed. The work includes a brief bibliography and an index.

200. Morrow, Lee Alan. *The Tony Award Book: Four Decades of Great American Theater.* New York: Abbeville Press, 1987. 274pp.

The history of the last four decades of American theater is presented here through the detailed description of plays and musicals that were Tony Awards nominees and winners. The author discusses plays and playwrights; actors, actresses, and directors; designers; and creators of musicals. The text is supplemented with many excellent illustrations and photographs. The book includes an index and a list of Tony Award nominees and winners from 1946–1987.

201. Oldenburg, Chloe W. *Leaps of Faith — History of the Cleveland Play House: 1915–1985.* Pepper Pike, Ohio: C. W. Oldenburg, 1985. 184pp.

This richly illustrated chronological study explores the history of the first American repertory company. The author presents the important role of the Cleveland Play House in the detailed context of the development of modern American theater. This book is a significant information source and useful tool for a researcher of contemporary repertory theater. It is well indexed and contains a bibliography; the Play House's repertory over the course of 70 years; and the list of the company members, its boards, and committees.

202. Poggi, Jack. *Theater in America: The Impact of Economic Forces, 1870–1967.* Ithaca, N.Y.: Cornell University Press, 1968. 328pp.

This diagnosis of the ailments of American stage was written in the sixties but may still be of interest for a researcher in theater after World War II. The author analyzes economic trends that, from his point of view, affected the quality of American theater, especially since 1945: centralization of theater life in New York City and the major decline of theatrical activities throughout the country because of the impact of movie industry, television, rising costs, etc. The book includes a series of tables, graphs, a bibliography, and index.

203. Poland, Albert and Bruce Mailman, eds. *The Off Off Broadway Book:*

The Plays, People, Theatre. Indianapolis: Bobbs-Merrill, 1973. 546pp.

This book is not much of the history and synthesis of the movement as is Stuart Little's study of Off Broadway. However, it is a useful combination of survey, criticism, and anthology that covers this significant phenomenon in the contemporary American theater called Off Off Broadway. The articles included discuss most of the important Off Off Broadway organizations, such as La Mama, The American Place Theater, etc. Origins, brief history, founders, philosophies, influences, listings of productions are provided. In the anthology section, the authors included selections from the foremost playwrights staged on Off Off Broadway, such as Ed Billins, Julie Bovasso, David Rabe, Ronald Tavel, etc. Brief biographical sketches are given for the playwrights. Included are also a bibliography and suggestions for further reading.

204. Savran, David. *Breaking the Rules: The Wooster Group, 1975-1985.* Ann Arbor, Mich.: UMI Research Press, 1988. 238pp.

This excellent book (first published in 1986) must be a required reading for any student or researcher interested in the historical and ideological development of contemporary American theater. The Wooster Group is at present the most extreme, important, and the best known of the experimental American theater companies. The author traces the Group's history from Richard Schechner's The Performance Group, and analyzes its productions that have included such disparate material as disco music, pornographic and TV films, lectures, and reconstructions of soap operas. The Group's purpose is a critical examination of theater classic, theme, or personal obsession done by juxtaposing, parodying, and deconstructing. The author himself considers the deconstruction revolutionary in its de-mythification of social structures and symbols. His book brings the reader closer to the Group's way of perceiving the art. Unfortunately, the lack of chronology may be confusing. However, the book does illuminate the important and very interesting period in our contemporary theater.

205. Schevill, James E. *Break Out! In Search of New Theatrical Environments.* Chicago: Swallow Press, 1973. 413pp.

This collection of essays deals with many aspects of contemporary theater experience. The coverage is international (Jerzy Grotovsky, Peter Brook) but the emphasis is on the experimental American theater (Bread and Puppet Theater, San Francisco Mime Troupe, etc.). The editor presented sensitive gathering of material from richly varied sources: criticism, short scripts, interviews, photographs, etc. The material covers street theater, open theater, black theater, new playing spaces in experimental theater, etc. The book is a valuable source of information for research in contemporary American theater.

206. Schneider, Alan. *Entrances: An American Director's Journey.* New York: Limelight Editions, 1987. 416pp.

Alan Schneider is known in the history of contemporary theater as an outstanding director who introduced to American audiences many unusual plays: Beckett, Pinter, Orton, and the like. His book is a picture of his life and work, but, at the same time, it has a much larger quality. The author presents a critique of the American theater, its history from the thirties to 1966. The book is also a detailed view of the process of directing various kinds of plays, and as such may be used by researchers interested in the history of contemporary American directorial theater. The author also highlights problems of American commercial theater; analyses the role of critics in American theater; describes in details the problems of producing non-realistic plays in the theater which is largely devoted to realism and in which commercial success is a major goal. This significant book might serve as an important tool for a scholar of modern American theater.

207. Shank, Theodore. *American Alternative Theatre*. New York: St. Martin's Press, 1989. 202pp.

This book is a valuable source for researching and understanding the history of the nontraditional, radical, iconoclastic movements of the 1960s and after in the American theater. The monograph is well illustrated with 120 photographs and focuses on such important for the contemporary theater groups as the Living Theatre, the San Francisco Mime Troupe, the Open Theatre, the Onthologic-Hysteric Theatre, the Bread and Puppet Theatre, and some others. The author provides detailed descriptions of the groups' and artists' philosophical positions and ideas and discusses their most significant efforts. Though first published in 1982 (by the Grove Press, New York), this study is still a very useful guide to the variety of alternative theater. It is important for understanding the development of an autonomous creative method in modern American theater, a shift from words to a visual emphasis, and the artistic philosophy of keeping the audience always aware of the real world. The book contains a useful bibliography.

208. Szilassy, Zoltan. *American Theater of the 1960s*. Carbondale: Southern Illinois University Press, 1986. 113pp.

This is a well-researched, scholarly monograph whose author tries to explore the diverse experimentations of the theater in the 1960s and to identify what was permanent in these often wild innovations. Szilassy employs an interdisciplinary method and offers an interesting historical analysis of the theater in the 1960s with its boundless energy and free spirit. The book includes bibliographical references and is indexed by play title and by person.

209. Van Erven, Eugene. *Radical People's Theatre*. Indiana University Press, 1988. 238pp.

This monograph provides a clear picture of an important segment of contemporary theater. The author describes a radical popular theater which appeared in the late 1960s in the United States and elsewhere. He provides synopses of plots used by the groups and covers their outdoor performances and the problems encountered by the actors and playwrights. The book contains an appendix that provides additional facts about the troupes and a bibliography. The numerous photographs provide good illustrations of the types of characters, costumes, or over-sized puppets used by the performers. Though this study is not comprehensive, and the author is not always objective in his evaluations of quality performances, *Radical People's Theatre* is an important and useful source for research in this interesting period in contemporary theater history.

210. Whiting, Frank M. *Minnesota Theatre: From Old Fort Snelling to the Guthrie*. St. Paul, Minn.: Pogo Press, 1988. 231pp.

 The author of this book, director of the University of Minnesota Theater for more than 25 years, helped to install the Guthrie Theater in Minneapolis. Whiting's monograph is a comprehensive and detailed survey of theaters, plays, and players in Minnesota from the 19th century to the present. The author covers the history of the theaters themselves, how they were organized and by who, the actors who acted on their stages, the plays that were presented, etc. Unfortunately, the author does not analyze the legacy of the historical productions, their artistry, or the significance of the theatrical past in relation to the present. However, this study presents essential information for anyone interested in American history, and is a valuable and an important source for studying the history of the American theater.

211. Wilk, John R. *The Creation of an Ensemble: The First Years of the American Conservatory Theatre*. Carbondale, Ill.: Southern Illinois University Press, 1986. 214pp.

 This study is an essential information source for all theater historians involved in studying contemporary American regional theater. The author provides detailed analyses of the historical and ideological development of ACT (American Conservatory Theatre)—this now recognized prototype of modern regional theatrical company. The study is well supported by personal interviews with company members, notes, bibliography, company roster, annual production schedules, numerous photographs, and the famous Statement of the Purpose written by the ACT's founder Bill Ball in 1965. The book gives a clear report of the complexities of the realization and survival of a new theatrical company in contemporary social and cultural environment.

212. Williams, Henry B., ed. *The American Theatre: A Sum of Its Parts*. New York: Samuel French, 1972, c1971. 431pp.

 This is a collection of addresses prepared for the symposium, "The American Theatre-A Cultural Process" (Washington D.C.). The essays provide a comprehensive look at the American theater in the historical context.

213. Zeigler, Joseph W. *Regional Theatre: The Revolutionary Stage.* New York: Da Capo Press, 1977. 283pp.

Though first published in 1973, Zeigler's book is a useful source of information for a researcher interested in the history of contemporary American theater. The author presented a skillfully written history and analysis of the problems which confronted the numerous nonprofit regional theaters, such as San Francisco's Actors Workshop, Washington D. C.'s Arena Stage, etc.

Guides and Bibliographies

214. Debenham, Warren. *Laughter on Record: A Comedy Discography.* Metuchen, N.J.: Scarecrow, 1988. 369pp.

The compiler based his research on access to university archives, private collections, record stores, etc. The bibliography consists of an alphabetical (by performer or by title) list of more than 4,000 LP recordings of comedy performances. There is also an extensive subject index, subjectively arranged. The author provides an especially useful list of sources of records and of out-of-print sources. The listings cover such well-known performers as Jack Benny, Richard Pryor, Will Rogers, and others. The book is a comprehensive and helpful reference source for those interested in studying contemporary American comic theater. Unfortunately, no listings are annotated.

215. Kaminsky, Laura J., ed. *Non-Profit Repertory Theatre in North America, 1958–1975: A Bibliography and Indexes to the Playbill Collection of the Theatre Communications Group.* Westport, Conn.: Greenwood Press, 1977. 268pp.

The arrangement of the main listing of productions is first by city, and then subdivided by theater and year. Followed are the numbered play entries that include information on author, title, and director. The set of indexes provides access to more than 3,000 theater programs held in the collection of the Theatre Communications Group, from productions staged by some 52 theater companies throughout the country. The indexes include titles, dramatists, directors, translators, adaptors, composers, lyricists, musical directors, and names of theaters. The editor does not make claim for completeness, since selection of programs for bibliography and indexes is restricted by the TCG collection. However, some researchers in contemporary American theater may find this reference tool useful.

216. King, Christine E., and Brenda Coven. *Joseph Papp and the New York Shakespeare Festival: An Annotated Bibliography.* New York: Garland Publishers, 1988. 369pp.

This important reference book provides a single source of information about Joseph Papp who has been an influential force in New York cultural life and American theater in general for the past thirty years. The book begins with an introduction describing Papp's artistic career and the development of the new York Shakespeare Festival — the institution almost synonymous with Papp's name. The bibliography itself is selective and consists of over 900 references from periodicals, newspapers, government documents, different subject bibliographies in this area, monographs on contemporary American theater, clipping files, and databases. There is also a chronologically arranged part of material by Papp himself: letters, interviews, articles, etc. The most detailed information comes from the section of writings about Papp and his Festival. The authors include a chronology of Papp's major productions from 1956 to 1986: plays directed by him as well as those produced by him and the Festival. The book is well indexed and includes an alphabetical listing of productions. This bibliography is a welcome and necessary source for research in modern American theater.

217. Leonard, William Torbert. *Broadway Bound: A Guide to Shows that Died Aborning*. Metuchen, N.J.: Scarecrow, 1983. 618pp.

This is a useful and very interesting reference tool for research in contemporary American theater written by the author of *Theatre: Stage to Screen to Television* (Scarecrow, 1981). The guide lists over 400 productions of commercial theater that were intended for opening on Broadway but were closed for different reasons during tryouts. The information provided for each production includes complete cast, when and where the first and last performances were given, a brief summary of the plot, a list of song for musicals, bibliography and some excerpts from reviews from local papers and *Variety*, and the author's own criticism of the production. This useful guide includes also detailed information on revivals, revisions, or different versions of these shows. Arrangement is alphabetical by show title. The book has several indexes: a chronological index; indexes for actors, playwrights, directors, choreographers, producers, designers, composers, etc.; and a title index. It is a helpful information source for researchers in contemporary theater interested in the commercial risk of the show business and in the supplementary cast and production credits for those shows than never made to Broadway.

218. Leonard, William Torbert. *Once Was Enough*. Metuchen, N.J.: Scarecrow, 1986. 282pp.

If in his *Broadway Bound*, Leonard lists shows that, after try-outs on the road, folded before going to Broadway; *Once Was Enough* is a guide to productions, that, aside from preview performances, lasted only through the opening night. The guide is arranged alphabetically by show titles and covers the time span from 1924 to 1983. For each show, the author provides summaries of the plot, selected criticism explaining why a production failed so swiftly, and discusses directors, actors, and playwrights involved. Especially interesting are the author's notes on other stage and film productions of the failed play and the production's try-out and preview history. There are helpful indexes on actors, choreographers, composers, costume and set designers, directors, lyricists, playwrights, etc. All of the indexes refer to the play titles, and a consolidated index refers to pages. Like his previous guide on failed shows, Leonard's *Once Was Enough* is an important research source in contemporary American theater and bridges a gap in theater history's reference tools.

219. Smith, Ronald L. *Comedy on Record: The Complete Critical Discography*. New York: Garland, 1988. 728pp.

In spite of the title of the book that promises the complete listing, the author provides only a discography of the comedy records that were issued in America between 1957 and 1987. The entries are arranged by names only, and there is no index. Most of the entries include the name of the comedian, the record label and number, samples of dialog from the recording, and a brief essay about the artist's career. It is difficult to locate comedians who appear in minor roles on one another's album; the dates of recordings are rarely provided. Scholars and serious collectors who are interested in comedy as an important aspect of the contemporary theater, perhaps would like to use the source with more bibliographic information. However, the book itself is an interesting, informing, and entertaining reading, because the author gives freely of his own opinions and includes a lot of examples of comedy routines.

220. Startman, Carl J. *Bibliography of the American Theatre Excluding New York City*. Chicago: Loyola University Press, 1965. 397pp.

Classified geographically and arranged by state and city, this systematic compilation treats the historical development of the theater in the United States (including ballet, opera, children's theater, technical aspects of theater arts, such as scenery, lighting, etc.). Among the materials included are books, monographs, articles (play reviews and references to motion pictures and television are omitted), dissertations, and theses. Not all the entries are annotated. Some library locations are indicated. There are author and subject indexes. Though the source provides a lot of useful information on regional theater, it is not easy to use for research in particular time periods in American theater due to lack of any chronological indication.

Indexes to Reviews

221. *New York Theatre Critics' Reviews Index, 1973–1986*. New York: Critics's Theatre Reviews, 1986.

Years 1940–1960 were indexed in 1960; years 1961–1972 in 1973.

These are indexes for reviews from a selection of New York newspapers (such as *New York Times, New York Daily News, New York Post*, etc.) duplicated in a weekly publication called *New York Theatre Critics' Reviews*. These indexes allows researchers in contemporary American theater to find and quickly compare comments of leading reviewers.

222. *New York Times Theatre Reviews Index*. New York: Arno Press, 1970–

   This is an index to *New York Times Theatre Reviews* that compiles reviews and background articles on theater, drama, playwrights, actors, and directors from the daily and Sunday *Times*. The index provides access to persons, titles, and theater companies.

223. *Selected Theatre Criticism. Vol. 3: 1931–1950*. Metuchen, N.J.: Scarecrow, 1986. 289pp.

   Edited by Anthony Slide, this volume presents reprints of contemporary reviews of New York theater productions – dramas, comedies, musicals, revues, etc. – during the years 1931–1950. As the editor indicated, the selection of shows was based on their contemporary and historical importance. The arrangement of the reviews is alphabetical by the play title. The playwrights, actors, directors, composers, theater name, and the opening dates are also provided. The editor included helpful indexes by critics, playwrights, actors, set designers, and composers. The reviews in the third volume are drawn mostly from the following periodicals: *America, Commonweal, Cue, Drama Magazine, Life, New Theatre, New Yorker, Newsweek, Rob Wagner's Script*, and some others – thus greatly reducing the difficulty of obtaining the full text of reviews published in these sources. The researchers involved in the history of New York theater after 1945 and interested in the first five years of this period may find Slide's book very helpful. Many libraries do not have access to periodicals from this period and would benefit from *Selected Criticism* as a full-text source. However, the narrow selection of periodicals and critics does not provide the necessary balance for evaluation of the show.

224. Stanley, William T. *Broadway in the West End: An Index of Reviews of American Theatre in London, 1950–1975*. Westport, Conn.: Greenwood Press, 1978. 206pp.

   This is a first-rate reference tool on an interesting subject produced by a member of the faculty of library science at the University of South California. The book consists of three main sections. The first one is a bibliography of reviews. It is arranged alphabetically by author, then the reviews of each author's plays are grouped together under the title of the play (there are more than 3,000 British reviews of 339 American plays and musicals presented in London during 1950–1975). Name of the theater, dates of the run, number of performances are also provided. The second section is a chronology of important dates, and the third is a title list of shows. There are several appendixes that provide data for the longest running American productions in London, and the seating capacities of theaters. The author also includes a well-written essay on American theater in London. This is an excellent source of secondary articles for comprehensive bibliographies of American playwrights.

Dictionaries and Encyclopedias

225. Bordman, Gerald. *The Concise Oxford Companion to American Theatre.* New York: Oxford University Press, 1987. 451pp.

This is an abridgment of the massive original book by the same author. Many entries on minor plays and figures are eliminated, while the most important articles are preserved. There are more than 2,000 entries total. Extensive coverage is given to the great tradition of the American musical. Detailed biographical sketches and play summaries are provided for such playwrights as David Mamet, David Rabe, Sam Shepard, and others. Updated information on many contemporary topics as well as many new articles make this source an excellent companion to the 1984 edition. This book is an outstanding reference tool for a researcher and an enjoyable reading for anyone interested in theater.

226. Bordman, Gerald. *The Oxford Companion to American Theatre.* New York: Oxford University Press, 1984. 734pp.

This is a comprehensive source of information on the American theater. There is a large number of biographical entries on persons important in American theater which were not included in Young's *Famous Actors and Actresses of the American Stage* or in Hartnoll's *The Oxford Companion to the Theatre.* Bordman provides information even on such peripheral figures as orchestrators, photographers, publicists, critics, scholars, and architects. Represented in addition to the legitimate stage are various forms of live theater, such as minstrel shows, vaudeville, and other forms of popular entertainment. The coverage of drama is very detailed. There are about 1,000 entries for individual plays and musicals that provide basic production data, brief summary of the plot, and some commentaries. There is also information on unions, scholarly societies, clubs, and other theater-related organizations. However, Hartnoll's *Companion* is much better source for current and past New York theaters. There are not enough topical entries, and this lack of topical survey somewhat reduces the book's usefulness. However, with its excellent, in general, coverage of the modern American theater, Bordman's is an extremely welcome resource for a researcher in theater after 1945.

227. Bronner, Edwin. *The Encyclopedia of the American Theatre, 1900–1975.* New York: A.S. Barnes, 1980. 659pp.

Arranged alphabetically by title, this work (not an encyclopedia in the true sense, but rather a dictionary) provides compendium of theatrical data for full-length non-musical plays by American or Anglo-American playwrights produced on Broadway or Off Broadway during the 1900–75 period. All entries give title, opening date, theater, length of the run, a brief statement of the play's theme, sometimes quotations from contemporary reviews, principal actors, author, producer, director, etc. Though musicals are not included, references to musical versions of the plays are provided in the notes. Playwrights are sometimes listed within the body of comments. Some of the author's critical evaluations are rather questionable. There are six appendixes: notable premieres; debut roles (with dates by year only); debut plays (non-musical); the 100 longest running productions (here, musicals are included); statistical records by season; and the listings of four major theatrical awards: Pulitzer Prize, New York Drama Critics' Circle (includes the best foreign play and the best musical), Obie, and Tony (includes only non-musical plays). In spite of its shortcomings, this work is a useful reference source for a basic research in American theater.

Directories

228. American Theater Association. *Annual Directory*. Washington, D.C.: American Theater Association, 1981–1985. Annual.

This directory provides information on membership and structure of the ATA. Continues the publication entitled, *Directory of Members*. The source arranged hierarchically and lists ATA's officers with their divisional affiliation and addresses, then committees, awards, ATA's constitution and by-laws. There is also a list of schools with addresses and telephone numbers in the United States and Canada offering theater programs. In addition, there is a brief list of theater books and publishers, and of theater equipment, services, and supplies. The information on ATA's publications is also provided.

229. Association of Theatrical Artists and Craftspeople. *The New York Theatrical Sourcebook*. New York: Broadway Press, 1984– . Annual.

This is a highly useful directory for all persons involved in theatre production or in display industries and also for those researchers who are interested in the contemporary American entertainment industry. The major portion of the book is the section "Products and Services" that provides listing of businesses supplying materials for props, stage designs, costumes, special effects, etc. The section is categorized by subjects, and within each category there is an alphabetical listing of establishments. Cross-references are given between the entries. The index includes references to all subject categories mentioned in the main section. There is also an appendix that provides information on design collections, special libraries, museums, etc.

230. Bainum, Mibs, Amy Miller, and Susan Levi Wallach, eds. *Summer Theatre Jobs*. New York: Theatre Crafts Books, 1984. 196pp.

This directory is compiled by the editors of *Theatre Crafts Magazine*. It offers full description of different summer jobs available in theaters throughout the country. For a historian of contemporary American theater, this book, along with Jill Charles' *Summer Theatre Directory*, may illuminate important aspects of summer theaters' day-to-day existence during the eighties.

231. Beecham, Jahnna, Zoaunne Leroy, and Adale O'Brien. *See the U. S. A. with Your Résumé: A Survival Guide to Regional Theatre.* New York: S. French, 1985. 256pp.

Serving similar purpose as the *Summer Theatre Jobs* directory, this book provides vocational guidance for actors and others seeking jobs in regional theaters. For a researcher of contemporary American stage, this directory, along with the annual *Regional Theatre Directory*, may be a detailed document of regional theaters' needs during the eighties.

232. Brooks, Jack. *Front Row Center: A Guide to Southern and Central California Theatres.* San Francisco, Calif.: Productions, 1984. 245pp.

The author — actor, director, theater critic, and entertainment editor for radio programs — presents a well-researched guide to repertory and facilities of 120 theaters in Southern and Central California. Each entry includes description of seating capacity, address of the theater, business phones, names of director, producing manager, brief history, and — for most major theaters — a seating plan. There are also a glossary and an index. This useful guide fills a gap in the contemporary theater history.

233. Charles, Jill. *Summer Theatre Directory: A National Guide to Summer Employment for Professionals and Students. . . .* Dorset, Vt.: Dorset Theatre Festival and Colony House/Theatre Directories. 1986–   . Annual.

This publication is a continuation of Leo Shull's annual, *Summer Theatres*. The work is arranged geographically. It is designed as a placement tool for both Equity and non–Equity professionals and students; and for each theater provides name and address, union affiliation and type of contract in use, hiring practices, salaries, the current producer, etc. The information presented is obtained through an annual mailing to various summer theaters and is alphabetically arranged by state under the headings Summer Theatre Directory and Summer Training Programs. A few Canadian theaters are also included. This publication is also a source of valuable information for a researcher in modern American theater for it provides some of the data often difficult to locate, such as the year a summer company was founded, number of years under the current director, the number and type of shows offered, description of theatrical philosophy supplied usually by the theater, etc.

234. Charles, Jill, ed. *Directory of Theater Training Programs: Profiles of College and Conservatory Programs Throughout the United States.* Dorset, Vt.: Theater Directories, 1989. 162pp.

This is the second updated edition of the best and most accessible source of information not only for students selecting a location for theater training but also for those researchers in modern American theater who are interested in comparative data of theater programs. The arrangement of the volume is alphabetical by state. The directory lists 250 institutions and additional 30 schools — from a liberal arts college to a professional conservatory. Each entry contains contact information, admission rules, degrees and majors, enrollment figures, number of graduates by degrees, statement of the department's philosophy of teaching, guest faculty and artists, etc. Included in the listings are schools that are members of the University/Resident Theatre Association, the National Association of Schools of Theatre, and the Association for Theatre in Higher Education. This source is very easy to use.

235. *Contact Book*. New York: Celebrity Service, 1958–   . Annual.
     This is a listing of names and addresses of people and organizations in New York and in Hollywood in all aspects of show business including drama theater. This source may be useful not only to people directly involved in show business but also to those researchers in modern theater who need to find contact with agents and managers or with various types of studios and producers.

236. Delaplaine, A. *The Dramatist's Bible*. Chicago: St. James Press, 1989. 222pp.
     This valuable source is a good companion to *Dramatists Sourcebook* (published by the Theatre Communication Group) and covers theaters, agents, dramatists' organizations, agents, publishers, competitions, grants, etc. The volume is a useful source for every outlet available to a writer or a dramatist who wants his work to be published and produced. The editor provides an alphabetical list of producing organizations on every level — professional or college theater — mostly in the United States, but also in Canada and the United Kingdom. The calendar of daily and monthly deadlines for submission of manuscripts is very helpful. The volume includes a comprehensive index.

237. Eaker, Sherry, comp. and ed. *The Back Stage Handbook for Performing Arts*. New York: Back Stage Books/Watson-Guptill, 1989. 239pp.
     This work is focused on the business side of the performing arts. It is a very useful directory of how-to and who-to contact in the world of entertainment industry. The arrangement of material is by six categories: training, basic requirements, finding job, getting the show on the road, working in the theater, and work for the back stage. Such important topics as resumes for theater professionals, photographers, auditions, agents, etc. are also covered. The editor also supplies trade list of dance studios, voice teachers, agents, and other different performance aids in New York and L. A. The book is indexed. This practical directory is of help to both a performer and a scholar of the contemporary

American theater interested in the state of the arts in the entertainment business.

238. Epstein, Lawrence S. *A Guide to Theatre in America*. New York: Macmillan, 1985. 443p.

This directory provides comprehensive information on theater's diverse service needs, and is intended for academic, amateur, and professional theater as well as for the general public. The listings include schools and colleges offering degrees in theater, library collections, producers, variety of theater-oriented services, entertainment lawyers, ticket agencies, unions, etc. Each of 18 chapters is arranged by city and state. Address and telephone numbers are provided for almost all entries. An especially useful feature is the Contact Index. Though there are some errors and omissions, this directory is a helpful sourcebook for any theater professional, researcher seeking an important address or telephone number, and the general public.

239. Goodrich, Anne. *Enjoying the Summer Theaters of New England*. Chester, Conn.: Pequot Press, 1974. 150pp.

This source provides basic directory-type information for 42 New England professional summer theaters: address, producer, telephone number, performance times, ticket prices and discounts, etc. In addition, the author gives information not always available otherwise, such as: travel directions, site of the theater, its history, popularity, architectural style and decorations, etc. It could be a useful finding tool in a study on contemporary summer theaters.

240. Handel, Beatrice, ed. *The National Directory for the Performing Arts/Educational*. 3d ed. New York: John Wiley, 1978. 669pp.

This work is designed as a companion to *National Directory for the Performing Arts and Civic Centers*. The volume is arranged as an alphabetical listing of schools by states with the emphasis on college and university programs. The information provided includes: arts areas, performing series and facilities, categories of class offerings, faculty and students, certification information, performance workshops, etc. However, some entries are incomplete. Those researchers who are interested in comparative data of theater programs in the seventies may find this source useful despite some of its omissions.

241. Handel, Beatrice, and Janet W. Spencer, eds. *The National Directory for the Performing Arts and Civic Centers*. 3d ed. New York: John Wiley, 1978. 1049pp.

This is a directory of organizations, civic centers and other facilities involved in the performing arts. It is arranged alphabetically by state and city, and then by categories, such as dance, instrumental music, vocal music, theater, etc. Performing series and facilities are listed alphabetically within each category. In case of the facilities, the type, number of seats, stage, architect, rental conditions, etc. are usually provided. The directory is indexed by facilities and categories. There are also a list of active (at the time of publication) Broadway producers with their phone numbers and another one of major symphony orchestras. The source is broad in scope but should be used with caution (perhaps with the aid of a standard telephone directory): there are some errors and omissions.

242. Helbing, Terry. *Theatre Alliance Directory of Gay Plays*. New York: JH Press, 1980. 122pp.
    This is a directory of plays (mostly American) that have gay characters and concentrate on homosexualism as a major theme. Entries are arranged alphabetically by title of the play and provide information on production data and a summary of the plot. There is a name index.

243. Henderson, Mary C. *The City and the Theater; New York Playhouses from Bowling Green to Times Square*. Clifton, N.J.: J. T. White, 1973. 323pp.
    This book provides history of New York's theaters (Off Broadway is excluded), extant or demolished. The major part of the work consists of chapters that trace development of various theatrical districts with a map and a list of theaters, and is illustrated with architects' drawings and photographs. About one third of the book is an alphabetically arranged historical directory of theaters with each entry providing brief account on the theater's past and present followed by an illustration of an exterior view. There are also a bibliography and index. The work can be used as a directory providing useful information for research in the history of New York theatrical life.

244. Hughes, Catharine, ed. *American Theatre Annual: Covering Regional Theatre and National Touring Companies and Incorporating the New York Theatre Annual*. Detroit: Gale Research, 1978/1979–1980. 280pp.
    Former *New York Theatre Annual*. The source mostly documents all plays opening On, Off, and Off Off Broadway and covers cast and production credits, plot summaries, opening and closing dates, excerpts from reviews, etc. There are also sections on awards for the year, on national touring companies, and reports on the seasons of the major resident companies around the country.

245. Kaplan, Mike. *Variety Presents: The Complete Book of Major U.S. Show Business Awards*. New York: Garland, 1989. 750pp.
    It is a well-designed and well-executed reference work on show business awards. The source is concerned with awards only and covers Oscars, Emmys, Grammys, Tonys, and Pulitzer Prizes for plays. Each award has its own section and a comprehensive index. There are no critical or evaluative commentaries given. The winners and runners-up are listed for each prize from the beginning through the end of 1987.

The book is well illustrated with black and white photographs. The tool provides a lot of facts on titles, casts, presenters, etc., which are accessed by a detailed index.

246. Kaye, Phyllis J. *American/Soviet Playwrights Directory*. Waterford, Conn.: O'Neill Theater Center, 1988. 140pp.

The result of the project of the American Soviet Theater Initiative (ASTI), this directory is a unique reference tool. It offers artists and theater scholars of both countries a source with which they can more easily discover information about each other's theatrical life. The directory provides data which is otherwise not available: about 100 of leading Russian playwrights, and, in the same manner, it will give information about selected American playwrights to those who are interested in the USSR. Each entry includes a short biographical sketch, list of an author's works, and brief synopsis of his major plays.

247. Levine, Mindy N. *New York's Other Theatre: A Guide to Off Off Broadway*. New York: Avon Books, 1981. 235pp.

This guide provides detailed discussions of the 84 theaters that were, at the time of the publication, members of the Off Off Broadway Alliance. The entries include a brief background, complete production lists for the 1978/79 and 1979/80 seasons, local restaurants and transportation information.There is also a well-written historically descriptive introduction by Joseph Papp. However, New York alternative theater has a rapidly transitional nature. As the author suggested in her "Explanatory Notes," her book may be used as a basis for exploring Off Off Broadway theaters along with the current sources for actual productions and new companies' names (such as weekly *Village Voice* or monthly *Theatre Times*). For a researcher interested in the history of New York alternative theater, this book can be used as a historical directory perhaps together with another detailed historical source, *Off Off Broadway Book*, published by Bobbs-Merrill in 1972 .

248. Novick, Julius. *Beyond Broadway: The Quest for Permanent Theatres*. New York: Hill & Wang, 1968.

This book is a directory to resident professional theaters in the United States (New York is excluded) and Canada. Material is organized by geographical locations and by type of theaters. Though twenty years old, this tool can be used by a researcher interested in the history of American residential professional companies.

249. Osborn, M. Elizabeth, ed. *Dramatists Sourcebook: Complete Opportunities for Playwrights, Translators, Composers, Lyricists, and Librettists*. 1989–90 ed. New York: Theatre Communications Group, 1989. 249pp.

This directory is intended for those theater professionals who are interested in having their work produced on the American stage. The

directory consists of two main sections. The first one, "Script Opportunities," gives list of theaters, prizes, publishers, and also information
on relevant workshops, conferences, festivals, etc. The second section
is called "Career Opportunities" and it provides listing of agents,
fellowships, grants, university programs, etc. There are more than 800
listing total. This is a useful information source for all those interested
in the American nonprofit theater market.

250. Perry, Jeb H. *Variety Obits: An Index to Obituaries in Variety,
     1905–1978*. Metuchen: N.J.: Scarecrow, 1980. 311pp.
        This directory provides references to obituaries published in *Variety*,
     the entertainment industry's premier trade journal. These obituaries
     were for those people who worked in different areas of performing arts,
     including the legitimate stage.

251. *Regional Theatre Directory: A National Guide to Employment in
     Regional Theatres*. Dorset, Vt: Dorset Theatre Festival and Colony
     House/Theatre Directories, 1985–   . Annual.
        This paperback book is a directory to the employment opportunities
     in regional theaters. It provides information on Equity contracts, union
     addresses, audition lists, listings of theaters by geographic region along
     with the contracts they offer and their hiring practices and salaries.
     There is also a description of computerized casting services in New
     York. This directory is a valuable placement aid for theater profes-
     sionals seeking employment in regional and dinner theaters. In the 1989
     volume, job market information for more than 400 theater companies
     is listed alphabetically by state. The five appendixes cover unions and
     their rules, theater services and information organizations, books that
     are useful for job-seeking actors and other theater professionals,
     bookstores that specialize in these materials, etc. The indexes list all the
     theater companies covered in the source and also categorize them by
     type, such as children's theater companies, musical, feminist's, etc. This
     tool is also a useful information source for those researchers in modern
     American theater who are interested in the employment opportunities
     and an atmosphere at the contemporary theatrical job market.

252. Stevenson, Isabelle. *The Tony Award: A Complete Listing, With a
     History of the American Theatre Wing*. New York: Crown, 1987.
     197pp.
        This directory provides information about people associated with the
     origin of the Tony award — this symbol of the excellence in the
     theater — and lists names of the recipients from 1956 up to the present.
     The book also includes a history of the American Theatre Wing, which
     administers the Tony, and a brief biography of Antoinette Perry — the
     late actress, in whose honor the award is presented. There is an appen-
     dix that lists regulations and the theaters eligible to participate.

253. Theatre Communications Group. *TCG Theatre Directory*. New York: Theatre Communications Group, 1981–   . Annual.

    This is a continuation of the previous title published by the Theatre Communications Group, *Theatre Directory*. The book is divided into three parts. The first part provides the alphabetical list of the TCG associated theaters. Each entry includes address, phone number, names of administrative and artistic heads, contact information, season dates, key personnel, performance schedule, etc. The second part provides a listing of names, addresses, and brief description of different theater services. In the last part, there is a state-by-state listing of the TCG theaters. The directory is of great use to theater professionals and to those researchers who are seeking information on TCG's constituent and associated theaters.

254. *Theatre Profiles: The Illustrated Guide to America's Nonprofit Professional Theatres*. New York: Theatre Communications Group, 1973–   .

    This important biennial directory provides an alphabetical listing of nonprofit professional theater companies in the United States. Each entry includes information for primary administrative personnel, address, telephone numbers, seating capacity, type of stage, other data for the theater's physical facilities, operating expenses for the last fiscal year, attendance figures, founding date, etc. There is also information for major productions, along with the list of directors, actors, set and costume designers, etc. The text is illustrated with the black and white photographs. The editors of the last volumes (volume 8 was published in 1988) provided also essays on various aspects of the nonprofit theaters. There are helpful title and name indexes.

255. *Theatrical Variety Guide*. Los Angeles: Issued on Behalf of the American Guild of Variety Artists by Theatrical Variety Publications, 1966–   . Irregular.

    This directory can be of use to those interested in the entertainment industry and theatrical market in the West Coast and of course to theater professionals who are considering employment opportunities. The source provides names and addresses of agents, producers, officers of Actors' Equity, lecture bureaus, recording companies, theaters, etc.

256. Wasserman, Paul *Awards, Honors, and Prizes: A Directory and Sourcebook*. 5th ed. Detroit: Gale Research, 1982. 2v.

    Volume 1 of this directory is devoted to the United States and Canada; volume 2 provides international and foreign coverage. The source is actually an international directory of various awards and their donors. It is arranged by sponsors. The directory is a good finding tool for those interested in the history of American theatrical awards.

257. Wasserman, Steven R. and Jacqueline Wasserman O'Brien, eds. *The Lively Arts Information Directory: A Guide to the Fields of Music,*

Dance, Theater, Film, Radio, and Television in the United States and Canada . . . 2d ed. Detroit: Gale Research, 1985. 846pp.

The importance and magnitude of this work is stated in its complete subtitle: ". . . covering professional and trade organizations, arts agencies, government grant sources, foundations, educational programs, journal and periodicals, consultants, special libraries, research and information centers, festivals, awards, and book and media publishers." The first edition appeared in 1982. The second one is over a third more enlarged and includes about 9,000 listings. Although some of the data was obsolete even before the publication, this is a valuable and useful source for any researcher concerned with various aspects of the performing arts.

258. *West Coast Theatrical Directory*. Los Angeles: California Theatre Council, 1987. 121pp.

This is an annual publication that since 1970 began to list companies connected with all aspects of theatrical film production. Includes classified section ("Translation Services," "Aerial Services," etc.) and many ads. This directory may be of use to those in the film industry rather than to researchers in theater.

259. Whillis, John. *Theatre World: 1986–1987 Season*. New York: Crown Publishers, 1988. 251pp.

This is a forty-third annual edition of *Theatre World*. It answers any question involving who did what in the field of theater in 1987. The volume provides complete listing of Broadway productions, including actors, directors, replacements, producers, playwrights, composers, costume and lighting designers, press agents, opening and closing dates, etc. The compiler also provides hundreds of short biographies and numerous photographs of the plays and the actors. The touring companies, Off Broadway shows, and regional theater productions are also included. This standard reference tool covers the theater world between 1 June 1986 and 31 May 1987.

260. Young, William C. *Famous American Playhouses, 1900–1971: Documents of American Theater History*. Vol 2. Chicago: American Library Association, 1973. 297pp.

This is an illustrated directory to the theaters from east to west Coast. There are four chapters: New York playhouses, regional, college and university, and summer theaters. Each section is arranged chronologically by opening dates and for each theater its history is summarized. The directory includes several indexes: geographical; alphabetical index of theater names; and index of persons involved in theater business, such as lighting and scene designers, directors, managers, owners, architects, etc. There are also two selective bibliographies; one for American theater in general, another for the playhouses. The book may be a valuable information source for those interested in the history of American playhouses.

Biographical Sources

261. Archer, Stephen M. *American Actors and Actresses: A Guide to Information Sources*. Detroit: Gale Research, 1983. 710pp. (Performing Arts Information Guide Series, vol.8)

   This annotated bibliography concerned with actors and actresses in the professional (legitimate) theater. There are over 3,200 entries to biographies of 226 stage performers in the U.S. theater history. The main part of the work is arranged alphabetically by the actor/actress' name. Sections of reference sources and general information tools (encyclopedias, collective biographies, etc.) precede individual coverage. Included are indexes of subjects, titles, and authors. Though selection of biographees can always be open to debate, the work is well thought out and is a valuable source for American theater historians.

262. Comtois, M.E. and Lynn F. Miller. *Contemporary American Theatre Critics: A Directory and Anthology of Their Works*. Metuchen, N.J.: Scarecrow, 1977. 979pp.

   This directory provides biographical information on major American theater critics, and, in many cases, sample pieces of their works. The main section, which is a biographical directory by itself, gives critic's name and his detailed personal and professional data, as it was provided by the returned questionnaire. Perhaps not many corrections were made by further research for there are some errors and omissions. The work has three useful indexes: geographical, an index of employers, and a title index of critiques covered in the book. In spite of some shortcomings, this is a helpful source of biographical information on important American critics.

263. Franklin, Joe. *Joe Franklin's Encyclopedia of Comedians*. Secaucus, N.J.: Citadel Press, 1979. 347pp.

   Joe Franklin's book is not an encyclopedia by any means. The book consists of alphabetically arranged essays on numerous — mostly American — comedians and comic writers. However, there is no standardization as to the information provided by the entries (some of them read like a gossip columns); and the book is not indexed.

264. Kaplan, Mike, ed. *"Variety's" Who's Who in Show Business*. New York: R. R. Bowker, 1989. 412pp.

   This is planned to be an annual publication. The current volume presents information complete up to the end of 1988 (persons deceased prior to June 30, 1988, are not included). The work covers biographical data of important figures in show business — more than 6,500 names total. The information provided in each entry is minimal and includes facts on birth date, place of birth, education, professional activities in different media — television, theater, movie industry, music, dance, etc. In spite of the evident lack of extensive information, this reference book is a valuable tool for locating the credits of currently alive and active entertainment industry personalities. The coverage is international with the emphasis on the United States show business.

265. *Notable Names in the American Theater*. Clifton, N.J.: James T. White, 1976. 1250pp.

This work is actually the second — updated and enlarged — edition of Walter Rigon's *The Biographical Encyclopedia and Who's Who of the American Theater* (1966). *Notable Names* is a comprehensive biographical dictionary of contemporary persons connected with different aspects of American theater. The work consists of nine sections. The first is "New York Productions" includes titles of the plays staged from 1900 through May 1974, type of production, name of the theater, open date and the length of run. However, names of the playwrights are not given. Then follows "Premieres in America" with title, author, premiere date, and the length of run; similar information is given in "Premieres of Americans Abroad." The main focus is the "Notable Names" section that provides concise but very detailed biographies of living American theatrical personalities. There are also "Theater Group Biographies"; a good summary article on "Stage Periodicals"; "Theater Buildings Biographies"; "Awards" section; "Biographical Bibliography" (lists books by and about significant personalities in American theater, but not criticism; there are 900 names and 2,900 titles); and "Necrology" (from the colonial time to the present). Individual biographical entries are well researched and carefully organized. This is an indispensable tool for any kind of basic research in modern American theater.

266. Robinson, Alice M., Vera Mowry Roberts, and Milly S. Barranger, eds. *Notable Women in the American Theatre: A Biographical Dictionary*. New York: Greenwood Press, 1989. 993pp.

This biographical dictionary is a comprehensive reference work that provides information on outstanding women in the history of American theater. The book is preceded by an introduction and is concluded by two appendixes: the listing by place of birth and the listing by profession. There is also a useful index. The main part of the dictionary is the "Notable Women" section that provides detailed biographies of the outstanding women connected with different aspects of theater: actresses and directors; critics, educators and scholars; children's theater specialists; designers; dancers and choreograpers; playwrights, lyricists, and librettists; producers, managers, and administrators; singers; even theater patrons. Entries generally run two or three pages and provide bibliographic references at the end. This new biographical source is an important and helpful reference tool for research in history of American theater.

267. Wearing, J. P. *American and British Theatrical Biography: A Directory*. Metuchen, N.J.: Scarecrow, 1979. 1007pp.

This guide provides an access to biographical information on nearly 50,000 people involved with the American and British theater from the earliest time to the present. It indexes over 200 works of collective biography, theater yearbooks, encyclopedias of the theater, and other related sources. Some foreign personalities who have contributed to the English-speaking theater are also included. Each entry contains a name with the cross-references to stage name or pseudonym, dates of birth and death, country of origin, theatrical occupation, and a code to the sources that will have fuller biographical information. Wearing's book is a good practical aid in researching for biographical information.

268. Young, William C. *Documents of American Theater History: Famous Actors and Actresses on the American Stage.* New York: Bowker, 1975. 2v.

These two volumes contain biographical information on 225 performers who appeared on the American stage from the beginnings until the publication time. For each performer there is a portrait, brief biographical data, and a number of extracts from contemporary reviews, interviews, memoirs, etc. The source is illustrated with prints and engravings. Included is a detailed index for names, characters, and play titles. However, the editor's decisions as to who is "famous" can be questionable as well as, sometimes, quality of the information provided: for example, "famous role" entry does not usually say where, for how long, and when it was played. There are not many contemporary performers; and though some scholars may find useful data in this source, it is not a serious information tool for research in modern American theater.

Dissertations

269. Litto, Frederic M. *American Dissertations on the Drama and the Theatre. A Bibliography.* Kent, Ohio: Kent State University Press, 1988, 1969. 519pp.

This comprehensive, computer-produced bibliography brings together references to all doctoral dissertations in the performing arts written in departments of English, foreign languages, history, music, speech and drama in the United States and Canadian universities. The cut-off date is 1965. The editor's approach was interdisciplinary, that is why the listing (about 4,500 entries) includes dissertations not only in drama criticism or theater history, but also in theater music, stagecraft, television and radio shows, etc. Though all dissertations are written in the United States and Canada, the subject matter is international. Entries are arranged by an author reference code. There are also conventional index of dissertation authors, keyword-in-context index, and a subject index that has geographical arrangement with chronological and subject divisions.

Part III.   Different Aspects of Theater Arts

5.   Visual Arts in Theater

Costume

270. Arnold, Janet. *A Handbook of Costume*. New York: S. G. Phillips, 1980. 336pp.

This scholarly tool presents discussions of various topics: visual and documentary sources for the study of costume, representation of fashion trends, archival and literary sources, technical manuals, problems and techniques of conservation of costumes, etc. There is a separate part that deals only with costume for the stage. The work is not indexed but a classified bibliography is included. The book is well illustrated.

271. Bruhn, Wolfgang, and Max Tilke. *A Pictorial History of Costume; A Survey of Costume of All Periods from Antiquity to Modern Times Including National Costume in Europe and Non-European Countries.* New York: Hastings House Publishers, 1973. 274pp.

This is a translation from the German book, *Das Kostuemwerk*. About 4,000 types of costume in color plates, drawings, engravings, and photographs represent historical fashion trends and the most important garments of various time periods.

272. Cassin-Scott, Jack. *Costume and Settings for Staging Historical Plays.* Boston: Plays Inc., 1979. 4v.

Volume 1 deals with the classical period; volume 2—with the medieval; volume 3 presents the Elizabethan and Restoration periods; volume 4—the Georgian. There is a general historical introduction to the period in each volume, with discussion of stage properties and stage settings. Each volume is separately indexed.

273. Kessler, Jackson. *Theatrical Costume: A Guide to Information Sources.* Detroit: Gale Research, 1979. 308pp. (Performing Arts Information Guide Series, 6)

This is a well-organized, valuable and usable bibliography for any costumer working in theater or for any researcher interested in theatrical costume. The source provides a classified annotated bibliography of

1,700 English-language titles published mostly after 1957 (though some of the foreign sources are included because of their superb illustrations). There are fourteen chapters covering respectively theater, dance, motion pictures, historical costumes that are arranged chronologically and regionally, fashion psychology and textile history, etc. Reference titles are subdivided into bibliographies, dictionaries, etc., and there are general works with special sections for Eastern costume and theater. There is an accessory section that deals with masks, makeup, hair style, militaria, ritual items, and even underwear. Author, title, and subject indexes are included.

274. Laver, James. *Costume in the Theatre*. New York: Hill and Wang, 1967. 212pp.

This is a good source of scholarly presented information on theater costume in various historical periods and dramatic art forms. A selected bibliography and index are included.

275. O'Donnol, Shirley Miles. *American Costume, 1915–1970: A Source Book for the Stage Costumer*. Bloomington: Indiana University Press, 1982. 270pp.

This work is very clearly written and well-documented, and is an essential reference tool for any professional costumer involved in staging a modern American play or a researcher in contemporary American theater interested in costumes. There are seven main parts that cover World War I (1915–1919), the twenties (1920–1929), Great Depression (1930–1939), World War II (1940–1946), the "New Look" (1947–1952), the fifties (1953–1960), and the unisex sixties (1961–1970). Each section provides a historical introduction to the period explaining fashion psychology and giving specifics on men's, women's, and children's costumes. Each subdivision includes such specific details as underwear, hats, footwear, etc. There are also detailed descriptions of materials most used at the particular period, colors, motifs, etc. Following is the list of the plays (about 40) set in the particular time period with the specific years covered. The source is illustrated with black and white photographs and drawings.

276. Owen, Bobbi. *Costume Design on Broadway: Designers and Their Credits, 1915–1985*. Westport, Conn.: Greenwood Press, 1987. 254pp. (Bibliographies and Indexes in the Performing Arts, #5).

The author, a specialist in costume design and history, presented a book that broadens our understanding of modern theater as a unique art form created by the contributions of many artists. One of the least appreciated groups — costume designers — is in the focus of the work. The author provides brief biographies and credits for 1,021 costume designers for shows staged on Broadway between 1915–1916 and 1985–1986 seasons. The illustrations (black and white photographs of nearly 100 costume sketches) all represent costumes in their original state. There are three appendixes that give information on designers who received Tony, Marharam, and Donaldson awards; recipients and plays are listed chronologically. There is also an alphabetical list of 7,000 plays with the name of the show's costume designer. This is a unique reference source for anybody seeking information on contemporary Broadway costume designer.

Furniture

277. Aronson, Joseph. *The New Encyclopedia of Furniture*. 3d rev. ed. New York: Crown Publishers, 1967. 484pp.

This encyclopedia may be a valuable reference tool for those researchers in theater interested, among other aspects, in furniture used for the show. The source is arranged alphabetically and includes discussions of period styles, definitions of terms, biographical entries for designers, and glossary for designers and craftsmen. There is also a selective bibliography.

Stage Makeup

278. Baygan, Lee. *Makeup for Theatre, Film, and Television: A Step by Step Photographic Guide*. New York: Drama Book Publishers, 1982. 182pp.

This book is written, first of all, for a performer or a makeup artist. However, it may serve as an information source for a researcher of visual aspects, including stage makeup, in today's theater arts (there are modern shows that involve hours of makeup for an actor, for example, part of Phantom in "Phantom of the Opera"). Each chapter deals with a certain type of makeup and repeats procedures or steps—if necessary—from the earlier chapters. Differences of makeup for black and white actors are considered. The book is not indexed, but there is a glossary that provides references to particular chapters.

279. Corson, Richard. *Stage Makeup*. 7th ed. Englewood Cliffs, N.J.: Prentice-Hall, 1986. 389pp.

This is a specialized handbook for use by makeup artists, instructors in makeup, actors, or anybody interested in techniques of makeup applications for contemporary shows. The work is well illustrated to support discussions of various types of stage makeup, such as grease-paint, artificial limbs, wigs, beards, etc. The information on hair styles and fashions is also included. This useful source helps in understanding of basic principles, planning, and applying the makeup.

Stage Design/Technology

280. Burris-Meyer, Harold and Edward C. Cole. *Scenery for the Theatre: The Organization, Process, Materials and Techniques Used to Set the Stage*. Rev. ed. Boston: Little Brown, 1971. 518pp.

This is one of the most complete books on theater scenery. There are fifteen chapters covering material on the state of the theater, planning, types of scenery, materials, tools and equipment for the scene shop, painting, properties, assembling and running the show, techniques and processes, etc. The book is well illustrated and includes numerous charts and graphs. There is an appendix on mechanics and mathematics. Selected bibliography and an index are included also. This one-volume encyclopedia of stage design is a valuable source for a researcher interested in contemporary American theater production and of course for all those directly involved in setting the stage.

281. Hainaux, Rene. *Stage Design Throughout the World Since 1950*. New York: Theatre Arts Books, 1964.
    _____. *Since 1960*. New York: Theatre Arts Books, 1973. 239pp.
    _____. *1970–1975*. New York: Theatre Arts Books, 1976. 159pp.
    The arrangement of this publication was originally by countries but in the last two volumes changed to playwrights. Numerous photographs and illustrations make the central and the major portion of each volume. There are also good indexes to the illustrations by designers, dramatists, composers, and choreographers. It is a useful pictorial reference tool to contemporary stage and scene design.

282. Heffner, Hubert C., Samuel Selden, Hunton D. Sellman, and Fairfax P. Walkup. *Modern Theatre Practice. With an Expansion of the Scenery Section by Tom Rezzuto and a Chapter on Sound by Kenneth K. Jones*. 5th ed. New York: Appleton, 1973. 660pp.
    This authoritative book deals with plays selection, their production and direction with attention paid to stage scenery designing, lighting, sound, costuming, etc. The glossary of professional terminology is included. There are also an annotated bibliography and detailed index. This is a good information source for those researchers interested in technical aspects of contemporary American theater practice.

283. Howard, John T. *A Bibliography of Theatre Technology: Acoustic and Sound, Lighting, Properties, and Scenery*. Westport, Conn.: Greenwood Press, 1982. 345pp.
    This useful bibliography is derived from the ongoing computer data base at the University of Massachusetts Computing Center. The source covers four main areas of theater technology. In 5,700 citations from books, periodical articles, dissertations, arranged by title within the five categories noted in the subtitle of the source, the authors provide full bibliographic information. There is also a section on research materials and collections. Some citations go back to the nineteenth century but the major emphasis is on the contemporary technology. A thorough subject index, organized according to the same five categories, provides topical access through the key words. There is also an author index. The bibliography is a good finding tool for researchers interested in modern American theater technology.

284. Izenour, George C. *Theater Technology*. McGraw-Hill, 1988. 552pp.
     This book deals with stage lighting, scenery, and with theater
     automation: programming and remote control of the stage machinery.
     The author provides an extensive historical background to his subject
     and gives very detailed descriptions. He includes more than 700 illustra-
     tions and nearly 300 bibliographic entries. This is an excellent reference
     source for any theater technician or researcher interested in modern
     theater technology.

285. Larson, Orville K. *Scene Design in the American Theatre from 1915 to
     1960*. Fayetteville, Ark.: University of Arkansas Press, 1990. 413pp.
     This book is a scholarly analysis of the stagecraft movement which
     changed attitudes toward play production: not anymore an assembly of
     individual parts but a cohesive whole dominated by a single artistic
     idea. The author attempts to chronicle the historical development of this
     important movement. The book is divided into seven chapters with the
     final chapter gathering together the previous statements. Illustrations
     form a substantial part of the book. The author also provides a useful
     bibliography and a year-by-year chronology of productions designed
     by forty most outstanding artists between 1915 and 1960. The book —
     based in part upon firsthand observations — presents an important seg-
     ment of American theater history.

286. Reid, Francis. *The Stage Lighting Handbook*. 3d ed. New York: Theatre
     Arts Books, 1987. 176pp.
     This frequently updated source provides useful information on equip-
     ment, rigging, wiring, etc., and discusses the basic steps in lighting
     design in modern theater. The author also considers the differences in
     creating lighting for musical and nonmusical productions. There is a
     glossary of professional terminology. The book is indexed. This is a
     good reference source for researchers in modern theatrical technology
     and, of course, for those professionals directly involved in creating
     lighting on the stage.

287. Rischbieter, Henning. *Art and the Stage in the 20th Century*. Greenwich,
     Conn.: New York Graphic Society, 1970. 306pp.
     This book is translated by Michael Bullok from the German *Buhne
     und Bildende Kunst im XX*. The work is a useful source for researchers
     interested in artists involved in modern theater design. The author
     discusses significant European and American painters and sculptors in
     their theatrical work. The material includes a catalog of productions,
     lists of exhibitions, and an extensive bibliography.

288. Stoddard, Richard. *Stage Scenery, Machinery and Lighting: A Guide to
     Information Sources*. Detroit: Gale Research, 1977. 274pp. (Perform-
     ing Arts Information Guide Series, v.2)
     The book focuses on readily accessible English-language sources

published from 1928 forward and covers books, periodical articles, pamphlets, unpublished theses, and a few exhibition catalogs (about 1,600 items total). There are three parts: part one deals with general reference tools on stage scenery and lighting; part two provides information on sources on stage scenery and machinery and is divided by geographical regions and chronological periods; part three lists chronologically arranged bibliography on stage lighting and projected scenery. There are also three indexes: author, subject, and person (as subject). The annotations provided are too brief but they convey the basic meaning of the source. It is an important tool for researchers interested in the development of scenic art and stage machinery.

289. Thurston, James. *The Theater Props Handbook: A Comprehensive Guide to Theater Properties, Materials, and Construction*. New York: Betterway Publications, 1988. 272pp.

The handbook treats the design, construction, and use of different type of props, bringing together in one volume information on wide variety of sources and techniques of using them. A glossary of professional terms and a list of material sources are included. The handbook is well illustrated with more than 650 photographs, drawings, and diagrams. It is a very helpful and essential resource tool for any theater technician and also for those interested in contemporary theater technology.

290. Warre, Michael. *Designing and Making Stage Scenery*. New York: Reinhold, 1966. 104pp.

The book was originally published in London and is focused mostly on the British stage. However, a good historical background of scenic design and major chapters dealing with the practical aspects of making stage sets can be useful for those interested in modern American theater. The introduction by Peter Brook is worth attention by itself.

291. Wehlburg, Albert F.C. *Theatre Lighting: An Illustrated Glossary*. New York: Drama Book Specialists, 1975. 62pp.

This specialized dictionary gives brief but clear definitions of more than 700 terms, some of them provided with good illustrations. It is a useful quick source of reference in the important field of modern stage technology.

Theater Architecture

292. American Theatre Planning Board. *Theatre Check List: A Guide to the Planning and Construction of Proscenium and Open Stage Theatres*. Middletown, Conn.: Wesleyan University Press, 1969. 72pp.

A wide variety of topics are discussed in this guide and directory to the planning, construction, and the uses of both types of theater: proscenium and the open stage. The guide deals with nature of the work of the theater architect; proportions of the stage; theater's entrances, exits, and trapdoors; necessary lines of vision in the modern theater; placement of seats, balconies, the orchestra; preparation and storage of the scenic elements; backstage areas; heating and ventilation; acoustics and loudspeakers, etc. The source is illustrated with drawings and can provide good information on all the elements of modern theatrical buildings.

293. Glaser, Irvin R. *Philadelphia Theatres, A-Z: A Comprehensive, Descriptive Record of 813 Theatres Constructed Since 1724.* Westport, Conn.: Greenwood Press, 1986. 277pp.

The focus of this book is on architecture of theater buildings in Philadelphia. There is an alphabetical annotated list of 813 theater buildings (both stage and movie theaters) built in Philadelphia from the early eighteenth century to the present time. Each entry provides information on theater name change (if it happened), its address, seating capacity, and of course name of the architect along with the detailed description of his work — interior and exterior. Dates of renovations are also mentioned. The work includes a glossary of architectural terms, an indexed map of theaters, and an alphabetically arranged list of theater architects. However, there are no indexes. This reference source can be used by researchers interested in the history of American theater architecture.

294. Schubert, Hannelore. *The Modern Theatre: Architecture, Stage Design, Lighting.* New York: Praeger, 1971. 222pp.

The book is translated by J. C. Palmer from the German work, *Moderner Theaterbau.* The author traces the history of theatrical architecture since 1945 focusing on acoustics, lighting, seating arrangements, and scenery changes. Modern theatrical buildings used for discussion are chosen from all over the world, including such important American theatrical complexes as the Lincoln Center in New York and the Alley Theater in Houston. The book is well illustrated by many indoor and outdoor photographs, drawings of floor-plans, etc. There are a selected bibliography and a name index. This work may serve as a useful reference source providing information on modern theatrical architecture.

295. Silverman, Maxwell. *Contemporary Theatre Architecture, An Illustrated Survey: A Checklist of Publications 1946–1964, by Ned A. Bowman.* New York: New York Public Library, 1965. 80pp.

The source provides a brief overview of theaters and auditoriums throughout the world with the emphasis on the American theater architecture. There is a subject index. The main feature of the book is an extensive bibliography of both books and periodical articles.

296. Stoddard, Richard. *Theatre and Cinema Architecture: A Guide to Information Sources.* Detroit: Gale Research, 1978. 368pp. (Performing Arts Information Guide Series, v.5)

This is an annotated bibliography of nearly 2,000 monographs, periodical articles, and specialized pamphlets covering various aspects of world theater and cinema architecture. The source provides sufficient coverage to modern as well as ancient, medieval, and Renaissance theater architecture. The emphasis is on English-language publications though some foreign titles were also included for their illustrations. General references, theater and cinema architecture are treated separately. The sections on theater and cinema architecture are arranged by countries and then divided by historical periods. There are indexes of architects, authors, designers, consultants, decorators, theaters, cinemas, and subjects. Though the scope of the source is not clear (what span of publication dates was selected), this guide is a useful reference tool for a researcher interested in the history of theater architecture.

297. Tidworth, Simon. *Theatres: An Architectural and Cultural History.* New York: Praeger Publishers, 1973. 224pp.

The author provides a survey history of theater architecture showing how it was influenced by the evolution of drama and its role in the society. The book is arranged chronologically; major architects of each historical periods are discussed and the theater buildings are compared. The author also discusses in details different problems of contemporary theater design. The work includes numerous illustrations and drawings. It is a good reference source on the history of theater architecture. However, the book's focus is on Western Europe, and researchers in American theater will find just a few examples of American theatrical buildings.

6. Stage Management and Producing

298. Baker, Hendrick. *Stage Management and Theatrecraft: A Stage Manager's Handbook*. 3d ed. New York: Theatre Arts, 1981. 384pp.

    This is a practical manual that provides discussions on the basic components of stage management, such as rehearsals, scenery, proprities, wardrobe, lighting, opening night, etc. A glossary of professional terminology and a bibliography on the subject are also included. The book is a helpful source of information not only for people involved in management but also for those researchers who are interested in contemporary American theater management.

299. Blaser, Cathy B. and David Rodger, eds. *The Stage Manager's Directory*. New York: Broadway Press, 1987. 174pp.

    This directory provides information on 267 stage managers working in different states throughout the country, including those in the commercial New York theater. The information given consists of each manager's credits and expertise and his related skills. There are several indexes: "Experience Index," "Foreign Language Index," and "Regional Index." It is a valuable source for establishing contacts and for better understanding the state of the arts in contemporary domestic theater management.

300. Dodrill, Charles W. *Theatre Management: Selected Bibliography*. Washington, D.C.: American Educational Theatre Association, 1966. 10pp.

    This source was prepared for Theatre Management Project and was intended to serve as an introduction to basic materials on front-of-the-house management. All entries provide a short summary of the text. Though this bibliography is more than twenty years old, some researchers of modern theater may find here citations to useful publications not listed in later sources.

301. Farber, Donald C. *From Option to Opening: A Guide for the Off Broad-*

way Producer. Rev. and updated ed. New York: Limelight Editions, 1988. 184pp.

The theatrical attorney's book covers every legal phase involved in producing a play on Off Broadway, all kinds of legal agreements, operating budgets, etc. The book includes useful information on options, leases, unions, and all the behind-the-scene steps. There are several appendixes with examples of forms and contracts and an index.

302. Farber, Donald C. *Producing Theatre: A Comprehensive Legal and Business Guide*. Rev. and updated ed. New York: Limelight Editions, 1987. 472pp.

This is a legal and business guide to producing plays, be it on Broadway, or in a resident theater. It covers all possible and probable aspects. Precise information is provided on contractual agreement along with samples of actual contracts. The source traces a commercial production from its legal acquisition to details of a long run, tours, and sale of movie rights. There are appendixes and general index. This is the most authoritative legal and business guide in theater field, and it could be of use to anyone interested in legal procedures involved in play production. This title updates and extends the author's book, *Producing on Broadway* (1969).

303. Georgi, Charlotte. *The Arts and the World of Business: A Selected Bibliography*. Metuchen, N.J.: Scarecrow, 1973. 123pp.

This classified bibliography provides a listing of legal, business, and social aspects of arts management, including the legitimate theater. The source is not annotated (except for the list of periodicals and the data for associations) and is not up-to-date. However, some researchers interested in theater management may find it useful.

304. Green, Joan. *The Small Theatre Handbook: A Guide to Management and Production*. Harvard, Mass.: Harvard Common, 1981. 163pp.

This book is a practical guide for managing a theater with a yearly budget of less than $100,000. The information provided deals with raising money, choosing the play, administration, budget, etc. in the small theaters. Though the work is most useful in providing practical directions, some researchers interested in organization and administration in contemporary theater may find it worth their attention.

305. Gruver, Bert. *The Stage Manager's Handbook*. New York: Drama Book Specialists, 1972. 215pp.

This handbook provides detailed information for stage managing from the prerehearsal period to the performance and touring, and illustrates all functions of the stage manager's role in his chaotic task. There are appendixes on selected Equity union rules, Off Broadway stage managing, etc. In the introduction there is a charting of the various unions and their relationship to the business of producing a play. Gruver's handbook is a good reference source for any professional in the theater arts interested in the process of staging.

306. Langley, Stephen. *Theatre Management in America: Principle and Practice; Producing for the Commercial, Stock, Resident, College, and Community Theatre.* Rev. ed. New York: Drama Book Specialists, 1980. 490pp.

This handbook deals with history, theory, and practice of theatrical producing in America and consists of four main parts: "Fundamentals of Theatrical Producing"; "Methods of Theatrical Producing"; "Business Management in Theatre"; and "The Theatre and Its Audience." A selective bibliography is included. This book is a good reference source for anybody interested in a comprehensive view of theatrical producing in America.

307. National Endowment for the Arts. *Conditions and Needs of the Professional American Theatre.* Washington, D. C.: National Endowment for the Arts, 1981. 131pp.

This book is a report provided by the Research Division of the National Endowment for the Arts. It is an analysis of the different economic aspects of the contemporary theater in the United States. This material may be a useful source of information for anybody interested in the various sides of modern theater, in theater management and producing.

Part IV. Alternate Theater Sources

7. Ethnic Theater

308. Seller, Maxine Schwartz, ed. *Ethnic Theatre in the United States.* Westport, Conn.: Greenwood Press, 1983. 606pp.

The book presents a collection of essays on the history of the theater of twenty different ethnic groups in the United States. The covered ethnic groups are Armenian, Black, Belorussian, Danish, Finnish, French, German, Hungarian, Irish, Italian, Jewish, Latvian, Lithuanian, Mexican, American Indian, Polish, Puerto Rican, Slovak, Swedish, and Ukrainian. Essays vary in length; all of them have individual bibliographies indicating high level of original research and the use of rare material, such as ephemeral or archival. Some essays present lists of all known performances by a particular ethnic theatrical company. Very little has ever been published on this topic. For example, *The Harvard Encyclopedia of American Ethnic Groups* (Belknap Press, 1982) gives almost no information on theatrical activities. Although the book does not claim to have a complete coverage of the subject to date and is not a standard reference tool per se, it may serve as an excellent source of information for researchers in modern American theater with any interest in ethnic or folklore studies.

Black Theater

Guides, Bibliographies, Directories, Biographical Sources

309. Arata, Esther S. *More Black American Playwrights: A Bibliography.* Metuchen, N.J.: Scarecrow, 1978. 321pp.

This is an additional volume to supplement the same author's bibliography *Black American Playwrights* (1976). Approximately 500 new names appear in this addition; the entries cover the years 1970–1978. The book has an arrangement similar to the earlier edition: an alphabetical listing of playwrights, their plays, critiques, and awards; a general bibliography; and a title index. Not all of the dramatists included in this bibliography have their vital statistics (birth and death dates, etc.) indicated. There are also some errors and omissions.

310. Arata, Esther S. and Nichola J. Rotoli. *Black American Playwrights, 1800 to the Present: A Bibliography*. Metuchen, N.J.: Scarecrow, 1976. 295pp.

This bibliography (over 1,550 entries total) offers resources for the study of American black playwrights. The book consists of three major sections: the first one is an alphabetical listing of more than 500 playwrights with criticisms, reviews, and awards listed under the author's title for individual play, musical, and script; the second section is a general bibliography that provides information on additional sources on black drama as a specific genre; the last section is a title index that refers the user to the play entries. Unfortunately, the publishers and dates of publications are not given for the plays indicated in this bibliography. There are also some errors in the authors' list. However, even used with caution, this tool is a valuable one for researchers in contemporary American theater engaged in black studies.

311. Davis, Thadious M. and Trudier Harris. *Afro-American Writers After 1955: Dramatists and Prose Writers*. (Dictionary of Literary Biography, vol. 38) Detroit: Gale Research, 1985. 390pp.

This important reference source provides accurate and detailed biographical and bibliographical data on 35 contemporary Afro-American writers, of whom 26 are primarily playwrights. Black plays of the period usually fall into two main categories: black revolutionary drama and plays of the black experience. The essays in this volume reveal the range of attitudes held by black writers and dramatists towards the black experience and the variety of responses to it in the crafting of plays. Each entry includes the following: personal data, scholarly accomplishments and awards, chronological list of writings, description of the works in progress, and biographical and critical sources. Unfortunately, there are few important omissions among the playwrights (August Wilson, for example). The book includes an appendix that brings together reprints of five essays on black theater and a listing of contemporary black theaters and theatrical organizations. There is also a cumulative index of the names of all writers who have so far appeared in the entire Gale's biographical series. As a whole, this volume is a very valuable resource for scholars interested in the black American theater.

312. French, William P. and Genevieve Fabre. *Afro-American Poetry and Drama, 1760–1975: A Guide to Information Sources*. Detroit: Gale Research, 1979. 493pp. (Performing Arts Information Guide Series, v.17)

The two genres are treated in different sections. This source contains "Afro-American Poetry, 1760–1975" by William P. French, Michael J. Fabre, and Amritjit Singh, and "Afro-American Drama, 1850–1975" by Genevieve E. Fabre. The drama section begins around 1850, the time of the first known black playwright, and it includes an introductory essay on the development of black drama as a specific genre. The book has a classified arrangement. Bibliographic references are listed under the following categories: "General Studies," "Critical Studies," "Anthologies/ Collections," etc. These bibliographic references constitute the first part of each section and include library resources, periodicals, play collections, criticism, etc. Individual authors belong to the second part of each section. The compiler of drama bibliography included those authors who had at least one work published. This reference tool is very comprehensive and includes even obscure authors. There are author, title, and subject indexes. This is a valuable source for those researchers in American theater who are interested in black drama as a genre.

313. Hatch, James V. *Black Image on the American Stage: A Bibliography of Plays and Musicals, 1770–1970.* New York: Drama Book Specialists, 1970. 162pp.
    This comprehensive bibliography provides a chronological author list of plays written or produced in America from 1767 to 1970 that either were written by black American playwrights, contain at least one black character, or have a black theme. Each entry has the author's name, the title of the play, its genre, date and publisher, or location of the manuscript if the work was never published. The scope of this source includes full-length and one-act plays, musicals, operas, and even dance dramas. There is a short bibliography of theses on the subject that precedes author and title indexes and a section of undated plays that follows the period in which they were probably written. This is an important reference source for researchers in black theater.

314. Hatch, James V. and Abdullah Omanii. *Black Playwrights, 1823–1977: An Annotated Bibliography of Plays.* New York: Bowker, 1977. 319pp.
    This is a very thorough author guide to more than 2,700 plays written by approximately 900 black American playwrights from 1823–1977. The list of plays is inclusive and the entries are careful and precise. Each entry provides information on the play's title, its genre, summary of the plot, dates for publication and production, cast, length, library sources, permissions, etc. There are three useful bibliographies: general references and research sources on black theater and black artists; anthologies; and dissertations and theses. There are also three appendixes: oral interviews; awards of the black artists; and directory of black artists, agents, and agencies with their addresses and telephone numbers. The source is indexed. It is an indispensable tool for any researcher in modern black American theater.

315. Mapp, Edward. *Directory of Blacks in the Performing Arts.* Metuchen, N.J.: Scarecrow, 1978. 428pp.
    The author, historian of the Negro Actors Guild, compiled a selected alphabetical listing of black performers of the past two centuries (with the emphasis on the present) from all areas associated with the performing

arts: theater, music, dance, opera, films, radio, television, even church. Each entry provides brief biographical information and includes birth and death dates, education, career data, recordings and films made, special interests, family relationships to others in show business, etc. A directory of organizations, bibliography, and a classified index are also provided. Selection techniques are not specified, and there are some errors and omissions. However, this directory is a helpful source of information in the area of modern black American theater.

316. Metzger, Linda, Hal May, Deborah Straub, et al., eds. *Black Writers: A Selection of Sketches from "Contemporary Authors."* Detroit: Gale Research, 1989. 619pp.

For any researcher of contemporary American theater with focus on black dramatists, this volume provides the latest and the most accurate bibliographical and biographical information. Fully updated essays cover more than 400 writers and playwrights of the twentieth century (300 entries are updated from *Contemporary Authors*, and 100 are originally written for this volume). Foreign black authors of interest to American audiences are also included (mostly African and Caribbean writers and playwrights). Each entry provides detailed information on the following: personal data (dates and places of birth and death, names of parents, spouses, children, colleges attended and degrees earned, political preferences, home, office, and agent's addresses, etc.); career data (scholarly accomplishments, honors, awards, memberships, etc.); writings (chronologically arranged bibliography of books and plays written, list of screenplays and other written works); sidelights (biographical essay, author's development; the critical reception during his/her career; revealing comments, often by the writers/playwrights themselves on their personal interests); bibliography of the secondary sources for research. It is a convenient and current source of information for research in contemporary black drama.

317. Peterson, Bernard L., Jr. *Contemporary Black American Playwrights and Their Plays: A Biographical Directory and Dramatic Index*. New York: Greenwood Press, 1988. 625pp.

This comprehensive reference work provides an alphabetical listing of more than 700 black American dramatists who were, or currently are, writing for the theater, film, television, and radio. The time span covered is from 1950 to the present. Also a new edition is already projected, this volume provides significant data not available elsewhere. The foreword to this book is written by James V. Hatch, a highly respected archivist in the field. The information in each entry includes a brief biography, career data, a mailing address for a dramatist, and an annotated list of plays. The plays are described by genre (drama, tragedy, tragi-comedy, domestic comedy, etc.), date of production, synopsis of plot, location of the scripts, and other information of value. Even those playwrights whose works were produced by nonprofessional groups are included. There is also an introductory essay that traces the development of black American theater. Peterson's directory is an essential reference tool for any researcher in modern American theater interested in black studies.

318. Pollack, Martin. *National Black Media Directory*. New York: Alliance Publishers, 1989. 135pp.

Designed to replace the *Black Media Directory*, this paper-back sourcebook contains data on black media not to be found presently elsewhere under one cover. This reference tool provides state-by-state listing of more than 1,000 daily and weekly newspapers, business, trade art, and show business magazines, television and radio stations that are black owned, offer black programming, or have a primarily black audience. The directory is aimed, first of all, at advertising media planners, but should also prove useful to anyone researching minority journalism (including theater criticism) and performing arts.

319. Reardon, William R. and Thomas D. Pawley. *The Black Teacher and the Dramatic Arts: A Dialogue, Bibliography, and Anthology*. Negro University Press, 1970. 487pp.

Still in print after eighteen years of its publication, this book serves as a guide for theater directors seeking plays with black themes and was originally designed for the training of black teachers in theater education. The bibliography presents mostly contemporary books, periodical articles, theses, and plays dealing with all aspects of black Americans life and creative dramatic activity. The anthology provides plays by significant black playwrights: C. B. Jackson, James Hatch, Ossie Davis, Loften Mitchell, and Ted Shine. The book is well illustrated with photographs.

320. Woll, Allen. *Dictionary of the Black Theatre: Broadway, Off Broadway, and Selected Harlem Theatre*. Westport, Conn.: Greenwood Press, 1983. 359pp.

This valuable reference work describes theatrical contributions related to the black experience. The book consists of two major parts. Part 1, "The Shows," lists the shows themselves and provides informative descriptions of more than 300 plays, revues, and musicals that have any relations to blacks. The time covered is from "A Trip to Coontown" in 1898 to "Dreamgirls" in 1981. Each entry includes summary of the plot, name of the playhouse, opening date, number of performances, cast, writing and major production credits, list of songs for musicals, and critical responses along with excerpts from the contemporary press. Part 2, "Personalities and Organizations," provides career information and full stage credits for selected individuals and organizations. There are cross references between these two parts. The book is supplemented by appendixes: a useful bibliography; play/film title index and a personal name index; the chronology of the shows; the discography, and a song index. The author also provides a well written historical introduction tracing the influence of black theatrical contributions and the process of acceptance of black artists. For any researcher in contemporary American theater with interest in black studies it is an important reference tool.

Histories and Critiques

321. Brown-Guillory, Elizabeth. *Their Place on the Stage: Black Women Playwrights in America.* (Contributions in Afro-American and African Studies, 117) New York: Greenwood Press, 1988. 163pp.

    This scholarly monograph will be useful to students and researchers in the fields of black and women's contemporary theater. The author starts with the analysis of the African origin of the black American theater, then continues with the study of the many women playwrights of the Harlem Renaissance who are usually rarely mentioned in other historical studies. The core of the book is the critical and historical analysis of the three major women playwrights: Alice Childress, Loraine Hansberry, and Ntozake Shange—those who, as the author asserts, made significant contribution to the American theater in the way of content, tonal and structural form, characterization, and dialog.

322. Euba, Femi. *Archetypes, Imprecators, and Victims of Fate: Origins and Development of Satire in Black Drama.* New York: Greenwood Press, 1989. 201pp.

    This is an excellent scientific study that traces the origins and development of black theater. In order to better understand modern American black drama and define a concept of black theater, the author aims to reach out into the traditional Afro-American culture and locate features of black expression. The book consists of two parts: Origins and Developments. The first part deals with the concept of fate and archetypes; the second analyzes satire and drama. The author also includes a selected bibliography, glossary of the specific terms, and an index. This is an essential source for understanding and studying contemporary Afro-American theater.

323. Fabre, Genevieve. *Drumbeats, Masks, and Metaphor: Contemporary Afro-American Theatre.* Translated by Melvin Dixon. Cambridge, Mass.: Harvard University Press, 1983. 274pp.

    This scientific study—though not a standard reference tool—is an excellent informational source for those involved in researching in contemporary black American theater. The author focuses on black drama since 1945 in historical and cultural context. There is a detailed analysis of two major tendencies in modern American black theater: the militant theater of protest (Amiri Baraka, Ted Shine, Douglas Turner Ward, and others) and the ethnic theater of black experience (James Baldwin, Ed

Billins, Edgar White, etc.). This book provides a researcher with thorough analysis of black theater's motives and a forecast of its future. The book is indexed and illustrated.

324. Gates, Henry L. *The Signifying Monkey: A Theory of Afro-American Literary Criticism*. New York: Oxford University Press, 1988. 290pp.

In the first part of his book the author defines a distinctive African-American literary tradition by offering a genealogy of black ways of speaking and black ways of writing. Gates treats the problem from a theoretical and a historical perspective and analyzes the African basis of Afro-American formal literary practice. In the second part Gates documents his theory with an exploration of contemporary black writings. This book is an indispensable source for understanding a great deal of modern Afro-American culture.

325. Grupenhoff, Richard. *The Black Valentino: The Stage and Screen Career of Lorenzo Tucker*. Metuchen, N.J.: Scarecrow Press, 1988. 188pp.

Though written as a biographical study, this book covers the historical development of black American theater and film in the course of more than sixty years. Lorenzo Tucker is not a well known name; yet during a span of sixty years, from 1926 to 1986, he acted in twenty films and performed a thousand times on stage as a theater actor, dancer, singer, and a vaudeville straight man. The author of this monograph approached Tucker as a representative figure in the history of contemporary black theater who was a first-hand witness to the evolution of black theater and film and who mirrored those of many black performers who came to Harlem in the 1920s. This book is a good source for studying the history of modern Afro-American theater. It is well-researched and well-written; has many black-and-white illustrations; a useful bibliography, and index.

326. Harrison, Paul C. and Bert Andrews. *In the Shadow of the Great White Way: Images from the Black Theatre*. New York: Thunder's Mouth Press, 1989. 150pp.

This unique book presents more than 200 photographs to visually document in dramatic and compelling images the Black Theater Renaissance that took place in New York from 1957 to 1985. The introduction is written by award-winning actress Cicely Tyson, and the photographs are provided with notes by playwright, critic, and director Paul Carter Harrison. The photographer Bert Andrews, born in Chicago and raised in Harlem, used to be a songwriter, singer, and dancer, and is acknowledged as the pre-eminent documentary photographer of the Black Theater. The book they created is an important record of the growth of the black theater in America as one of the vital forces in our cultural life.

327. Haskins, James. *Black Theater in America*. New York: Crowell, 1982. 184pp.

This is an important historical survey of black artists' contributions to the theater. The study begins with pre–Civil War black productions and closes with a balanced critique of today's black American theater. There are some errors or occasional impositions of the author's view point. However, the book is very valuable in the author's consistency to make connections between the strategies and motives of the black theater and the changing status of the blacks in the society. The study is organized by decade, and within each chapter the author moves from social, political, and economic climate to biographies of the most prominent black artists and analysis of the most influential black theater companies. The book is well illustrated with black and white photographs and indexed. This monograph is a very important source on social and artistic history of the contemporary black theater.

328. Sanders, Leslie Catherine. *The Development of Black Theater in America: From Shadows to Selves*. Baton Rouge: Louisiana State University Press, 1988. 280pp.

This academic study is not a comprehensive historical survey, but the author gives a thoughtful scientific analysis of three major periods of black theater. She presents discussion of the most representative playwrights and their works: Willis Richardson, Randolph Edmonds, Langston Hughes, LeRoi Jones, Ed Billins, and others. It is well researched, well organized, and clear written work. A bibliography and index are included. This study may be a helpful source for a researcher in modern American black theater.

329. Williams, Mance. *Black Theatre in the 1960s and 1970s: A Historical-Critical Analysis of the Movement*. Westport, Conn.: Greenwood Press, 1985. 188pp.

In his scientific study, the author provides an analysis of the major tendencies in black American theater during the indicated period. He describes individual theater companies, the audience, the producers and directors, the major actors, etc. At the same time, the author analyses the philosophical and ideological context within which modern black theater exists. The work is indexed and there is a selected bibliography. It is a very useful informational source in the history of the black theater movement.

330. Woll, Allen. *Black Musical Theatre: From "Coontown" to "Dreamgirls."* Baton Rouge: Louisiana State University Press, 1989. 301pp.

This is an impressively extensive study of black musical theater beginning with *Clorindy* and *A Trip to Coontown*, 1898, through the next hundred years to *Dreamgirls*, 1981. While acknowledging the contributions of white producer Lew Leslie and white composer George Gershwin, the author rescues from oblivion some of the great black performers and musicians — Bob Cole, Will Cook, J. Rosamond Johnson, Florence Mills, and others. Allen Woll provides plot summaries and quotations from both black and white critics. The book is well illustrated with photographs and well indexed. There is a useful bibliography. This is an important source for the study of black theater history in the field that until now was neglected by theater historians.

Jewish Theater

Guides, Bibliographies, Biographical Sources

331. Cohen, Edward. M., ed. *Plays of Jewish Interest*. Rev. ed. New York: Jewish Theatre Association, 1982. 126pp.

This is the revised and enlarged version of the first edition published in 1980. The author presented a guide to plays relevant to Jewish interest. Plays are arranged alphabetically by the following categories: plays from the National Foundation for Jewish Culture Playwriting Competition; plays from catalogs such as, for example, the Dramatists' Play Service, Inc.; plays performed at the 1980 Jewish Theater Festival; plays translated from Yiddish and Hebrew; and unpublished plays. Each entry provides the name of the playwright, composer, lyricist, translator; number of characters in the cast — males, females, and children; set; and a summary of the plot. The book has title and name indexes. This useful guide proves to be an important source of information for a researcher in modern American theater interested in ethnic or Jewish studies, in particular.

332. Fried, Lewis, ed. *Handbook of American-Jewish Literature: An Analytical Guide to Topics, Themes, and Sources*. New York: Greenwood Press, 1988. 539pp.

This detailed, near-encyclopedic guide provides a collection of eighteen essays on the most significant aspects of American-Jewish literary and drama culture from the 1880s to the present. The topics discussed include the development of drama, the evolution of fiction, poetry, Yiddish literary and drama criticism, autobiography, Zionism, Holocaust studies, and American trends in Judaic theology. Though authors vary in their critical and theoretical approaches, each of the essays is organized on bibliographical lines, offering the user an assessment of individual works and authors. Also, each essay provides a discussion of the topic in a comprehensive cultural context, giving a historical account of the major philosophical and literary tendencies of the time. From the reference point of view, the handbook has strong bibliographical features. In general, all eighteen essays presented in this volume provide an in-depth interpretation of the spirit and ideological basis of American Jewish culture. The research value of this analytical guide to themes and topics in American-Jewish culture is greatly enhanced by the bibliographies of relevant subject. The work is indexed.

333. Lyman, Darryl. *Great Jews on Stage and Screen*. Middle Village, New York: Jonathan David Press, 1987. 279pp.

Most of the information included in this book may be easily found in *Current Biography*. However, this source provides an ethnic overview that is not available in other reference books. The author presents more than a hundred biographies of Jewish performers from the theater, film, and television. The length of the entries range from one to three pages. Each biography includes an essay, a photograph, and a list of a performer's shows. The book is well indexed.

Histories and Critiques

334. Backalenick, Irene. *East Side Story: Ten Years with the Jewish Repertory Theatre*. Lanham, Md.: University Press of America, 1988. 197pp.

    This book is a detailed historical analysis of the Jewish Repertory Theatre (JRT) — a pioneering professional American Jewish company. From its birth in the mid-1970s in New York to its present leading role in American Jewish theatrical community, the author chronologically depicts the company's development. She also studies JRT audience and its theatrical tastes. In her historical monograph, the author surveys Jewish attitudes toward theatre through Jewish history and analyses significant Jewish playwrights and their themes. A bibliography and some illustrations are included, but, unfortunately, the book is not indexed. Backalenick's scholarly monograph is a significant contribution to the study of contemporary ethnic American theater.

335. Cohen, Sarah Blacher. *From Hester Street to Hollywood: The Jewish-American Stage and Screen*. Bloomington: Indiana University Press, 1983. 278pp.

    Though not a standard reference tool, Cohen's insightful work is a valuable source for a researcher in filing a gap in the knowledge about the importance of Jewish contribution to the performing arts in the United States. The book consists of eighteen essays on the Yiddish theater; Tin Pan Alley; Jewish comics; careers of Elmer Rice, Cliford Odets, Lillian Hellman, Arthur Miller, and Neil Simon; the plays and films of Jules Feiffer, Paddy Chaevsky, Woody Allen, and Mel Brooks; the dramatic works of the famous Jewish writers, such as Isaak Bashevis Singer and Saul Bellow; and other related subjects. The author covers the time period from 1920 to the present. Unfortunately, there are no illustrations or pictures.

336. Harap, Louis. *Dramatic Encounters: The Jewish Presence in Twentieth-Century American Drama, Poetry, and Humor and the Black-Jewish Literary Relationship*. New York: Greenwood Press, 1987. 177pp.

    Published in cooperation with the American Jewish Archives, this work is a socioliterary study that maintains the standards for thoroughness and scholarship previously established by Lois Harp. The book gives half of its space to drama furnishing both a historical and a literary context. Providing perhaps the most comprehensive and inclusive treatment in English of the Jew in American modern drama, Harp's valuable study becomes an excellent informational and insightful source for the expert.

337. Lifson, David S. *The Yiddish Theatre in America*. New York: Thomas Yoseloff, 1965. 659pp.

The author traces the development of the Yiddish theater from its beginning in Rumania in 1876 to the 1960s in the United States. The work and career of notable directors, actors, and dramatists are analyzed. Lifson also describes how major European theatrical theories and discoveries were first brought to American stage by the Yiddish companies. The book is well illustrated with photographs. Not a reference tool in a standard meaning, Lifson's book may serve as an important source of information for any researcher in modern ethnic American theater.

Spanish-Speaking American Theater

Guides and Bibliographies

338. Allen, Richard. *Spanish American Theatre: An Annotated Bibliography Teatro Hispanoamericano: Una Bibliografia Anotada*. Boston: G. K. Hall, 1987. 633pp.

This is one of the major tools in identifying and locating Spanish American plays for any researcher in modern ethnic American theater. This guide is written by a professor of Spanish at the University of Houston and is based, in general, on the special collection at the University of Houston Libraries, supplemented by works in major U.S. libraries. The guide provides a list of more than 3,500 Spanish American plays published individually, in anthologies, or in periodicals. Arrangement is geographical, by country and, within each country, alphabetical by author. Locations for every item are provided. The guide is in English and Spanish, and for each play analytical and descriptive annotations are provided. There are also author and title indexes.

339. Hepplethwaite, Frank P. *A Bibliographical Guide to Spanish American Theater*. Washington: Pan American Union, 1969. 84pp.

This guide provides information on historical and critical works about the Spanish American theater (including the Spanish-speaking theater in the United States). Monographs or essays on individual playwrights, plays, or history of playhouses are not included in the guide's scope. Most entries are annotated. The sources considered are books, pamphlets, and periodical articles. The guide consists of five major parts: books — general sources; books — sources by country; articles — general sources; articles — sources by country; a bibliography and an author index. It is a well-organized and easy-to-use reference tool that could be of interest to any researcher in the Spanish-speaking theater in the United States.

340. Rela, Walter, comp. *A Bibliographical Guide to Spanish-American Literature: Twentieth-Century Sources*. (Bibliographies and Indexes in World Literature, 13) New York: Greenwood Press, 1988. 381pp.

The author—a well-known Uruguayan bibliographer—states in the introduction that this bibliography of almost 2,000 entries will serve as an initial point of of departure for serious scholarship. The bibliography covers all genres of Spanish-American literature and drama, including Spanish-language plays written in the United States through the mid-1980s. The arrangement is by type of publication: bibliographies, dictionaries, history and criticism, and anthologies. These categories are then subdivided by country and by genre. The author focuses on works published after 1945. Annotations are provided when the work title is not self-explanatory. The guide contains a useful author index. This publication can serve as a helpful reference source for a researcher interested in the area of Spanish-language literature and drama.

Biographical Sources

341. Kanellos, Nicolas, ed. *Biographical Dictionary of Hispanic Literature in the United States: The Literature of Puerto Ricans, Cuban Americans, and other Hispanic Writers*. Westport, Conn.: Greenwood Press, 1989. 374pp.

This dictionary concentrates on contemporary Hispanic authors within the United States and focuses primarily on Puerto Rican and Cuban writers and playwrights active in the United States from 1959 to the present. The arrangement is alphabetical by name of writer. Each entry provides biographical information about an author, a brief discussion of his major works, and an analysis of critical literature about this writer. The editor also provides a summary of the importance of the author's major themes. The book also contains an introduction presenting the context of the volume and providing an analysis of Hispanic literature and drama; a three-page general bibliography on Hispanic literature of the United States; an author-title index; and a listing of contributors (most of them are professors of literature, Spanish, foreign languages, or Hispanic studies at the universities). This dictionary is a useful tool for researchers interested in Hispanic literature and drama.

342. Lomely, Francisco A. and Carl R. Shirley, eds. *Chicano Writers*. (Dictionary of Literary Biography, vol. 82) Detroit: Gale Research, 1989. 388pp.

This Gale's dictionary is an indispensable source for students and scholars in modern American ethnic theater. This reference tool provides the latest and the most accurate biographical and bibliographical information on major Chicano writers and playwrights. Each entry includes personal data of a writer or a playwright, a bibliographical checklist of works by and about the author as well as a short analyses of the most significant secondary sources. Visual material such as photographs of the writers and playwrights and their families, manuscript pages, book jackets, etc. add to the immediacy of the text and enhance the book's value.

Histories and Critiques

343. Collins, J. A. *Contemporary Theater in Puerto Rico: The Decade of the Seventies*. Rio Piedras, P. R.: Editorial Universitaria, Universidad de Puerto Rico, 1982. 265pp.

The author, who has been the drama critic for the *San Juan Star* for a long time, has amassed a tremendous amount of information pertinent to contemporary Puerto Rican theater. This book presents 135 of the author's articles, essays, and reviews in chronological order, providing a comprehensive view of contemporary Puerto Rican theater and its historical development. The author includes a detailed essay on the background and history of the island's theater, providing also a broad historical perspective on the current island scene. This is a valuable and informative research source.

344. Huerta, Jorge A. *Chicano Theater: Themes and Formes*. Ypsilanti, Mich.: Bilingual Press, 1982. 274pp.

This is a comprehensive and well-organized study that presents an excellent historical account of the development of Chicano theater since the late 1960s. The author (who was a founder of El Teatro de la Esperanza — one of the most important Chicano theater groups) organizes his book following what he considers to be the dominant themes emerging from his examination of major drama. The study consists of six chapters, and each of them focuses on one of the major themes of Chicano theater placing the analysis in theatrical, social, and historical context. In his treatment of the subject, especially of the contributions of the Teatro Campestino and Luis Valdez, the author indicates his thoroughness and attention to detail. This comprehensive study is a valuable research tool for a researcher interested in the Spanish-speaking modern American theater.

345. Kanellos, Nicolas, ed. *Hispanic Theatre in the United States*. Houston, Tex.: Arte Publico Press, 1984. 79pp.

This is a collection of scholarly essays that document the vibrant tradition of the Hispanic theater in the United States. The authors approach their subject from different perspectives: historical, anthropological, literary, political, etc. The first essay written by Nicolas

Kanellos provides a historical overview. Unfortunately, the book is not indexed, but it is illustrated with reproductions of rare photographs. This collection of essays is an important source for studying the history of the Hispanic theater in America.

346. Kanellos, Nicholas, ed. *Mexican American Theatre: Then and Now.* Houston: Arte Publico Press, 1983. 120pp.

The book is a collection of essays, sketches, and interviews, and originally was written for an exhibit entitled "Two Centuries of Hispanic Theatre in the Southwest." The purpose of both the book and the exhibit was to motivate scholars interested in ethnic Spanish-speaking American theater and to engage them in further research in this field. The topics covered include the history of theater in the Southwest; actors, acting styles, and theatrical companies; the impact of Latin American theater on contemporary Mexican American theater; the role of women in the development of Chicano theater; etc. In the editor's essay, the history of the Southwest theater is traced, and touring companies, locations, actors, types of plays produced are all reviewed. There are two interviews that present major contemporary figures in Chicano theater—Luis Valdez (who after his "Zoot Suit" became successful in the mainstream theater) and Rodrigo Duarte. Though the book does not provide much analysis of selected works, it does, however, give a researcher a valuable overview of the history and modern trends of Mexican American theater. Unfortunately, this work is not indexed.

347. Pottlizer, Joanne. *Hispanic Theatre in the United States and Puerto Rico.* New York: Ford Foundation, 1988. 85pp.

This book was originally thought of as a report on Hispanic theater in the United States to acquaint the Ford Foundation with the scope of Hispanic theatrical activities. It grew to become an interesting and important book in which the author analyses Hispanic theater in a broad historical and cultural context. Chapter one presents diversity of cultures within American Hispanic theater. Chapters two and three cover the historical development of theatrical movements. Chapter four discusses current theatrical activities. In the last chapter, the author offers recommendations for increasing the stability of Hispanic theater in the United States as a rich art form. There are also two appendixes: one presents a directory of organizations in the field throughout the United States and Puerto Rico, and the second appendix offers the theater survey data for 1985. This small book may be an important information source for those scholars who are interested in contemporary Hispanic theater.

8. Musical Theater

Histories and Show Reference Sources

348. Bordman, Gerald. *American Musical Comedy: From "Adonis" to "Dreamgirls."* New York: Oxford University Press, 1982. 244pp.

   In the preface to the first edition of this author's *American Musical Theatre: A Chronicle* (1978), Bordman promised a volume that would provide information on "every fact and figure" (p.vi) mentioned in the book. In his *From "Adonis" to "Dreamgirls,"* the author attempts to fulfill this promise. He analyzes the history of this specific genre of the American theater — a musical, and traces its development in form, style, and subject from 1884 to 1980. The book is indexed and illustrated with good black and white photographs. It may serve as an important source for the researcher interested in the contemporary American musical and its history.

349. Bordman, Gerald. *American Musical Revue: From "The Passing Show" to "Sugar Babies."* New York: Oxford University Press, 1985. 184pp.

   The principal authority on the American musical today, Gerald Bordman thinks of the operetta as a more formal variant of the musical comedy or an earlier manifestation of this genre. Whereas musical revue, according to Bordman, is another form of musical which is more of a stage entertainment without a plot. His trilogy of volumes — comedy, operetta, and revue — represent a significant contribution to the history of musical theater in the United States and is one of the most important reference sources for any researcher interested in the contemporary American musical.

350. Bordman, Gerald. *American Musical Theatre: A Chronicle.* Expanded ed. New York: Oxford University Press, 1986. 787pp.

   The first edition of this book was published in 1978, and was the first attempt to narrate the history of the American musical: minstrel shows, burlesque, comic opera, operetta, etc. The 1986 edition expands this chronicle from the colonial period to 1985–86 season. The author provides a very detailed season-by-season coverage, supplemented by three indexes: "Shows and Sources," "Songs," and "People." There is also an appendix list of major persons — creators and performers and the productions associated with them. For the theater historian or researcher involved in American musical theater, it is an important source of information.

351. Bordman, Gerald. *American Operetta: From "H.M.S.Pinafore" to "Sweeny Todd."* New York: Oxford University Press, 1981. 206pp.

352. Ewen, David. *Composers for the American Musical Theatre.* New York: Dodd, Mead, 1968. 270pp.

    Not a standard reference tool, Ewen's book is, nevertheless, a good informational historical source even over twenty years after its publication. The author traces the history of the modern American musical theater, describing its roots in European influences, the minstrel show, farce, and burlesque. He analyzes works of composers who actually created the modern American musical as a genre: Cohan, Berlin, Kern, Gershwin, Porter, Rodgers, and others. The book is illustrated with photographs and indexed.

353. Ewen, David. *New Complete Book of the American Musical Theater.* New York: Holt, Rinehart & Wilson, 1970. 800pp.

    In this work, Ewen presents an encyclopedic history of the American musical from "The Black Crook" in 1866 to "Applause" in 1970, 'in chronological order. The book consists of two major parts and two appendixes. Part one is in alphabetical order by title, and provides information on plays: their background and production history, creators of the show and a brief synopsis. Part two gives biographies of librettists, lyricists, and composers. There is a chronology of the musical theater and famous songs in the appendixes. The book is well indexed and may serve as a helpful reference source for any researcher in modern American musical.

354. Engel, Lehman. *The American Musical Theatre.* Rev. ed. New York: Macmillan, 1975. 266pp.

    The first edition of this book was entitled, *The American Theater: A Consideration* and published in 1967. This historical study of the American musical is written by a famous Broadway musical conductor. Lehman Engel presented a comprehensive book about the musical — this specific theater genre without which contemporary American stage cannot be understood. The book is well illustrated. There are also a discography, a list of published librettos and vocal scores, selected bibliography on the subject, and index. *The American Musical Theatre* is not a regular reference tool, but is a good source for anyone interested in the contemporary American musical.

355. Ganzl, Kurt. *Ganzl's Book of the Musical Theatre.* New York: Schirmer/ MacMillan Books, 1989. 1353pp.

This book provides information on more than 300 shows, arranged by country or region: Austria, France, Germany, Great Britain, Hungary, Spain, and the United States. The cut-off date is 1987 (*Phantom of the Opera*). Each section begins with the introduction describing the historical development of the musical theater in that country and includes a listing of the musicals in chronological order by date of first performance. The author provides the following detailed information for each title: plot summary, names of performers, revivals, list of characters. The date and location of the first production are also identified. Black-and-white photographs of stage scenes or of the newspapers and other publicity material enhance the text. The listing of musicals is selective, and some major American musicals are missing. There are two useful indexes: first one includes titles, authors, lyricists and composers; the second index lists song titles. The discography follows the same geographical and chronological arrangement as the other sections. In spite of the several omissions, this reference source on musical theater may prove a valuable tool for researchers.

356. Green, Stanley. *Broadway Musicals Show by Show*. 2d ed. Milwaukee, Wi.: H. Leonard Books, 1987. 368pp.

This work updates the same author's *Encyclopedia of the Musical Theatre* (1980). The book is arranged chronologically by shows. Each of the entries (over 300 total) provides a brief summary of the plot, names of creators of the musical, original cast, credits, lists of songs, length of run, etc. There are also detailed indexes for show, composer/lyricist, director, choreographer, major actors, and theater names. This is a valuable, quick reference tool.

357. Green, Stanley. *Encyclopedia of the Musical Theatre: An Updated Reference Guide to Over 2,000 Performers, Writers, Directors, Productions, and Songs of the Musical Stage, both in New York and London*. New York: Da Capo Press, 1980. 492pp.

This clear, easily read volume provides comprehensive information on the musical theater from the late nineteenth century to 1979. Coverage includes musical comedy, play, farce, revue, and operetta (Gilbert and Sullivan, vaudeville, revues that are not really musicals are not discussed). There are alphabetical entries with brief professional biographies for actors, actresses, composers, lyricists, librettists, directors, choreographers, and producers—people involved in creation and production of musicals. The real and stage names are provided, and all the productions in which each person was involved are listed chronologically. For an alphabetical list of musicals the author gives information about the plots, casts, opening dates of both London and New York openings, names of the theaters in which the musicals were played, number of performances, etc. If appropriate, the author also provides titles of films based on the musicals listed, year of the film's production, director, major actors, etc. A list of over 1,000 songs from musicals with brief descriptions (who sang them, composers, lyricists, the song's theme, etc.); a section on awards and prizes; a chapter entitled "Long Runs"; bibliography of various shows' books; and a discography are also included. For any researcher in modern American musical theater this is a very valuable source of information.

358. Green, Stanley. *The World of Musical Comedy: The Story of the American Musical Stage as Told Through the Careers of Its Foremost Composers and Lyricists.* 4th rev. and enl. ed. New York: Da Capo Press, 1984. 480pp.

   In this well illustrated book the author discusses the careers and musical productions of the most important contemporary American composers and lyricists — creators of musicals. There is an appendix that provides production information for every Broadway and Off Broadway musical with scores written by persons discussed in the book. This work, together with Green's *Encyclopedia* and his *Broadway Musicals*, provides a comprehensive picture of contemporary American musical stage.

359. Guersney, Otis L., ed. *Broadway Song and Story: Playwrights, Lyricists, Composers Discuss Their Hits.* New York: Dodd, Mead, 1985. 447pp.

   This interesting book contains dialogues and panel discussions on both plays and musicals by people who were directly involved in creating Broadway musicals. The work may be a useful source of information for a researcher in modern American musical theater, and it is also compelling reading for all those interested in contemporary commercial theater.

360. Hall, Charles J., comp. *A Twentieth-Century Musical Chronicle: Events 1900–1988.* Westport, Conn.: Greenwood Press, 1989. 358pp.

   In this expansive reference work, the compiler brings together various information about music, musicians, composers, musicologists, and performers and presents it in the context of general cultural climate of the time — events and developments in theater, arts, and literature. For each year there is a listing of cultural highlights, musical events, prizes and honors, new books on different musical genres, new musical compositions. For his sources, the compiler used magazines, newspapers, reference dictionaries, recognized authorities in the field, insights offered by composers or musicians themselves. Though not directly concerned with the theatrical musical as a genre, this chronological guide may prove useful reference source for researchers interested in American musical and general musical background in which they came into being.

361. Hirsch, Foster. *Harold Prince and the American Musical Theatre.* New York: Cambridge University Press, 1989. 187pp.

   The author, who teaches theater and film at Brooklin College, with his monograph on Prince adds the 13th volume to the Cambridge University Press' "Directors in Perspective" series. Though he does not intend to study every show in which Prince was ever involved, Hirsch maintains topical approach, and through nine chapters traces Prince's career: from his apprenticeship under George Abbott, to the first show produced by Prince, *Pajama Game* (1954), through first directing experience in *A Family Affair* (1962), to his success with Webber's musicals, such as *Evita* (1978) or *Phantom of the Opera* (1986). The first chapter of the book provides an excellent overview of the historical development of the American musical. The foreword is written by Prince himself. The monograph is well illustrated with photographs. There are also a chronology of Prince's career, a useful bibliography, and an index. With its many perceptive insights, Hirsch's book may become a good source for understanding and studying the development of the American musical of this century.

362. Hummel, David. *The Collector's Guide to the American Musical Theatre*. Metuchen, N.J.: Scarecrow, 1984. 2v.

Volume One of this work consists of an alphabetical listing of the shows: musical comedies, reviews, operettas, etc. Each entry provides information on the creators of the show, the book the show is based upon, the premiere theater and date, the number of performances, when the first London production took place (if appropriate), etc. There is also a listing of songs in show order; even those songs that were added or cut prior to New York opening are included. Continuing is a listing of the recordings of the show. They may range from those of the original and touring casts — foreign and American, sound track film cast to excerpts from the show found on other recordings or sung in tribute to the composer or lyricist. Hummel's work is the only place where many of the Off Off Broadway musicals documented for the first time. Volume Two is actually an index that lists all persons mentioned in Volume One: composers, lyricists, playwrights, performers, etc. These two volumes are a quality publication, an important reference source for researchers in American modern musical as well as for collectors interested in this genre.

363. Ilson, Carol. *Harold Prince: From "Pajama Game" to "Phantom of the Opera."* (Theatre and Dramatic Studies, 55) Ann Arbor, Mich.: UMI Research, 1989. 443pp.

The author, who has taught at Queen's College and performed and directed in different theaters, maintains her focus on Prince through every show in which he had a hand. The book consists of an introduction and twenty chapters, where Prince's career and the development of the musical as a theatrical genre traced in details. There is also an epilogue that describes Prince's activities since *Phantom*. The author provides an extensive bibliography, a detailed index, and illustrations. The thoroughness of Ilson's monograph makes it a useful reference tool for

studying the American musical and one of its most important and innovative directors.

364. Inge, Thomas, ed. *Handbook of American Popular Culture*. Westport,
     Conn.: Greenwood Press, 1989. 1613pp. 3v.
          This extensive reference source traces the history of one of the most
     vital forms of American contemporary art—popular culture—and
     treats it as an important expression of American society. The handbook
     is divided into 55 chapters where the leading authorities on the subject
     analyze different aspects of popular culture, such as catalogs, com-
     puters, dance, graffiti, musical theater, etc. Each section provides a
     chronological description of the development of the topic and a critical
     essay on most useful reference sources, bibliographies, histories, critical
     studies, etc. For the historian of contemporary American theater, this
     work offers a unique view on musical theater and the revue as the
     cultural phenomena that expresses mass appeal and which purposes are
     entertainment and recreation—the fulfillment of common needs. The
     work has a useful bibliography and an index.

365. Jackson, Arthur. *The Best Musicals: From "Showboat" to "A Chorus Line,"*
     Off Broadway, London. Rev. ed. New York: Crown, 1979. 208pp.
          This is a historical survey of the Broadway musical. The author pro-
     vides abundant information concerning each show: creators of the
     musical, summary of the plot, list of songs, length of the run, films and
     records done after the show, etc. The work is well illustrated and con-
     tains a detailed index, selected bibliography, and several appendixes.

366. Laufe, Abe. *Broadway's Greatest Musicals*. Rev. ed. New York: Funk &
     Wagnalls, 1977. 519pp.
          The author thoroughly examines the history and development of the
     Broadway musical as a specific theater genre. The narrative history
     covers the period from 1884 ("Adonis") to 1976 ("A Chorus Line"). The
     basic arrangement is chronological. Information provided for each
     musical includes background events, the history of the show's develop-
     ment, synopsis of the plot, production costs and budget, total income,
     number of performances, who made a hit, persons involved in the pro-
     duction, etc. Throughout his narrative, Laufe shows the place of each
     musical, both original production and Broadway revivals, in the history
     of the genre, and points out how the show corresponded with the taste
     of the time and the cultural climate. The most momentous musicals—
     "Show Boat," "Oklahoma!," "My Fair Lady," "Fiddler on the Roof,"
     etc.—are treated in separate chapters. The appendix provides a list of
     musicals that ran for more than 500 performances with their authors,
     composers, lyricists, cast members, etc. (Laufe has chosen length of run
     as the criterion). The work is indexed by titles and personal names.
     While not an encyclopedia, Laufe's book is a scientific historical survey
     of the genre and an important reference source.

367. Lerner, Alan Jay. *The Musical Theater: A Celebration*. New York: McGraw-Hill, 1986. 240pp.

This book is not, by any means, a scientific study of the genre. This entertaining and informal history of the musical theater was written by the lyricist of "My Fair Lady" and "Camelot" shortly before he died. Though Lerner's anecdotes about his own career are the major feature of the work (thus complementing his autobiography, *The Street Where I Live*), the book is structured chronologically, and presenting a relatively complete history does a good job of relating the theater to the social climate of the time. The period covered is from the late nineteenth century to 1985. The author's concentration is on the New York stage with some consideration of London. The work is well illustrated and includes a short bibliography and an index. Though this book does not replace other standard reference sources in the field and has errors and omissions, it can offer some useful information and insights for a researcher.

368. Lynch, Richard C., comp. *Broadway on Record: A Directory of New York Cast Recordings of Musical Shows, 1931–1986*. Westport, Conn.: Greenwood Press, 1987. 347pp.

This comprehensive source provides detailed coverage of 459 show albums from *The Band Wagon* (1931) to *Me and My Girl* (1986) with some 4,000 song titles. The arrangement is alphabetical by the musical title. Each entry includes the following information: opening date and name of theater, revivals, composer and lyricist, conductor and his credits, cast members, and the title of each song and who performs it. The discography is complete and includes record label and number of the original and any reissues or multiple recordings, type and mode of recording — disc, tape, etc. There is an index of performers that identifies the albums on which each performer appears. There are also separate indexes for composers, lyricists, and musical directors. The comprehensive coverage of this directory makes it an invaluable research source.

369. Mast, Gerald. *Can't Help Singing: The American Musical on Stage and Screen*. New York: Overlook Press, 1987. 389pp.

The author, professor of English at the University of Chicago who has previously written several books on cinematography, provides in this work a history of the American stage and film musicals. The book is not a comprehensive overview, but provides a reader with a different perspective on the subject: how the requirements of stage or film affected or changed the individual shows. Included are a selected bibliography and an index. The work includes numerous illustrations. Mast's book, being an enjoyable reading by itself and an interesting source of information and insights into the subject, supplements the major historical tools (Bordman's or Green's) but cannot replace them.

370. Mates, Julian. *America's Musical Stage: Two Hundred Years of Musical Theater*. Westport, Conn.: Greenwood Press, 1985. 252pp.

In his well documented scientific study, the author provides wealth of information on the long tradition of musical theater in America showing its roots in opera, melodrama, circus, ballet, vaudeville, minstrel shows, and burlesque. The book includes illustrations, a bibliographical essay and an index. However, the title of the work is somewhat misleading: the author's emphasis is on early theater and he is much stronger in the pre–twentieth century stage. For a researcher in modern American musical theater, this source could be helpful in clarifying the long tradition of musical, but it should be supplemented with other major historical tools on the subject to achieve balance.

371. Simas, Rick. *The Musicals No One Came to See: A Guidebook to Four Decades of Musical Comedy Casualties on Broadway, Off Broadway and in Out-of-Town Try-Out, 1943–1983*. New York: Garland Publishers, 1987. 637pp.

This unique guide documents 577 shows that were staged in New York between 1948 and 1983. All shows are divided into four categories: Broadway shows, Off Broadway productions, shows that closed in try-outs or preview, and shows that ran longer than 300 performances but are currently unavailable for production. Under these categories, entries provide information on the musical: title, facts about the production, the availability of associated material, location of additional information, and critical responses. There are useful indexes that provide access by show title, opening date, names of authors, librettists, composers, and lyricists. Though this volume aims to interest theater companies (regional, educational, or community) to produce musicals commercially unsuccessful in New York, it may be a useful reference tool for a researcher interested in the development and history of the American musical.

Production and Direction

372. Lunch-Burns, Carol. *Musical Notes: A Practical Guide to Staffing and Staging Standards of the American Musical Theatre*. Westport, Conn.: Greenwood Press, 1986. 581pp.

The author discusses 145 popular American musicals in alphabetical arrangement. Each entry provides information on the musical's creators — authors, composers, lyricists, and source. The history of the original production: date, the name of the theater, the length of the run, number of performances, director, choreographer, cast, brief synopsis, etc. follows. The author also provides production information on the required vocal types and chorus numbers, technical problems with staging the musical and their possible solutions, casting, adaptation guides, etc. Instrumentation specifications, discography, and availability of the script are also included in every entry. There are several appendixes that list, chronologically, long-running and award-winning musicals; a bibliography, and an index. Written for actors and theater groups, this guide is also a useful and convenient reference tool for any researcher interested in concise, thorough, and practical treatment of musicals.

373. Lynch, Richard Chigley. *Musicals! A Directory of Musical Properties Available for Production.* Chicago: American Library Association, 1984. 197pp.

This guide provides information on more than 400 musicals available (at the time of the book's publication) from the major agencies that control production rights to most American musical theater properties. Entries are arranged alphabetically by title and each of them provides the following information: creators of the musical (composer, lyricist, librettist); the source of adaptation; a brief synopsis; the availability of libretto (published separately or in an anthology); vocal selections, piano-vocal score, and recordings; dates of major productions (unfortunately, there is no information on original cast); cast requirements; and the name of the licensing agent. A name index and a list of the addresses of licensing agents are included. The coverage is not comprehensive; there are some omissions. However, though written primarily for amateur theater groups, Lynch's book is a very useful reference tool for information relating to the most enduring musicals.

374. Tumbusch, Tom. *The Theatre Student Guide to Broadway Musical Theatre.* Rev. ed. New York: Richard Rosen Press, 1983. 264pp.

This guide outlines 114 Broadway musicals. The information provided for each show includes: summary of the plot; authors' names; original source of the musical; dates of opening and number of performances; cast and costume requirements; list of scenes and sets; licensing agent; availability of published text and recordings; lighting and special effects; notes on the type of audience for which the show is best suited, etc. There are special sections with the names and addresses of agents for the musicals listed and with suggestions for acquiring productions not easily available. In spite of some errors and omissions, this guide is a good source for anyone interested in the production aspects of musicals.

Song Reference Sources

375. Bloom, Ken. *American Song: The Complete Musical Theatre Companion.* New York: Facts on File, 1985. 2v.

Volume One of this important reference work provides information on approximately 3,000 American musicals staged between 1900 and 1984. Some of them are not well known and some never made it to Broadway. Each entry lists songs from this musical; place and date of the opening; names of composer, lyricist, and others associated with the show's production; director, conductor, and principal cast. Volume Two provides three indexes to the information in Volume One: name index (22,000 persons involved in the production of the musicals); title index for more than 42,000 theater songs; and a title index for the shows. Bloom's work is an important reference source for anybody involved in studying American musical theater.

376. Krasker, Tommy. *Catalog of the American Musical: Musicals of Irving Berlin, George and Ira Gershwin, Cole Porter, Richard Rodgers, & Lorentz Hart*. Washington, D.C.: National Institute for Opera and Musical Theater, 1988. 442pp.

The author's aim is to locate and restore the librettos, scores, and lyrics of the musicals by popular American composers. The volume provides lists of the songs and musical numbers for musicals written by Berlin, Gershwins, Porter, and others. Shows are listed chronologically, and detailed information is given about each of them. Brief critical essays and short biographies are provided for each composer. The book includes an index of songs and addresses for the repositories. It is a very useful tool for research in contemporary American musical theater.

377. Lewin, Richard and Alfred Simon. *Songs of the Theater*. New York: H. W. Wilson, 1984. 897pp.

This book consists of two major parts. Part One provides a listing of 17,000 theater songs from musicals dating from 1891 to 1983. The second part lists the musicals themselves, with detailed production information: name of the theater and the date of the opening; number of performances and length of the run; major cast and director; composer, author, lyricist, and song titles. Includes bibliography and an index. It is a good reference source for verification and identification of less known and obscure theater songs.

Biographical Sources

378. Kasha, Al and Joel Hirschhorn. *Notes on Broadway: Intimate Conversations with Broadway's Greatest Songwriters*. New York: Simon & Shuster, 1987. 365pp.

This is a reprint of the original edition published by Contemporary books in Chicago, 1985. This work consists of a series of interviews with many famous Broadway songwriters. Though not a standard reference source, the book provides detailed biographical information (combining it with anecdotes) and offers an inside view of what it is like to work in the American musical theater today and produce contemporary musicals.

379. Mordden, Ethan. *Broadway Babies: The People Who Made the American Musicals*. New York: Oxford University Press, 1983. 244pp.

The work follows a rough chronological arrangement and provides detailed biographical information on people important in the history of American musicals. The title of the book is misleading though. The author is not very much concerned with actors or actresses; his main focus is on composers of American musicals. The work provides a researcher with many acute, defining observations on the subject. The author enlivens his narration with many anecdotes about the musicals and their creators, but often he supplies neither documentation nor bibliography. There are, however, an extensive discography and an index. As a whole, Mordden's book presents the history of the musical as a complex, dynamic process, not just a series of random facts. The work also shows us the lives of musicals' creators and performers as a constant struggle with the conventions of popular theater. The author gives a reader a different perspective on the subject.

380. Suskin, Steven. *Show Tunes, 1905–1985: The Songs, Shows, and Careers of Broadway's Major Composers*. New York: Dodd, Mead, 1986. 728pp.

The author discusses biographies of thirty major composers who made a difference in the development of the American musical: from Irving Berlin to Stephen Schwartz. The information provided on each composer includes also list of the shows with which he was involved, a brief description of each show, the length of its run, and its significance and place in the history of the genre. The book includes a bibliography and indexes for persons associated with the discussed musicals, and for song titles and shows themselves. There are also appendixes: a chronological list of productions and a collaborator list. Suskin's book may serve as a good source of biographical information on major Broadway composers.

Part V. Other Resources

9. Periodicals

Guides to Periodicals

381. Gerstenberger, Donna L. and George Hendrick. *Fourth Directory of Periodicals Publishing Articles on English and American Literature and Language*. Chicago: Swallow Press, 1975. 234pp.

This is an annotated guide to periodicals that publish material dealing with English and American literature, including drama. It provides information regarding submitting manuscripts for each periodical. The guide is indexed by subject.

382. *Guide to the Performing Arts*. New York: Scarecrow Press, 1960– . Annual. Absorbed: *Guide to Dance Periodicals*, 1965.

This guide provides an annual subject index to selected periodicals in the performing arts with the emphasis on the American publications.

383. *Magazines for Libraries*, 6th ed., Bill Katz and Linda Sternberg Katz, eds. New York: R. R. Bowker, 1989. 1159pp.

This standard reference tool is an excellent guide to research oriented and scholarly periodicals. The latest edition reflects the evaluations of titles listed in the fifth edition and a 30 percent addition of titles never listed in this publication before. For the first time, there is a detailed Subject Index to the book's 6,521 titles, complete with cross references. The coverage of English-language journals on theater and drama is very good.

384. *Modern Language Association Directory of Periodicals: A Guide to Journals and Series in Languages and Literature*. New York: Modern Language Association of America, 1979– . Biannual. Publication Center, Modern Language Association of America, 162 Fifth Ave., New York, NY 10011.

Being a companion to the MLA international bibliography, this publication is a guide to periodicals in languages and literature, including drama. The 1988–89 edition (Eileen M. Mackesy and Dee Ella Srears, compilers) is available in two versions. The complete, hardbound edition, which has been published biennially since 1979, includes all

3,146 titles that are screened regularly for their inclusion in the *MLA International Bibliography*. The paperback edition, published since 1984, is limited to 1,170 journals and series that are issued in the United States and Canada. Near the front of each volume is a list of all the publications covered. The directory portion is arranged by the title of the periodical in alphabetical order. Complete bibliographic information is given for each entry (similar to the information in *Ulrich's International Periodicals Directory*): editorial address, beginning date of publication, ISSN, subscription and advertising information, editorial description, submission requirements, etc. *MLA Directory* also includes indexes to editorial personnel, languages, subjects, and sponsoring organizations. This reference source continues to be the most comprehensive and detailed listing available of current journals and series dealing with language, literature, drama, and folklore.

385. Patterson, Margaret C. *Author Newsletters and Journals: An International Annotated Bibliography of Serial Publications Concerned with the Life and Works of Individual Authors*. Detroit: Gale Research, 1979. 497pp.

This guide includes serials dealing with the bibliographical research, analysis of works, textual studies, etc. on the live and creations of one author or dramatist (for example, *Tennessee Williams Review*). Entries are arranged by the author's name. The guide is annotated and includes various appendixes and a title index.

386. Stratman, Carl Joseph. *American Theatrical Periodicals, 1798–1967: A Bibliographical Guide*. Durham, N.C.: Duke University Press, 1986, 1970. 133pp.

This bibliographical guide is arranged chronologically by the first year of the initial publication with titles then following alphabetically within the year. The guide covers nearly 700 serials — from newspapers to annuals — published in 122 cities in 31 states. Locations are given in 137 libraries in the United States, Canada, and Great Britain. Complete bibliographical information is provided for each periodical: original title, editor, place of publication, address of the publisher, frequency, dates of first and last issues, etc. The guide is indexed by names, titles, locations, and organizations. Even over twenty years after its publication, the guide remains a valuable research tool for a scholar in modern American theater.

Periodicals

387. *American Theatre*. New York: Theatre Communications Group, 1984– .
Monthly. Theatre Communications Group, 335 Lexington Ave., New York, NY 10017. Ed. Jim O'Quinn. Circ. 14,000.

This monthly forum for news and opinions features reviews and essays on the modern American theater.

388. *The Arts Calendar Quarterly*. New York: The Arts Calendar, Inc.,
     1985– . Quarterly. The Arts Calendar, Inc., 600 W. 58th St., Suite
     9217, New York, NY 10019. Ed. Kathi R. Levin.
     This publication serves as a guide to major events in theater, music,
     and dance.

389. *Arts Management*. New York: Radius Group, Inc., 1962– . 5/yr.
     Radius Group, Inc., 408 W. 57th St., New York, NY 10019. Ed. Alvin
     H. Reiss. Circ. 12,000.
     This publication features articles on contemporary aspects of manage-
     ment in the performing arts. Also available in microfiche form from UMI.

390. *ASTR Newsletter*. Greenvale, New York: Dept. of English, C. W. Post
     College, 1957– . Biannual. Dept. of English, C. W. Post College,
     Greenvale, NY 11548. Ed. P. T. Dircks. Circ. 600.
     This publication covers news of the American Society for Theatre
     Research.

391. *Broadside*. New York: Theatre Library Association, 1940– . Quarterly.
     Theatre Library Association, 111 Amsterdam Ave., New York, NY
     10023. Ed. Alan J. Pally. Circ. 500.
     This is a newsletter of the Theatre Library Association.

392. *Bulletin of Bibliography*. Westport, CT: Meckler Publishing, 1897– .
     Quarterly. 11 Ferry Lane, Westport, CT 06880. Ed. Anthony Abbott.
     Circ. 1,300.
     An indispensable tool for researchers and book collectors, this jour-
     nal provides annotated bibliographies on varied writers, playwrights,
     and different subjects. This bulletin offers guidance for both general and
     scholarly research.

393. *California Theatre Annual*. Beverly Hills, CA: Performing Arts Net-
     work, 1981– . Annual. 9025 Wilshire Blvd., Suite 210, Beverly Hills,
     CA 90211.
     This journal is directed to those interested in the theater in California.
     Being a good source of information about the current theater events out-
     side New York, *California Theatre* covers theatrical history or deals
     with the companies and their shows.

394. *Comparative Criticism*. New York: Cambridge University Press,
     1979– . Annual. 32 E. 57th Street, New York, NY 10022. Ed. E. S.
     Shaffer.
     Each of these 400-page, hardbound volumes deals with specific
     topics, such as comedy as a dramatic genre, Hamlet and mourning,
     science and literary genres, texts and reader, translation, boundaries of
     literature, etc. This publication is very useful for researchers interested
     in comparative analysis of literature and drama.

395. *Comparative Drama*. Kalamazoo, Mich.: English Dept. Western Michigan University, 1967–   . Quarterly. English Dept. Western Michigan University, Kalamazoo, MI 49008. Eds. Clifford Davidson, C. J. Gianakaris, and John H. Stroupe. Circ. 900.

   This scholarly publication is intended for the researchers and students of drama and theater. There are articles on all aspects of the subject. Coverage is international and often interdisciplinary. Book reviews are also included.

396. *Critical Digest*. New York: Critical Digest, 1984–   . Semimonthly. 225 W. 34th St. Rm. 918. New York, NY 10001.

   This is a newsletter that provides current news on the New York and London theater scene, followed by the digest of critical comments about these shows. There are also brief discussions on controversial productions.

397. *The Cue*. Upper Montclaire, N. J.: Dept. of Speech/Theatre, Montclaire State College, 1928–   . Semiannual. Dept. of Speech/Theatre, Montclaire State College, Upper Montclaire, NJ 07043. Ed. Gerald Lee Ratliff. Circ. 3,500.

   This is the official magazine of Theta Alpha Phi, National Theater Honors Fraternity. Covers different aspects of the performing arts.

398. *Daily Variety*. Hollywood, CA: Daily Variety Ltd., 1933–   . Daily (except Sat., Sun., & holidays; special edition last week in Oct.). Daily Variety Ltd. 1400 N. Cahuenga Blvd., Hollywood, CA 90028. Ed. Thomas M. Pryor. Circ. 19,049.

   Dedicated to the news of the show world, this publication provides reviews on musicals, plays, movies, and television shows.

399. *Drama Review*. Cambridge, MA: MIT Press, 1988–   . Quarterly. Continues *The Drama Review* (1968–1987). MIT Press, 55 Hayward St., Cambridge, MA 02142. Ed. Richard Schneider. Circ. 4,000.

   This scholarly publication is one of the basic sources of articles covering contemporary and historical trends in avant-garde American and international drama: from Peter Brook's "Mahabharata" to what is going on at "Downtown Beirut." *Drama Review* is a journal of performance with a strong intercultural, intergeneric, and interdisciplinary focus. The journal combines scholarship and journalism in the form of essays, interviews, letters, and editorials. There are usually excellent and numerous illustrations and photographs.

400. *Dramatists Guild Quarterly*. New York: Dramatists Guild, Inc., 1964–   . Quarterly. Dramatists Guild, Inc., 234 West 44th St., New York, NY 10036. Ed. Otis L. Guernsey, Jr. Circ. 8,200.

   This journal is dedicated to professional playwriting, theater music composition, and lyric writing. Though almost each issue is devoted to

the business of the Guild, it covers, at the same time, the present state
of American drama.

401. *Educational Theatre News*. Whittier, CA: Southern California Educational Theater Association, 1954–   . Bimonthly. Southern California
Educational Theater Association, 9811 Pounds Ave., Whittier, CA
90603. Ed. Lee Korf. Circ. 3,100.

This official publication of the American Educational Theatre
Association covers different aspects of contemporary theater education
in the United States.

402. *Equity News*. New York: Actors' Equity Associations, 1915–   . Monthly.
165 W. 46th Street, New York, NY 10036. Ed. Dick Moore. Circ.
38,000.

Though this publication is directed to the members of the professional
stage actors' union, it is also an important source of information for the
historians and researchers of contemporary American theater interested
in professional theater productions, salaries, union news, etc.

403. *Essays on Theatre*. Guelph, Canada: University of Guelph, 1982–   .
Semi-annual. Department of Drama, University of Guelph, Guelph,
Ontario, Canada, N1G2W1. Eds. Donald Mullin and L. W. Conolly.

This publication covers Canadian, British, and American drama in
five or six scholarly articles in each issue. The journal is dedicated to the
research in theater and drama and covers such areas as dramatic theory,
aesthetics, dramatic literature, dramatic criticism, theater history, and
performing arts.

404. *High Performance*. Los Angeles, CA: High Performance Inc., 1978–   .
Quarterly. 240 S. Broadway, Los Angeles, CA 90012. Ed. Linda Burn-
ham. Circ. 3,000.

This is a documentary journal about performing art that contains
material on performing art pieces from all over the world—including,
of course, the United States—written by the artists who performed
them. The magazine also features interviews. The primary audience for
this publication is an avant-garde art world, researchers in modern
theater, art and theater students.

405. *The Journal of Arts Management and Law*. Washington, D.C.: Heldref
Publications, 1982–   . Quarterly. Continues *Performing Arts Review*.
Heldref Publications, 4000 Albemarle St., N.W. Washington, D.C.
20016. Ed. Joseph Taubman. Circ. 1,000.

This is a journal of theater and business and it fits both research
theater collection and the law and social studies areas. There are articles
on financial problems of the theater business written by lawyers or ac-
countants balanced by interviews with actors and directors, critical
essays, and theater books reviews.

406. *Journal of Drama Theory and Criticism.* Lawrence, KS: University of Kansas, 1986– . Semi-annual. Department of Theater and Media Arts, Murphy Hall, University of Kansas, Lawrence, KS 66045. Ed. John Gronbeck-Tedesco.

   This publication covers dramatic theory as exhibited on stage, thus bringing together drama and performing arts in an unusual way. There are six to twelve articles in every issue analyzing dramatic technique in plays, characters in drama, theatrical companies and their productions, etc. The journal also provides a few play reviews mostly of American and English regional theater companies.

407. *Modern Drama.* Downsview, Canada: University of Toronto Press, 1958– . Quarterly. University Of Toronto Press, Journals Department, 5201 Dufferin Street, Downsview, Ontario, Canada M3H 5T8. Ed. John H. Ashington. Circ. 2,500.

   Though published in Canada, this scholarly journal has an international scope and deals primarily with American and British drama. There are usually ten to twelve articles covering many aspects of contemporary drama as literature. The annual bibliography is published in the June issue.

408. *NATO News and Views.* New York: National Association of Theatre Owners, 1967– . Semimonthly. National Association of Theatre Owners, 1560 Broadway, Suite 714, New York, NY 10036. Ed. Wayne R. Green. Circ. 2,500.

   This publication is published by the National Association of Theatre Owners and features the latest aspects of the theater management and operation.

409. *The New Calliope.* Lake Jackson, TX: Clowns of America Intl., Inc., 1983– . Bi-monthly. P. O. Box 570, Lake Jackson, TX 77566-0570. Ed. Ruth Erkkila.

   Though primarily oriented to members of Clowns of America International, this publication is a good source of information for those historians and researchers of contemporary American theater who are interested in clowning as a specific theatrical and show business genre.

410. *New York Theatre Critics Review.* New York: Critics' Theatre Reviews Inc., 1943– . Weekly. Critics' Theatre Reviews, Inc., Four Park Ave., Suite 21 D, New York, NY 10016. Eds. John Marlowe and Betty Blake.

   This valuable publication contains compilations of reviews from *New York Times, New York Daily News, Wall Street Journal, Time, New York Post, Women's Wear Daily, Christian Science Monitor, Newsweek,* and ABC, CBS, and NBC television. It allows a researcher in contemporary theater to quickly compare comments of leading reviewers.

411. *NTQ. New Theatre Quarterly*. New York: Cambridge University Press, 1985– . Quarterly. Continues *Theatre Quarterly*. Cambridge University Press, 32 East 57th St., New York, NY 10022. Eds. Clive Barker and Simon Trussler. Circ. 3,900.

    This is a scientific publication that features material devoted to all aspects of theater, historical and contemporary. The emphasis is on a practical rather than theoretical nature: documentation, source material, rehearsal logs, etc. Extensive bibliographies on various aspects of theater can be frequently found in this publication. Most of the material centers around the Great Britain and the United States.

412. *Performance Practice Review*. Claremont, CA: Claremont Graduate School, Music Department, 1988– . Semi-annual or annual with a double issue. 150 E. 10th Street, Claremont, CA 91711. Ed. Roland Jackson.

    This journal deals with performance practice which is an important topic interest in several of the performing arts. Though the primary concern of the publishers is music, there are serious studies in this journal analyzing dance and or drama. This publication can be useful to those researchers and students of American theater who are interested in musical aspects of contemporary dramatic performance.

413. *Performing Arts*. New Canaan, CT: News Bank, Inc., 1975– . Monthly. 58 Pine Street, New Canaan, CT 06840.

    This title is one of four parts of a larger series, *Review of the Arts* — the collection of reviews and articles on microfiche that provides an access to a lot of different newspapers and magazines throughout the country on theater, dance, and other performing arts. Because of its scope and coverage, this microfiche publication is an essential reference tool.

414. *Performing Arts Journal*. New York: PAJ Publications, 1976– . 3/yr. PAJ Publications, 325 Spring St., Rm. 318, New York, NY 10013. Eds. Bonnie Marranca and Gautam Dasgupta. Circ. 4,500.

    This journal covers all aspects of the performing arts from modern drama and dance to video and cabarets. The scope is international. There is a new play in each issue, together with interviews and dialogues between artists or directors. There are usually excellent book reviews. It is an imaginative, substantial and serious publication.

415. *Play Source*. New York: Theatre Communications Group, 1980– . 5–6/year. Theatre Communications Group, Inc., 355 Lexington Ave., New York, NY 10017. Ed. Ray Swetman.

    This publication is a good source of information on new plays and an opportunity for promoting their production. *Play Source* is a newsletter that provides descriptions of full-length, one-act, and musical theater scripts, as well as addresses where and who to contact for permission to present them and to learn about the newer, not yet licensed by the agencies, plays.

416. *Playbill Magazine*. New York: Playbill Inc., 1964– . Monthly. Playbill Incorporated, 71 Vanderbilt Ave., New York, NY 10169. Ed. Joan Alleman. Circ. 1,000,000.

 Established in 1884, this small magazine is given to the theater-goers in New York right in the theater. It serves as a program of the show and also provides a number of interviews with New York stage personalities, articles and reviews on current productions in New York.

417. *Resources for American Literary Study*. College Park, MD: University of Maryland, 1970– . Semi-annual. Department of English, University of Maryland, College Park, MD 20742. Eds. Jackson Bryer and Carla Mulford. Circ. 500.

 This publication is dedicated to research in different genres of American literature, including drama. It provides evaluative and annotated bibliographies and checklists, bibliographic and critical essays, writers' and critics' personal papers, etc.

418. *San Francisco Theatre*. San Francisco, CA: Heirs Inc., 1977– . Quarterly. Heirs, Inc., 408 Columbus Ave., San Francisco, CA 94133. Eds. Durand Garcia and Douglas Corwin.

 This publication is directed to those interested in the theater in and around San Francisco, and sometimes features even a Bay area theater directory. The articles may cover theatrical history or deal with the companies in the San Francisco area. This journal is a good source of information about the theater life outside New York.

419. *Secondary School Theatre Journal*. Washington, D.C.: American Theatre Association, 1962– . 3/year. 1000 Vermont Ave. N.W., Washington, D.C. 20005. Ed. David Grote. Circ. 900.

 Though directed, first of all, to the drama and theater arts teachers, this magazine might also appeal to those scholars who are interested in new ideas in theatrical pedagogy and innovative theater programs across the country.

420. *Show Business*. New York: Leo Shull Publications, 1941– . Weekly. Leo Shull Publications, 1501 Broadway, New York, NY 10036. Ed. Leo Shull. Circ. 82,000.

 This publication is the entertainment weekly and features interviews and news of the show world.

421. *Special Collections*. New York: Haworth Press, 1981– . Quarterly. Haworth Press, 149 Fifth Ave., New York, NY 10010. Ed. Lee Ash.

 This journal surveys special collections in the various fields of the humanities, sciences, and arts. The very first issue of this publication was entitled, "Theater & Performing Arts Collections," Louis A. Rachow, guest editor. The issue included an informative introductory essay on the state-of-the-art followed by articles on theater materials in the Library of Congress, the New York Public Library's Billy Rose Theater Collection, the Players Library, the William Seymour Theater Collection at Princeton, the Hoblitzelle Theater Arts Library at the University of Texas (Austin), the Wisconsin Center for Film and Theater Research, the theater department at the Metropolitan Toronto Library, etc. Essays on bibliographic control and recent reference works in the field were also included. Other issues of this journal have a similar arrangement. Usually, there is a concluding article written by an editor on general publications of interest to special collections librarians and researchers that use them.

422. *Stages*. Norwood, NJ: Curtains Inc., 1984– . 10/year. 8 Frasco Lane, Norwood, NJ 07648. Ed. Seymour Isenberg. Circ. 12,000.

This is a theater magazine of record that provides theater reviews of Broadway, Off Broadway, and Off Off Broadway productions and articles on artists and directors. Also there are book and film reviews. May be used by researchers of New York theater history as a source of sketchy information on lots of plays and theater not covered in one place.

423. *Studies in American Drama, 1945–Present*. Erie, PA: Humanities Division, The Behrend College, Pennsylvania State University, 1986– . Annual. J. Madison Davis, Humanities Division, The Behrend College, Pennsylvania State University, Erie, PA 16563. Eds. Philip C. Kolin and Colby H. Kullman.

This is an excellent scientific publication that presents scholarly articles on theater history and dramatic influences, theater documents, bibliographies, and interviews. International theater reviews are also included.

424. *TDR: The Drama Review: A Journal of Performance Studies*. Cambridge, MA: MIT Press, 1955– . Quarterly. 55 Hayward Street, Cambridge, MA 02142. Ed. Richard Schechener. Circ. 5,400.

The major concern of this unusual journal is contemporary gender conflict as it regards theater people—a touch on feminist views of theater. Every issue consists of seven or eight articles that are lively and controversial, and bring into a regular academic discussion more than the traditional view of theater production.

425. *Tennessee Williams Review*. Ann Arbor, MI: University of Michigan, 1981– . Semiannual. University of Michigan, 1079 Engineering Bldg., Ann Arbor, MI 48109.

This scholarly publication is dedicated to Tennessee Williams studies.

426. *Theatre*. New Haven, CT: School of Drama, Yale University, 1977– . 3/yr. Continues *Yale/Theatre*. Yale University, School of Drama, 222 York St., New Haven, CT 06520. Ed. Joel Schechter. Circ. 2,300.

This publication is intended for theater-creators, theater-scholars, and theater-goers. It covers recent performances in the U.S. and Europe, retrospective of individual and company work, scholarly essays on modern theater theory and practice, etc. There are usually excellent illustrations. Also available in microfiche form from UMI.

427. *The Theatre Annual.* Akron, Ohio: Dept. of Theatre Arts, University of Akron, 1942– . Annual. Dept. of Theatre Arts, University of Akron, Akron, Ohio 44325. Ed. John V. Falconieri.

This is a publication of information and research in theater both historical and contemporary. The journal publishes essays on American and world theater, critical analyses, scenography, history of theatrical companies and playhouses, etc.

428. *Theatre Crafts.* New York: Theatre Crafts Association, 1967– . 9/yr. Theatre Crafts Association, 135 Fifth Ave., New York, NY 10010. Ed. Patricia MacKay. Circ. 29,809.

This journal contains material on all technical aspects of the theater (video and film also). There are articles on makeup, scenic design, theater architecture, costume, lighting, etc. Included usually are the news on theater personalities, and some notes on books, material on theater festivals and street theater.

429. *Theatre Design and Technology.* New York: U.S. Institute of Theatre Technology, Inc., 1965– . Quarterly. U.S. Institute of Theatre Technology, Inc., 330 W. 42 St., Suite 1702, New York, NY 10036. Eds. Arnold Aronson and Kate Davy. Circ. 3,200.

This publication is intended for technicians and production people in the theater and also for those researchers who are concerned with the physical aspects of the theater art: architecture, design, lighting, sound, etc. The articles presented are of theoretical as well as of practical nature. Also available in microfiche form from UMI.

430. *Theatre History Studies.* Grand Forks, ND: University of North Dakota Press, 1980– . Annual. Department of Theatre Arts, University of North Dakota, Grand Forks, ND 58202. Ed. Ron Engle. Circ. 1,000.

This is an official publication of the Mid-America Theatre Conference. The journal is international in scope with the major emphasis on American theater. Every issue has seven to nine scholarly articles dealing with different aspects of contemporary theater.

431. *Theatre Journal.* Baltimore, MD: Johns Hopkins University Press, Journals Publishing Division, 1979– . Quarterly. Continues *Educational Theater Journal.* Johns Hopkins University Press, Journals Publishing Division, 701 W. 40th St., Suite 275, Baltimore, MD 21211. Ed. Sue-Ellen Case. Circ. 6,200.

Emphasis of this extremely valuable publication is on scholarly articles dealing with areas of theater history and theatrical theory and criticism. There is also a theater reviews section (edited by Steven E. Hart, New York University, 50 West 4th St., 829 Shimkin Hall, NY, NY 10003). The journal is intended for scholars and students of theater. Also available on microfiche form from UMI.

432. *Theatre News*. Washington, D.C.: American Theatre Association, 1968– . Monthly. 1010 Wisconsin Ave., N.W., Washington, DC 20007. Circ. 8,000.

This monthly publication is issued by the American Theatre Association and covers different aspects of contemporary American theater world.

433. *Theatre Research International*. Oxford, United Kingdom: Oxford University Press, 1975– . 3/yr. Formed by the union of *Theatre Research* and *New Theatre Magazine*. Oxford University Press, Walton St., Oxford OX2 6DP, UK. Ed. C. Schumacher. Circ. 1,500.

Though this is a British publication, the journal may be of use for a researcher in American theater because it provides international coverage in the historical, critical, and theoretical study of contemporary drama with the emphasis on English-speaking theater. The aim of this publication is to keep in touch with what is new and exciting in modern theater. Particularly useful are numerous book reviews. Also available in microfiche form from UMI.

434. *Theatre Studies: The Journal of the Ohio State University Lawrence & Lee Theatre Research Institute*. Columbus, OH: Ohio State University Press, 1955– . Semi-annual. Jerome Lawrence & Robert Lee Theatre Research Institute, Ohio State University, 1430 Lincoln Tower, 1800 Cannon Drive, Columbus, OH 43210–1230. Ed. Patricia Adams.

The journal is dedicated to publishing a wide variety of scholarly articles on special topics in American theater: theater history, critical and literary studies in drama, theoretical studies in theater, etc. It focuses on articles by graduate students in theater departments around the United States with the purpose of fostering theater scholarship.

435. *Theatre Survey*. Albany, NY: American Society for Theatre Research, State University of New York at Albany, 1960– . Semiannual. American Society for Theatre Research, State University of New York at Albany, PAC 266, Albany, NY 12222. Ed. Roger Herzel. Circ. 1,250.

The primary aim of this journal is to publish scholarly articles on different aspects of theater history: acting and directing styles, playwriting, stage and design, audience and cultural climate, etc. Essays on dramatic criticism are not usually included. The coverage is international. This publication is also available in microfiche form from UMI.

436. *Theatre Three*. Pittsburgh, PA: Carnegie Mellon University Press, 1986–

Semi-annual. Department of Drama, Carnegie Mellon University Press, Pittsburgh, PA 15213. Ed. Brian Johnson. Circ. 300.

This semi-annual scholarly magazine is dedicated to publishing articles on the drama and theater of the modern world. The coverage ranges from text and textuality to dramaturgy to playwrights. There are also two special sections in the journal, "Performance in Review" and "Books in Review" that provide essays on productions in regional theaters and new books in the field.

437. *Theatre Times.* New York: Alliance of Resident Theatres, 1982– . Bimonthly. 325 Spring St., Rm. 315, New York, NY 10013. Ed. Mindy Levine. Circ. 2,500.

This is a publication of the Alliance of Resident Theatres in New York and it covers news in the New York theatrical world: interviews with stage personalities, controversial shows, etc.

438. *TheaterWeek: A Comprehensive Guide to American Theater.* New York: TheaterWeek, 1987– . Weekly. 28 W. 25th Street, 4th Floor, New York, NY 10010. Ed. Charles L. Ortleb.

This is a theatergoers' guide to New York theater. The publication provides useful information on New York theater companies, actors and directors, some popular articles on theater history. Also there are columns of theatrical gossip and news. Though the title is misleading, and the journal is directed primarily to tourists, a researcher in contemporary American theater might find this publication useful along with *Playbill* and *Stages*.

439. *USITT Newsletter.* New York: United States Institute for Theatre Technology, 1965– . Quarterly. 330 W. 42nd St., New York, NY 10036. Ed. Tina Margolis. Circ. 2,500.

This is a publication of the United States Institute for Theatre Technology. It covers material on different aspects of modern theater management and technology.

440. *Variety.* New York: Variety, Inc., 1905– . Weekly. Variety, Inc., 154 W. 46th St., New York, NY 10036. Ed. Syd Silverman. Circ. 36,076.

This is the official publication (and one of the oldest) of American show business and it provides complete coverage of all areas of the entertainment world. There are sections on "legitimate" theater with reviews of on and Off Broadway shows, information on casting, budget, and touring companies. Coverage also includes movie, radio, television, music, records, book reviews, etc. This publication is also available in microfiche form from MIM.

441. *West Coast Plays.* Los Angeles, CA: California Theatre Council, 1977– . Quarterly since summer 1981. California Theatre Council, Eastern Columbia Bldg, 849 S. Broadway, Suite 809, Los Angeles, CA 90014. Ed. Robert Hurwitt. Circ. 1,500.

The primary aim of this publication is to cover modern drama and theater of the Pacific states.

442. *Women & Performance: A Journal of Feminist Theory*. New York: Women & Performance Project, Tisch School of the Arts, New York University, 1983– . Semiannual. Women & Performance Project, New York University, Tisch School of the Arts, 51 W. 4th St., Rm. 300, New York, NY 10012. Ed. Jill Dolan.

The focus of this publication is on the role of women in the different fields of the performing arts — theater, television, and motion pictures.

Abstracts and Bibliographies

443. *Annotated Bibliography of New Publication in the Performing Arts*. New York: Drama Book Shop, 1970– . Quarterly. Drama Book Shop, 150 West 52nd St., New York, NY 10019. Ed. Ralph Newman Schoolcraft.

This publication began in 1970 as a supplement to the same editor's *Performing Arts Books in Print: An Annotated Bibliography*. This serial provides a classified, annotated list of books on different aspects of theater and other fields of the performing arts published in the United States and Great Britain. There is also a list of drama recordings.

444. *Critics' Guide to Films and Plays*. New York: Critics' Guide, 1967–1969. Monthly. Ceased after #6, v.2.

This short lived publication provided excerpts from current (to the time of its existence) reviews in New York newspapers and in some periodicals not indexed elsewhere. The remaining two volumes may still be of use for a researcher in modern American theater.

445. *Theatre/Drama Abstracts*. Pleasant Hill, CA: Theatre, Drama, and Speech Information Center, 1975– . 3/yr. Continues *Theatre/Drama & Speech Index*. Theatre, Drama, and Speech Information Center, 1 Erin Court, Pleasant Hill, CA 94523. Ed. Paul T. Adalian. Circ. 600.

This triannual publication (with annual cumulation) provides abstracting and indexing services to articles, essays, book and drama reviews, scripts, etc. that were published in journals in the theater field. Each entry is given a complete bibliographical citation. The coverage is international.

10. Major Databases

Directories

446. *Directory of Online Databases*. Oxford, England: Elsevier Advanced Technology Group, 1989. Quarterly.

This is an indispensable reference source that gives the most current information about the content and availability of nearly 4,600 databases, accessible through more than 650 online sources. With its comprehensive, authoritative summaries of online databases which are updated quarterly, the *Directory* helps a user to identify new databases of interest, discover alternate sources for accessing databases, find databases in the subject area of interest, or guide a searcher to new information resources. The source contains helpful indexes to make the search easy. The *Directory* is also available on line.

447. *Directory of Portable Databases*. Oxford, England: Elsevier Advanced Technology Group, 1990. Semi-annual.

This new semi-annual publication contains nearly 600 databases available on CD-ROM, diskette, or magnetic tape. The publication is designed to provide full coverage of all types of product information, such as bibliographic, referral, numeric, full text, images, software, etc. The *Directory* also contains complete addresses and telephone numbers of information providers or vendors. There are helpful indexes by name, medium, subject, vendors or distributors, plus two special indexes for identifying portable databases that have corresponding online databases.

Databases

448. DIALOG Information Retrieval Service. LC MARC. Files 426, 427. Miami, Fl.: Knight-Ridder Corporation.

The LC MARC stands for *Library of Congress MAchine Readable Cataloging*. This database contains records representing monographic works cataloged by the Library of Congress. Library of Congress Cataloging Distribution Service provides the content of this database. LC MARC covers all subject areas—including American theater and drama — of the monographic collection of the Library of Congress. File 426 contains monographs that were published from 1980 forward. It is updated monthly; approximately 11,000 records are added per each update. File 427 includes monographs with publication years prior to 1980. It is also updated monthly with nearly 7,000 new or revised records per update. Each citation provided by this database includes the basic bibliographic data from the standard MARC fields.

449. DIALOG Information Retrieval Service. REMARC. Files 423, 424, 425. Miami, Fl.: Knight-Ridder Corporation.

The REMARC stands for *Retrospective MAchine Readable Cataloging*. This database contains bibliographic records representing the works cataloged by the Library of Congress (LC) which were not included in the MARC–database (also LC–generated). These are the entries made in the Library of Congress shelflist from 1897 to December 31, 1978. Researchers in American theater and drama after WWII have to use the following files: 423–includes works published during 1940–1959; 424–works published in 1960–1969; and 425–works produced in 1970–1980. REMARC contains citations to all works in subject areas — including, of course, American theater and drama — cataloged by the Library of Congress prior to 1980 (these records are not in the MARC database). Each REMARC citation contains all of the major bibliographic elements from the LC catalog cards which are the source for this database.

450. EPIC Information Retrieval Online Reference Service. Dublin, OH: OCLC Online Computer Library Center, Inc.

The EPIC service is the new online reference system that provides complete subject access to the OCLC Online Union Catalog. This is a unique, comprehensive, and indispensable information retrieval system for any serious research. There are 28 points of access to each of almost 20 million OCLC Online Union Catalog records: title or author name, publication year or type, subject area, etc. With complete subject searching, a librarian or a scholar can find and use the information contained in almost all fields in all records. One can search the notes fields of movies and videos for cast listings, directors, producers, and writers, for example. For sound recordings, one can locate individual songs or movements on any album, disc, or tape. If there is a need to find a play compiled in a collected work, the information is there and searchable. One can also find out who holds the necessary item; OCLC database contains more than 330 million location listings. It is a user-friendly system and easy to use for both beginners and sophisticated searchers.

451. MLA INTERNATIONAL BIBLIOGRAPHY on *Wilsondisc*. New York: H. W. Wilson Company, 1987–   . Quarterly.

The Wilson indexes, familiar to all reference librarians and available online for some time, are now also available in CD-ROM format. This new retrieval system offers its users the convenience of local CD-ROM searching and unlimited online access for a fixed cost. A relatively unsophisticated user can search now a large database without the knowledge of special commands. MLA International Bibliography on *Wilsondisc* covers current scholarship in the modern languages, literature, drama, and folklore. It provides bibliographic data on nearly 3,000 periodicals, monographs, and book collections. Like all databases on *Wilsondisc*, it is updated quarterly. Users can search by author or subject heading or by journal name.

11. Theater Organizations, Research Centers, and Associations

Theater Research

452. Bank, Rosemarie K. and Harold J. Nichols, eds. *The Status of Theatre Research*. Lanham, MD: University Press of America, 1986. 59pp.

This book is the result of the special project of the Commission on Theatre Research of the American Theatre Association. This study illuminates the state of the art in the field of theatrical teaching and studies and provides information on research grants.

Organizations

453. Actors Studio (AS). 432 West 44th Street, New York, NY 10036. Frank Cursaro, Artistic Director. Phone: (212) 757-0870.

The purpose of this organization of professional actors, playwrights, and directors is to experiment with new forms in theater. The AS consists of the following sections: Actors, Directors, and Playwrights. Conducts theater workshop and maintains special theatrical library of 500 volumes.

454. Alliance of Resident Theatres/New York (ART/NY). 325 Spring Street, Room 315, New York, NY 10013. Kate C. Busch, Executive Director. Phone: (212) 989-5257.

The members of this organization are nonprofit professional theaters in New York City area and also those associations that are theater related. The ART was founded in 1972 with the major purpose to promote recognition of the nonprofit theaters. The ART operates a real estate project to assist theaters in their search for performance space; it also acts as advocate on behalf of its members with government or corporate founders; facilitates discussion among the theaters, serves as a source of information for general public. Career counseling, placement services, seminars, and internship programs are among the ART's activities and functions. *The Theatre Member Directory* is published periodically. The organization also issues a newsletter entitled *Theatre Times, Get Me to the Printer, How to Run a Small Box Office*, different handbooks, and guides.

455. American Alliance for Theatre and Education (AATE). Theatre Arts Department, Virginia Tech. University, Blackburg, VA 24061. Roger L. Bedard, Executive Secretary. Phone (703) 961-7624.

The organization promotes theater and drama education for young people. It was founded in 1987 as an association of drama and theater teachers, theater artists, directors, playwrights, and other theater professionals interested in theater for youth. The AATE sponsors and conducts workshops and festivals, and maintains historical archives of artifacts, pictures, and various documents. The AATE consists of three committees: Curriculum, Professional Theater, and Research. *AATE Membership Directory* is published annually. Also publishes *The Drama/Theatre Teacher* three times a year and *A Model Drama/ Theatre Curriculum* four times a year.

456. American Association of Community Theatre (AACT). C/o James C. Carver, 329 S. Park Street, Kalamazoo, MI 49007. James C. Carver, Manager. Phone: (616) 343-1313.

The AACT was founded in 1986 by individuals involved in community theater with the purpose to offer networking opportunities and to promote community theater. This organization sponsors travel for community theater groups for participation in various festivals. Special awards and the placement services are among the AACT's activities. The *AACT Directory of Community Theatres in the United States* is published periodically. The AACT also issues *Theatre Crafts* and bimonthly newsletter, *Spotlight*.

457. American Center for Stanislavski Theatre Art (ACSTA). 485 Park Ave., 6th Floor, New York, NY 10022. Sonia Moore, Pres. Phone: (212) 755-5120.

ACSTA was founded in 1964 by and for persons interested in introducing into the American theater the Stanislavski System. The organization sponsors and conducts research into refinements and clarification of the Stanislavski's Method. Also sponsors seminars, lectures, and demonstrations; trains actors, directors, and drama teachers. Publication: *Stanislavski Today and the Logic of Speech on the Stage*. ACSTA meets annually.

458. American Conservatory Theatre Foundation (ACTF). 450 Geary Street, San Francisco, CA 94102. John Sullivan, Managing Director. Phone: (415) 771-3880.

The ACTF was founded in 1965 for providing resources for the American Conservatory Theatre. This repertory theater is also an accredited acting school. The activities of the Foundation extend beyond the San Francisco area: usually in February, the ACTF sponsors the auditions for the Master of Fine Arts program in New York, Chicago, and Los Angeles. The ACTF also organizes student matinee performances, various school outreach programs, discussions between the theater company members and the audience, productions for younger children, and other programs geared towards education. The organization maintains a special library of more than 8,000 volumes and an archive. The ACTF publishes *ACT Bulletin*, *Act Preview Magazine* (three times a year), *Performing Arts* (eight times a year).

459. American Directors Institute (ADI). 248 West 74th Street, Suite 10, New York NY 10024. Geoffrey C. Shales, Artistic Director. Phone: (212) 924-8415.

   The ADI is an organization of professional stage directors. It was founded in 1985. The goal of the ADI is to advance and revitalize the art of theatrical stage directing. The organization sponsors three professional seminars a year; publishes annually *Directors Directory* and *Directors Sourcebook*, semiannually *Symposium Transcript*, quarterly *Directors Notes*, and a newsletter. Among the ADI's regular activities are the survey projects, compilation of statistics, bestowing of awards, and maintaining of the speakers' bureau.

460. The American Mime Theatre (TAMT). 24 Bond Street, New York, NY 10012. Paul J. Curtis, Founder and Director. Phone: (212) 777-1710.

   This organization functions as a theater company also. The TAMT travels extensively throughout the country to promote the American mime art. It offers classes, lectures, and demonstrations. The TAMT was founded in 1952 with the purpose to promote the American mime and to foster its development as a distinct art form. The TAMT maintains its own archive and the special library.

461. American Place Theatre (APT). 111 West 46th Street, New York, NY 10036. Mickey Rolfe, General Manager. Phone: (212) 840-2960.

   The APT was founded in 1964 with the major goal of providing the opportunity for the talented American playwrights to write and produce outstanding plays. The best dramatists are chosen by the APT, the directors must be approved by the playwrights themselves, and the actors are usually drawn from the New York City area. Productions are scheduled four times a year for a run of four or even eight weeks. The APT offers early collaboration with a playwright and professional consultations. The audience for the year series is usually a heterogeneous one: a single ticket subscription is sold for all the plays.

462. American Society for Theater Research (ASTR). Theatre Arts Program-

D1, Univ. of Pennsylvania, Philadelphia, PA 19104. Cary M. Mazer, Secretary. Phone: (215) 898-7882.

ASTR was founded in 1956 for scholars of the theater in order to promote better knowledge of the history of the theater. Affiliated with International Federation for Theater Research. Sponsors research projects and awards annual scholarship to graduate students in the theater. Publishes: *Theatre Survey*, semiannual; *Newsletter*, semiannual; *International Bibliography of Theatre*, annual; *Membership List*, annual. The society provides annual conferences with exhibits.

463. American Theatre Arts for Youth (TAFY). 1429 Walnut Street, Philadelphia, PA 19102. Laurie Wagman, Executive Director. Phone: (215) 563-3501.

The purpose of this organization is to provide the teachers countrywide with the curriculum-related professional theater as an important motivating and stimulating educational medium. The TAFY consists of the following sections: Magazine, Media and Methods. The TAFY maintains the special library of original musicals the subject of which is history or literature.

464. The American Theater Association. 1010 Wisconsin Ave., Washington, D.C. 20007.

This association is concerned with all phases of educational theater. It consists of the following divisions: American Community Theater Association, Army Theater Arts Association, Children's Theater Association, Secondary School Theater Association, University and College Theater Association, and University Resident Theater Association. The association publishes *Theatre News*, *Placement Service Bulletin*, its convention program, and an annual directory.

465. American Theatre Critics Association (ATCA). C/o Clara Hieronymus, The Tennessean 1100 Broadway, Nashville TN 37202. Clara Hieronymus, Executive Secretary. Phone: (800) 351-1752.

The ATCA was founded in 1974 to promote freedom of expression in the theater criticism, advance its standards, and encourage greater communication among American theater and drama critics. The ATCA also nominates regional theater productions for special Tony Award. Among the ATCA's publications are: *Critics Quarterly*, and the *Newsletter*.

466. American Writers Theatre Foundation (AWTF). 145 W. 46th Street, New York, NY 10036. Linda Laundra, Artistic Director. Phone: (212) 869-9770.

This performing and literary arts organization was founded in 1975 for encouraging writers to work for the theater. The members of the AWTF are theater professionals, dramatists, regional and university theaters. The AWTF sponsors producing of original plays and different adaptations for the stage. There is speakers' bureau and a special library. The AWTF is also known as The Writers Theater. The Foundation publishes *Newsletter, Stagewright*, fact sheets, and a reference book, *Adaptations*.

467. ASSITEJ/U. S. A. C/o Harold R. Oaks, Theatre and Film, Brigham Young University, Provo, UT 84602. Harold R. Oaks, President. Phone: (801) 378-4674.

   This organization is the American chapter for International Association of Theatre for Children and Youth. The ASSITEJ consists of 44 similar chapters throughout the world comprised of professional theatrical companies playing exclusively for young audience and also of other organizations actively interested in the theater for children. The ASSITEJ was founded in 1965 with the major goal to promote research and development opportunities in children theater field. Among the organization's activities are the Project entitled International Playscript Exchange; regular participation in international congresses; sponsoring seminars and lecture series, etc. The ASSITEJ publishes *Theatre Enfance et Jeunesse-Paris* (semiannually); *Theatre for Young Audiences Today* (three times a year); book reviews, calendars of events, and directory of new scripts for children theater.

468. Association for Puerto Rican–Hispanic Culture (APRHC). C/o Peter Bloch, 83 Park Terrace, West, New York, NY 10034. Peter Bloch, President. Phone: (212) 942-2338.

   The APRHC was organized in 1965 for promotion and preservation of Puerto Rican–Hispanic artistic work, primarily in the performing arts area. The organization funds and sponsors drama theater performances, concert, and other cultural events. Pamphlets and *Newsletter* are published periodically.

469. Association of Entertainers (AE). P. O. Box 1393, Washington D. C. 20013. Donna Howell, Director. Phone: (202) 546-1919.

   The AE was founded in 1981 by and for theater managers, producers, performing artists, lawyers actively engaged in performing arts areas, theater technicians, and support personnel. The purpose of the AE is to provide the opportunities for professionals of the entertainment business to meet and discuss their work. Among the AE's publications: *Talent Spotlight* (quarterly), *VICA Professional Journal* (quarterly). Meetings and conventions are organized semiannually in Washington, D. C.

470. Association of Hispanic Arts (AHA). 173 E. 116th Street, 2nd Floor, New York, NY 10029. Jane Delago, Executive Director. Phone: (212) 860-5445.

   The AHA supports presentations of theater performances, dance and music concerts that reflect Hispanic cultural history. This organization was founded in 1975 in order to promote Hispanic performing arts as an integral part of the arts in the United States. The AHA maintains special library and a mailing list of arts organizations and funding sources. The activities of the AHA include individual technical assistance, referral services on different legal or administrative matters, and private funding. *AHA!—Hispanic Arts News* covers Hispanic cultural activities in the area of performing arts and is issued ten times a year. The *Directory of Hispanic Arts Organizations* is published periodically.

471. Audience Development Committee (AUDELCO). P. O. Box 30, Manhattanville Station, New York, NY 10027. Vivian Robinson, Executive Director. Phone: (212) 534-8776.

    The purpose of this organization founded in 1973 is to build an educative and appreciative audience for the black theater. The AUDELCO maintains black theater archives and speakers' bureau. Among the organization's activities are bestowing awards to the black theater professionals, offering a low-cost ticket programs, etc. The AUDELCO publishes *Black Theatre Directory* (updated periodically); *Intermission* (monthly); *Overture* (monthly magazine). The AUDELCO organizes and sponsors annual Black Theatre Festival.

472. Bilingual Foundation of the Arts (BFA). 421 North Avenue, 19, Los Angeles, CA 90031. Carmen Zapata, Mng. Producer. Phone: (213) 225-4044.

    Founded in 1973 by Hispanics and non–Hispanics interested in professional Hispanic-American theater, the BFA produces and performs contemporary and classic Hispanic-American drama in Spanish and English. Producing four to five plays annually, the BFA seeks to promote Hispanic theatrical heritage and share it with non–Hispanic Americans. The organization sponsors new translations and offers professional training in theater. The BFA also organizes and funds a special touring theater program for children, Teatro Para Los Ninos, and various low-cost ticket programs.

473. Burlesque Historical Society (BHS). C/o Exotic World, 29053 Wild Road, Helendale, CA 92342. Jennie Lee, President. Phone: (619) 243-5261.

    Founded in 1963, the BHS maintains and preserves a collection of various materials related to burlesque: books, magazines, photographs, programs, costumes, films, and videos, etc. The organization also supports Burlesque Hall of Fame. Among its activities are sponsoring of specialized education and offering of placement services. The BHS publishes semiannual *Bulletin*, the magazine, *Jennie Lee, the Bazoom Girl*, and *Legend of Jennie Lee*.

474. Catholic Actors Guild of America (CAG). 165 West 46th Street, Suite 710, New York, NY 10036. Suzanne Richardson, Executive Secretary. Phone: (212) 398-1868.

The CAG was organized in 1914 by and for theater professionals with the goal of maintaining welfare of people working in theater and entertainment industry. The CAG presents awards and scholarships in performing arts.

475. Center for Safety in the Arts. 5 Beekman Street, Suite 1030, New York, NY 10038. Michael McCann, Ph. D., C.I.H., Executive Director. Phone: (212) 227-6220.

Research activities of this independent, nonprofit, and educational organization is concentrated in the areas of different hazards in the performing and visual arts. The Center supports and conducts studies on hazards of specific materials used in arts, crafts, and theaters. The Center's publication *Art Hazards News* is issued ten times per year. The organization also maintains a library of 500 volumes.

476. City University of New York Center for Advanced Study in Theatre Arts (CASTA). 33 West 42nd St., New York, NY 10036. Prof. Edwin Wilson, Director. Phone: (212) 690-5415.

CASTA was founded in 1978 as an integral unit of Graduate School and University Center of City University of New York. The organization conducts research in theater arts, including studies in dance and film. There are projects on video series on American theater and on Black popular music; computer uses in the arts, etc. Sponsors exhibitions, conferences, and symposia. Publishes bibliographies, translations, conference proceedings, etc.

477. Committee for National Theatre Week (CNTW).

The goal of the CNTW is to develop and maintain better communication and understanding between the audience and the theater professionals. The organization maintains resource library, bestows special awards, and sponsors National Theater Week in order to advance the cause of theater and enlighten public opinion.

478. Drama Desk (DD). C/o Alvin Klein, 722 Broadway, New York, NY 10003. Alvin Klein, Contact. Phone: (212) 674-4436.

Founded in 1949, this organization has 1,000 current members who are drama and theater critics from New York television and radio stations, magazines and newspapers. The DD periodically holds press conferences, monthly discussions and luncheons with prominent theatrical personalities, and organizes after-theater salutes to actors, directors, producers, etc. The Drama Desk also presents annual awards for outstanding performances.

479. Dramatists Guild (DG). 234 W. 44th Street, New York NY 10036. David E. Levine, Executive Director. Phone: (212) 398-9366.

Founded in 1920 by and for playwrights, lyricists, and theater composers, the DG currently consists of 8,300 members. The organization bestows annual Hull-Warriner award, organizes seminars and symposia, and maintains reference library. Among the DG activities is advisory and consulting program for members. The DG publishes *Dramatists Guild — Newsletter*, ten times a year, and a quarterly *Magazine*.

480. Eugene O'Neill Memorial Theater Center (EOMTC). 305 Great Neck Rd. Waterford, CT 06385. George C. White, President. Phone: (203) 443-5378.

The Center was founded in 1963 as a permanent memorial to one of the greatest American playwrights. The EOMTC organizes and sponsors the annual National Playwrights Conference with the staged readings of new plays and discussions with directors, producers, agents, and other theater professionals. The organization also sponsors O'Neill National Opera/Theater Conference which offers young and talented American composers and librettists the opportunity to experiment and develop new works for the musical theater. The EOMTC holds training and exchange programs with theatrical school in Europe and maintains the National Theater Institute and professional theater program for studying theater, dance, music, and films under a faculty of distinguished critics. The Center owns an extensive Theater Collection which includes books, magazines, newspapers, pictures, and various memorabilia dealing with O'Neill and American theater. Among the EOMTC's publications are *The O'Neill*, semi-annually, and *National Playwrights Directory*.

481. FEDAPT. 270 Lafeyette Street, Suite 810, New York, NY 10012. Mr. Nello McDaniel, Executive Director. Phone: (212) 966-9344.

The purpose of this organization founded in 1967 is to provide guidance and consultation to professional performing art companies in the United States in the various areas of art management. The FEDAPT publishes *Challenge of Change, In Art We Trust, Market the Arts*, and plans to issue *No Quick Fix*.

482. Friars Club (FC). 57 E. 55th Street, New York, NY 1002. Jean Pierre Trebot, Executive Director. Phone: (212) 751-7272.

The Friars Club was organized in 1904 by and for theatrical writers and drama critics, show business performers and executives, theatrical agents, and public relations professionals. The FC offers scholarships and grants to students attending performing arts programs in colleges; maintains theatrical research library of 3000 volumes and several thousand photographs; dispenses also gifts and toys to underprivileged children.

483. Hispanic Institute for the Performing Arts (HIFPA). P. O. Box 32249, Calvert Station, Washington D. C. 2007. Myrna D. Torres, Executive Director. Phone: (202) 289-8541.

The HIFPA was founded in 1981 to promote an understanding and appreciation of Hispanic performing arts. The organization conducts educational and cultural activities: workshops, lectures, dramatic performances, concerts, etc. The HIFPA plans to open a national Hispanic cultural center in Washington, D. C. The organization provides consulting and referral services.

484. Hospital Audiences (HAI). 220 W. 42nd Street, New York, NY 10036. Michael Jon Spencer, Executive Director. Phone: (212) 575-7676.

The purpose of the HAI is to promote the cultural enrichment for patients in hospitals, nursing homes, mental health facilities, and the like. The organization brings theatrical performances and art workshops into the institutions for those who are disabled and unable to leave. The HAI's activities are focused in advocacy of the utilization of the performing arts in health and rehabilitative settings. Among the HAI's publications are books, including *The Healing Role of the Arts: A European Perspective; The Healing Role of the Arts: Working Papers*; and *The Provision of Cultural Services to Physically and Mentally Impaired Aged in Long Term Care Facilities.*

485. Institute for Advanced Studies in the Theatre Arts (IASTA). 310 West 56th St., New York, NY 10019. John D. Mitchell, President. Phone: (212) 581-3133.

IASTA was founded in 1958 to increase the American theater artist's chances of studying the best styles and techniques of foreign theater. Sponsors research in intercultural relations, organizes lectures, seminars, and commissions translations of foreign classical plays. Makes it possible for foreign theater practitioners to come to the United States and work with American actors and directors. Maintains archives of films and tapes, library of rare theater books, and publishes books on different theater styles.

486. Institute for Outdoor Drama (IOD). CB 3240, Graham Memorial, University of North Carolina, Chapel Hill, NC 27599. Mark R. Summer, Director. Phone: (919) 962-1328.

Founded in 1963 as an integral unit of the University of North Carolina (but with its own board of control), the IOD functions as a research and advisory agency for all phases of producing outdoor drama. The organization assists writers and academic researchers; sponsors research and bibliographical work for outdoor drama, including studies in music, scene design, lighting, etc.; maintains placement services for theater professionals; and holds annual auditions for summer jobs. Among the IOD's other activities are sponsoring conferences for promoters, playwrights, architects, etc. The organization owns an extensive collection of various materials on outdoor drama projects: playscripts, slides, photographs, videotapes, letters, etc. The IOD publishes *Conference Notes, Institute of Outdoor Drama – Drama List* (annual), *Institute of Outdoor Drama – Newsletter*; also periodically issues bibliographies, bulletins, and booklets on outdoor drama and amphitheater design.

487. International Foundation for Theatrical Research (IFTR). P. O. Box 4526, Albuquerque, NM 87196. Mario Dellamadonna, Secretary. Phone: (505) 843-7749.

    IFTR was founded in 1978 for the promotion of "new theatrical orientations to be gathered from the inspiration of the great classics in world literature." (*Encyclopedia of Associations*, 23rd ed., 1989, vol. 1). The organization conducts research, sponsors teaching, tryouts, and performances.

488. International Society of Dramatists (ISD). P. O. Box 1310, Miami, FL 33153. Mr. A. Delaplaine, President. Phone: (305) 674-0722.

    The organization consists of more than 4,000 members — dramatists, artists, and stage directors. The purpose of the ISD is to provide marketing information and to support dramatists working in all areas of the performing arts. The Society publishes directories, newsletters, monthly *The Globe*, and annually *The Dramatists Bible*.

489. International Theatre Institute of the United States (ITI/US). 220 West 42nd St., Suite 1710, New York, NY 10036. Martha W. Coigney, Director. Phone: (212) 944-1490.

    ITI/US was established by UNESCO in 1948 to serve as an international organization in the field of theater and as a forum for an international exchange of ideas and techniques. Consultation services and different research programs are conducted. The Institute consists of the following committees: Dance, Musical Theater, New Theater, Playwrights, Study, and Third World. Publishes special monographs on theater subjects and *International Directory of Theater*. Sponsors conventions and conferences.

490. International Theatrical Agencies Association (ITAA). 1123 N. Water Street, Milwaukee, WI 53202. Paul A. Mascioli, President. Phone: (414) 276-8788.

    The purpose of the ITAA is to assist theatrical agencies to book actors and international theatrical acts and to provide placement services. Among the organization's other activities are educational seminars, workshops, and computerized information service linking theatrical agencies. The ITAA holds annual conventions and publishes *Newsletter*.

491. League of American Theatres and Producers (LATP). 226 W. 47th Street, New York, NY 10036. Harvey Sabinson, Executive Director. Phone: (212) 764-1122.

    The members of the LATP (founded in 1930) are producers and theater owners. The principal purpose of this organization is negotiation of labor contracts and government relations. The famous Tony Awards for outstanding theatrical performances are annually presented by the LATP. The League also compiles statistics, conducts audience development, research and educational activities.

492. League of Historic American Theaters (LHAT). 1600 H St., N.W. Washington, D.C. 20006. Deborah E. Mikula, Executive Director. Phone: (202) 783-6966.

LHAT was founded in 1977 by and for professional theater managers, community organizations, art councils, individuals involved in restoration of historic theaters as well as scholars in theater history. LHAT maintains the Chesley Collection on American historic theaters at Princeton University; offers free consultations, conducts annual conferences, sponsors workshops, seminars, and research programs. The League publishes: monthly *Bulletin*; annually *Theater Classics*; *National Directory of Historic Theater Buildings*.

493. League of Off Broadway Theatres and Producers (LOBTP). C/o George Elmer Productions, Ltd. 130 W. 42nd Street, Suite 1300, New York, NY 10036. George Elmer, Secretary-Treasurer. Phone: (212) 730-7130.

The LOBTP was formed in 1957 with the major goal to represent its members interests in collective bargaining and other labor relations negotiations. The organization seeks to further and support the development of Off Broadway productions. The LOBTP holds annual conventions for its members.

494. League of Resident Theatres (LORT). C/o Tom Hall, Old Globe Theatre, P. O. Box 2171, San Diego, CA 92112. Tom Hall, Managing Director. Phone: (619) 231-1941.

Founded in 1965 by and for professional regional theaters, the LORT seeks to further the development of the regional theaters in the United States. The organization assists and consults its members in labor relations and in their artistic and management needs. The meetings and conventions are held semiannually.

495. National Association of Dramatic and Speech Arts (NADSA). P. O. Box 20984. Greensboro, NC 27420. Dr. H. D. Flowers, II, Executive Director. Phone: (919) 334-7852.

Area of interest of the NADSA is black and ethnic contemporary American theater and playwrights. The organization was founded in 1936 by and for individuals involved in educational, children's, community, and professional theaters. Among the NADSA's regular activities are placement services, bestowing of special achievement awards, organizing annual Playwrighting Contest, and publishing of *Encore* (annual journal), *NADSA Conference Directory*, and quarterly *Newsletter*.

496. National Corporate Theatre Fund (NCTF). 22 Cortland Suite 1079, New York, NY 10007. Sandra S. Swan, President. Phone: (212) 393-6252.

This Fund was formed in 1977 by and for regional theaters with the objective to support and foster partnership and better communications between business organizations and regional theaters. The NCTF publishes quarterly *NCTF News*.

497. National Critics Institute (NCI). C/o Ernest Schier, Eugene O'Neill Memorial Theater Center, 234 W. 44th Street, New York, NY 10036. Ernest Schier, Director. Phone: (212) 382- 2790.

The NCI is one of the projects of the Eugene O'Neill Memorial Theater Center. The NCI organizes and sponsors conferences and workshops for film and theater critics, and offers placement services. The major objective of the NCI is to foster the development of new trends in theater and drama criticism.

498. National Foundation for Advancement in the Arts (NFAA). 3915 Biscayne Blvd., 2nd Floor, Miami, FL 33137. Dr. Grant Beglarian, President. Phone (305) 573-0490.

The Foundation was organized in 1981 with the purpose to identify and support young aspiring artists in various art forms, including theater, writing and playwriting, dance, music, etc. The NFAA sponsors annual Arts Week and conducts the so called ARTS project – Arts Recognition and Talent Search. The National Endowment for the Arts, the Kennedy Center for the Performing Arts, and some other important art organizations, including the White House Commission on Presidential Scholars join the NFAA in its program activities. The Foundation publishes *NFAA Newsletter*, *NFAA Arts Alumni Directory*, and *NFAA Annual Report*.

499. National Mime Association (NMA). P. O. Box 148277, Chicago, IL 60614. Susan Pudelek, Secretary. Phone: (312) 871-6179.

The purpose of the NMA is to educate the public and to heighten people's awareness of mime as an important and professional art form. The organization offers workshops, professional performances, compiles statistics, and maintains speakers' bureau. The NMA holds annual conferences for its members and publishes quarterly *Newsletter*.

500. National Performance Network (NPN). Dance Theatre Workshop, 219 W. 19th Street, New York, NY 10011. David R. White, Project Director. Phone: (212) 645-6200.

The organization was founded in 1984 as a program of Dance Theatre Workshop with the purpose to increase touring opportunities for talented young artists in all areas of the performing arts. The NPN seeks to bring innovative artists to the attention of the American audience throughout the country. The Network publishes *Newsletter* (semiannual), *NPN Brochure* (annual), and holds conventions for its members every year.

501. National Playwrights Conference (NPC). Eugene O'Neill Theater Center, 234 W. 44th Street, New York, NY 10036. Lloyd Richards, Artistic Director. Phone: (212) 382-2790.

The NPC—a program of the Eugene O'Neill Memorial Theater Center—is organized annually for four weeks to offer young talented American playwrights an opportunity to work on their new plays with the outstanding professional artists and directors. There are usually more than 1,500 plays and scripts are submitted annually to the NPC and 12–14 are selected for work at the conference.

502. National Theater Conference (NTC). C/o Prof. William A. Allman, Art and Drama Center, Baldwin-Wallace College, Berea, OH 44017. Prof. William A. Allman, President. Phone: (216) 826-2239.

The NTC was formed in 1925 with a membership limited to only 120 voting members who are academic and nonacademic theater professionals. The NTC assisted in creating American Association of Community Theatre and other regional theater conferences and was instrumental in establishing first fellowships for young outstanding playwrights. The major concern of this organization—a leader of nonprofit American theaters—is the development and advancement of American drama and theater arts. The NTC serves as a liaison between noncommercial American theaters and major theatrical organizations, such as American National Theatre and Academy, and various federal government agencies dealing with performing arts. The NTC's archives are deposited in the Theatre Collection in Baldwin-Wallace College, Berea, Ohio, and in the Eli Lilly Library at Indiana University, Bloomington, Indiana.

503. National Theatre of the Deaf (NTD). Hazel E. Stark Center, Chester, CT 06412. David Hays, Artistic Director. Phone: (203) 526-4971.

Founded in 1967 and partially subsidized by the United States Department of Education, the NTF is a professional international touring theater group which presents in its productions a heightened extension of sign language combined with the spoken one. The company makes the Broadway appearances and tours U. S., Canada, Europe, Australia, and the Orient. The NTF assists other countries in establishing performing arts companies for the deaf audience. In the United States, the NTF operates professional theater school and maintains placement services. The organization was a winner of 1977 Tony Award.

504. New Dramatists (ND). 424 W. 44th Street, New York, NY 10036. Tom Dunn, Executive Director. Phone: (212) 757-6960.

The purpose of the ND (founded in 1949) is to further the development of new drama for the contemporary American stage. The ND offers a comprehensive studying program in a laboratory setting: readings of works in progress, script distribution, play panels, playwriting classes, research library of more than 2,000 volumes, etc.

Among the ND's publications are *On Stage* (annually), *Readings* (bi-monthly), and *Members Bulletin* (monthly).

505. New England Theatre Conference (NETC). 50 Exchange Street, Waltham, MA 02154. Marie L. Philips, Executive Secretary. Phone: (617) 893-3120.

The NETC was founded in 1952 by individuals and theater groups in New England with the objective to support, develop, and expand theatrical activities in all levels — professional, educational, and community. The NETC offers placement and consulting services, organizes auditions for summer theater jobs, maintains speakers' bureau, owns research and reference library and archives. The organization sponsors five-day Drama Festival for community theaters, workshops on various aspects of theatrical work — performance, administrative and technical. The NETC bestows special awards, such as annual Award for Outstanding Creative Achievement in the American Theater; annual John Gassner Memorial Play Writing Award for one-act and full-length plays; annual Community Theater Drama Award for the best play entered in annual drama competition, etc. Among the NETC's publications are annual *Membership Directory*; *News*, eight times a year; *Proceedings of Annual Convention*; and a periodical *Resource Directory*.

506. New York Critics Drama Circle (NYDC). C/o Richard Hummler, Variety, 475 Park Avenue, S., New York, NY 10016. Richard Hummler, Secretary. Phone: (212) 779-1100.

The NYDC is the organization of theater and drama critics working for major magazines and newspapers in New York City. With the objective to further the development of contemporary drama and uphold the standards of theater criticism, the NYDC bestows annual awards for best play and best musical. The organization holds semiannual meetings for its members.

507. North American Regional Alliance of IATA (NARA). 2735 W. Warren, Detroit, MI 48208. Dr. Shirley Harbin, Secretary. Phone: (313) 898-6340.

The NARA was formed in 1974 as a section of the International Amateur Theatre Association to support and further the development of theater and drama in the North America. The NARA maintains three centers for the North America: Detroit, Toronto, and Mexico City. The organization holds congresses, festivals, conferences, workshops, and quarterly publishes the *Newsletter*.

508. Northwest Drama Conference (NWDC). Western Oregon State College, Monmouth, OR 97361. Richard Davis, President. Phone: (503) 838-1220.

The NWDC was founded in 1946 by individuals and theater groups interested in exchange of ideas in all aspects of theater arts and dedicated to fostering the development of contemporary theater. The NWDC bestows special awards, holds auditions, and offers workshops.

509. Ohio State University Jerome Lawrence and Robert E. Lee Theatre Research Institute. 1430 Lincoln Tower, 1800 Cannon Drive, Columbus, Ohio 43210-1230. Alan Woods, Director. Phone: (614) 292-6614.

The Institute was founded in 1972 as an integral unit of Theater Department and University Libraries, but with its own board of control. It conducts research in the following fields: American and English theater of the 19th and 20th centuries; theatrical activities in Western Europe, 15th-19th centuries, such as festivals; historical and modern theater architecture; machinery designs; costume; commedia dell'arte materials; etc. The Institute maintains the following special collections: on post–World War II American theater centered in the collections of the dramatists Jerome Lawrence and Robert E. Lee, and actress Eileen Heckart; on Burgtheater (Austria) and Sadler's Wells (England); special collections of theater artifacts from various sources in Ohio state. Publishes scholarly monographs and dissertations, and *Theater Studies*, annual. It also sponsors annual conferences.

510. Outer Critics Circle (OCC). C/o Margorie Gunner, 101 W. 57th Street, New York, NY 10019. Margorie Gunner, President. Phone: (212) 765-8557.

The OCC is the organization of theater and drama critics who write about New York theater for regional (out-of-town) magazines and newspapers. The OCC presents various awards for outstanding work on New York stage, including Lucille Lortel Award to best director or John Gassner Award to a new author of a best play. The organization holds annual meeting for its members.

511. The Paper Bag Players (PBP). 50 Riverside Drive, New York, NY 10024. Judith Liss, Managing Director. Phone: (212) 362-0431.

The PBP was founded in 1958 with the support of National Endowment for the Arts, New York State Council on the Arts, and private contributions. The purpose of this organization is to assist and foster the development of the theater for children's audiences. The PBP create original plays with music for children, give their performances in public schools, offer lecture demonstrations and workshops on children theater, and tour the country and abroad. The PBP holds annual meeting for its members.

512. The Players. 16 Gramercy Park, New York, NY 10003. Roger Bryant Hunting, Secretary. Phone: (212) 475-6116.

The Players were founded in 1988 as a private club for theater professionals — actors, directors, playwrights, critics, composers, etc. The organization maintains research library (Hampden-Booth Theatre Library) with the materials relating to the history of American and British theater.

513. Performing Arts Research Center. New York Public Library at Lincoln Center. 111 Amsterdam Avenue, New York, NY 10023. Mrs. Heike Kordish, Acting Chief. Phone: (212) 870-1630.

This research archive of the New York Public Library was founded in 1965 with the purpose to collect, process, catalog, and maintain published and unpublished materials dealing with performing arts. The Center houses the following special collections: the Dance Collection (covers ballet, modern, ethnic, folk, etc. dance with the aid of videotapes and films of life performances, and also through manuscripts, newspapers and magazines, costume and set designs for the shows, taped interviews, etc.); the Music Collection (contains autograph scores of classical music and theoretical works); TOEFT Collection—the Theater on Film and Tape (consists of over 1,000 films and tapes of life performances and musicals from the early ones to the latest shows on Broadway); the Rogers and Hammerstein Archives of Recorded Sound (serves as a repository of 460,000 recordings and videotapes, plus catalogs, periodicals, etc.); and the famous Billy Rose Theater Collection (covers the entertainment and show business world and professional theater, including drama, film, radio, television, vaudeville, magic shows, etc.). The purpose of the Center is to provide reference services, to answer letters and telephone inquiries, and to provide materials for professional theater related research for which prior arrangements are necessary.

514. Performing Arts Resources (TAP). 270 Lafayette Street, Suite 809, New York, NY 10012. Donna E. Brady, Director. Phone (212) 966-8658.

Founded in 1960, this organization (formerly: TAP—Technical Assistance Program) of theater professionals in the field of production management, stage management, tour coordination, arts project administration, etc. offers various production and administration services in the theater, consultations on general practices of theater companies and on arts projects: such as management of outdoor festivals or special Broadway seasons. The library maintains technical data on theaters and performance halls throughout the country and the New York City area and lists of rental and purchase sources of different theatrical equipment. The *Newsletter* is issued eight times a year.

515. Producers Group (PG). 630 Ninth Avenue, Suite 808, New York, NY 10036.

The PG is the organization of theatrical producers who founded the group in 1985 with the purpose of improving the quality of commercial shows and exchanging information on the cost of theatrical productions. The PG holds monthly meetings for its members.

516. Professional Arts Management Institute (PAMI). 408 W. 57th Street, New York, NY 10019. Alvin H. Reiss, Director. Phone: (212) 245-3850.

The PAMI was founded in 1957 with the idea of providing intensive training for students and professionals in the performing arts field interested in arts management. The Institute sponsors and conducts seminars, compiles statistics, and houses the library.

517. Save the Theatres (STT). 165 W. 46th Street, New York, NY 10036. Curt Hagedorn, Acting Executive Director. Phone: (212) 764-7647.

The STT was formed in 1982 in order to protect Time Square area theaters from being torn down and obtain for them landmark status. The organization maintains speakers' bureau, conducts land-use studies, compiles statistics, and bestows special awards. Among the major STT's activities are the educational programs and exhibits about the theater preservation. One of the STT's objectives is to develop national program on theater preservation to help identify and preserve historical theaters throughout the country. The organization publishes bimonthly *Save the Theatres Newsletter*.

518. Society for the Arts, Religion, and Contemporary Culture (ARC). C/o Rev. Howard M. Fish, Box 6194, Lawrenceville, NJ 08648. Rev. Howard M. Fish, Chairman. Phone (212) 737-6522.

The purpose of this society is to build bridges between the various arts and religion. The members of the society include scholars and critics, playwrights, musicians, artists, and theologians. The ARC publishes *SEEDBED* biennially. There is also semiannual program meetings.

519. Southeastern Theatre Conference (SETC). 311 McIver Street. University of North Carolina—Greensboro, Greensboro, NC 27412. Marian A. Smith, Administrative Director. Phone: (919) 272-3645.

Among the SETC's 3,000 members are individuals and theater organizations from ten southeastern states involved in professional as well as in university, community, children's, and secondary school theaters. The major objective of this organization (founded in 1949) is to promote high standards and stimulate the development of contemporary theater in all of its aspects. The SETC maintains central office for business and communication; provides job contact service; holds annual auditions for summer jobs and for professional theaters; sponsors design competition; compiles statistics; bestows special awards and scholarships. The SETC also sponsors and organizes various festivals, such as American College Theatre; Children's Theatre; Community Theatre, etc. Among the SETC's publications are *Job Contact Bulletin* (periodical); *Southeastern Theatre Conference—Newsletter* (bimonthly); and *Southern Theatre* (quarterly). The SETC meets annually.

520. State Historical Society of Wisconsin, Archives Division. 816 State Street, Madison, WI 53706. Harold Miller, Reference Archivist. Phone: (608) 262-3338.

Founded in 1848, this organization is concerned with social and cultural history of Wisconsin and the U. S., including the modern history of mass communications, film, and theater. The collections — business records, personal papers, photographs, etc. — are available for public screening. The organization also provides reference services to students and scholars.

521. Theatre Authority (TA). 16 E. 42nd Street, Suite 202, New York, NY 10017. Helen Leathy, Executive Secretary. Phone: (212) 682-4215.

The purpose of the TA is to regulate the appearances of artists on benefits or telethons and to assist in enlisting the services of professional performers for these events. The Theatre Authority West is located at 6464 Sunset Blvd., Hollywood, CA 90028.

522. Theatre Communications Group (TCG). 355 Lexington Ave., New York, NY 10017. Peter Zeisler, Director. Phone: (212) 697-5230.

TCG was founded in 1961 to foster cooperation and interaction between nonprofit professional theaters, theater artists, administrators, technicians, and other members. Other objectives include: to develop public appreciation of the modern theater's role in society, and act as a resource for the press and funding sources. TCG conducts research projects, sponsors seminars and conferences. It also operates National Computer Project for the Performing Arts and maintains research library of theater materials. Among TCG's publications are: *Art Search*, biweekly; *American Theater*, monthly; *Plays in Process*, bimonthly; *Dramatists Sourcebook*, annually; *Theater Directory*, annually; and *New Plays, USA*, biennially.

523. Theatre Development Fund (TDF). 1501 Broadway, New York, NY 10036. Henry Guettel, Executive Director. Phone: (212) 221-0085.

The TDF was founded in 1967 as a nonprofit organization with the major objective to stimulate the production of outstanding plays on the commercial stage. The TDF's present activities include support of every area of professional theater. Among the TDF's programs are low-cost admissions to plays, dance, and concerts; subsidized and nonsubsidized ticket distribution; half-price tickets on the day of show at the Times Square, Brooklyn, and Low Manhattan Theatre Centers; and national services to assist other cities in similar programs. The TDF publishes *New York on Stage* (annual) and *TDF Sightlines* (quarterly).

524. Theatre Guild (TG). 226 W. 47th Street, New York, NY 10036. Philip Langner, President. Phone: (212) 869-5470.

The TG was formed in 1919. At the present time, it is the theatrical producing organization of 105,000 members, whose major objective is to promote and encourage attendance at theatrical performances of high standards. The TG sponsors American Theatre Society, a national subscription service for major Broadway productions touring the big cities throughout the country, and cultural exchange program through Theatre Guild Abroad.

525. Theatre Historical Society (THS). 2215 W. North Ave., Chicago, Ill 60647. William T. Benedict, Jr., Archives Director. Phone: (312) 252-7200.

THS was founded in 1969 as an independent, nonprofit research organization to preserve the history of American theater, to encourage studies in this field, and to promote preservation of important theater buildings. Supports research of members and non-members by providing information from its archives on American theater (photographs, clippings, theater programs, postcards, etc.). Maintains speakers' bureau and museum, sponsors conventions. Publishes: *Marquee*, quarterly; and special material related to the field.

526. Theatre for Ideas (TFI). C/o Shirley Broughton, 14 Diamond E., Palm Desert, CA 92260. Shirley Broughton, President. Phone: (619) 568-1261.

The TFI was founded in 1962 by Miss Broughton, a choreographer and a dancer, as a "salon for intellectuals." The purpose of this theatrical organization is to provide theater shows and entertainment in home and in theaters for different parties.

527. Theatre Library Association (TLA). 111 Amsterdam Ave., Rm. 513, New York, NY 10023. Richard M. Buck, Secretary-Treasurer. Phone: (212) 870-1670.

TLA was founded in 1937 by and for curators, librarians, theater scholars, writers, actors, and others interested and involved in performing arts research. Affiliated with American Library Association; American Society for Theatre Research; Council of National Library and Information Associations; and International Federation for Theater Research. Annually presents Freedley Memorial Award for an outstanding published work in the field of legitimate theater. Publishes: *Broadside*, quarterly; *Performing Arts Resources*, annual; and *Membership List*.

528. Theatre of Latin America (TOLA). C/o Center for Inter-Amer. Relations, 680 Park Avenue, New York, NY 10021. Fatima Bercht, Contact. Phone: (212) 249-8950.

The TOLA was formed in 1966 with the goal of providing to the audience in the United States Latin American theater, film, music, and other arts. The programs of the TOLA of various theater productions, exhibitions, university presentation of theater artists and musicians make available to artists in the United States new creative ideas and techniques developed in Latin America. The organization is working on information and translation exchange services, maintains research and reference library on contemporary Latin American theater; publishes *Newsletter* three times a year.

529. University of Kansas International Theatre Studies Center. 339 Murphy

Hall, Lawrence KS 66045. Dr. Andrew T. Tsubaki, Director. Phone: (913) 864-3534.

The center was founded in 1968 as an integral unit of the University of Kansas for research in drama and theater activities around the world. Conducts interdisciplinary historical, critical, and artistic studies on modern theater. Participates in producing plays. Research results published in scholarly journals and monographs.

530. University of Wisconsin-Madison, Wisconsin Center for Film and Theatre Research. Vilas Communication Hall, 821 University Ave., Madison, WI 53706. Dr. Donald Crafton, Director. Phone: (608) 262-9706.

The center was founded in 1960 as an integral unit of University of Wisconsin-Madison, Department of Communication Arts, but with its own board of control in collaboration with State Historical Society of Wisconsin. Conducts research projects in American theater, film, radio, and television. Maintains collection of primary source material.

531. U. S. Center for: Organizations of Scenographers, Technicians, and Architects of Theatre (USITT). 330 W. 42nd Street, Suite 1702, New York, NY 10036. Richard M. Devin, Executive Officer. Phone: (212) 563-5551.

Among the 3,000 members of the USITT (founded in 1964) are professionals involved in technical theater and scene design: architects, acousticians, engineers, educators, lighting designers, and others. The purpose of the organizations is mainly to exchange information on advances in the field and to support and promote high standards in these areas. The USITT publishes *USITT Directory* (annually); *Theatre, Design & Technology* (quarterly); and *Newsletter* (monthly). The USITT holds periodical regional conferences as well as annual convention.

532. United States Institute for Theatre Technology (USITT). C/o Richard Devin, School of Drama, DX-20, University of Washington, Seattle, WA 98195. Richard Devin, President. Phone: (206) 543-5140.

This organization was founded in 1960 for individuals, colleges, theater groups, researchers and students interested in the advancement of theater technique and technology. The goal of the USITT is to conduct research projects in the field and to provide consulting services on practices in the areas of theater planning, design, construction, presentation, and operation. The USITT sponsors a costume symposium. Among the USITT's publications are: *Theatre Design and Technology,* quarterly; *Newsletter,* monthly; *Project Report,* periodically; *Membership Directory,* annually.

533. Video Alliance for the Performing Arts (VAPA). The purpose of this organization is to develop special material that will give the broadest scope to the American cultural heritage: theater, dance, visual arts,

architecture, etc. The VAPA collects and distributes educational multi-visual presentations, tapes, and films to the Public Broadcasting Service, colleges, and libraries.

534. Wolf Trap Foundation for the Performing Arts (WTFA). 1624 Trap Road, Vienna, VA 22180. Charles A. Walters, Jr., Executive Vice President. Phone: (703) 255-1900.

Wolf Trap Farm Park was created by an Act of Congress in 1966 as the first National Park dedicated to the performing arts. The Foundation was established in 1968 at the request of the Secretary of the Interior with the purpose to fund and support programs in the park. The programs include drama theater, musicals, opera, modern and classical dance, and pop concerts. The organization is committed to the advancement of talented young American artists; and organizes theater workshops and master classes. The WTFA publishes its brochures periodically.

535. Yiddish Theatrical Alliance (YTA). 31 E. Seventh Street, New York, NY 10003. Seymour Rexsite, Executive Secretary. Phone: (212) 674-3437.

The YTA is affiliated with Hebrew Actors Union. The organization was formed in 1917 to provide care for sick and poor members of the Yiddish theater. The YTA bestows special wards; maintains research and reference library and biographical archives. Conventions for the YTA members are held annually.

536. Young Audiences (YA). 115 E. 92nd Street, New York, NY 10128. Warren H. Yost, Executive Director. Phone: (212) 831-8110.

The organization was founded in 1952 with the major purpose to increase the creative and imaginative capacities of school age children through participating in performing arts. The YA organizes professional theatrical companies to perform for children and thus help to educate future audiences for the contemporary theater and to develop the performing arts resources of communities. The YA supports research and development of new program techniques and concepts. The organization owns 200 volumes special library and a collection of materials for arts education. *Newsletter* is published bimonthly.

Author Index